GUILTY AS SIN

An addictive and heart-pounding crime thriller

BILL KITSON

DI Mike Nash Book 16

Joffe Books, London
www.joffebooks.com

First published in Great Britain in 2023

Cover art by Nick Castle

ISBN: 978-1-80405-655-4

To my beautiful wife and partner in crime.

CHAPTER ONE

The screams shattered the silence. As the last echo died away, it was replaced by a variety of other sounds. Gasps, moans, cries, muttered imprecations, and running footsteps merged together in reaction to the noise that had disturbed the night.

A hurried conversation alerted others to the crisis. 'It's Mr Donaldson again, Doctor. Can you come immediately?'

The ward had been quiet, the occupants sleeping. The culprit lay staring at the ceiling, his face still registering the panic that had induced the screams, as a nurse bent anxiously over him.

One of her colleagues went in turn to each of the other patients, attempting to calm them. 'There's nothing to worry about,' she told them. 'It's only Mr Donaldson having a nightmare — again. Doctor will be here soon to give him a sedative so you can all go back to sleep.'

The nurse charged with comforting the distressed patient told him, as she had on several occasions previously, that he had nothing to fear. 'You're in hospital, Mr Donaldson. Can you remember what happened to you? Would you like to tell me what it was that made you cry out like that?'

Despite her efforts, she failed to persuade him. Eventually, the doctor arrived, and a strong sedative enabled the patient to return to the semi-comatose state he'd been in prior to the scream. Even then, the nightmare of what he'd seen remained, subdued and silent, in the dark recesses of his mind. Lurking in the shadows of his memory like the bogeyman of a children's terror story, waiting to pounce and devour its innocent victim.

It was the fourth occasion this had happened during his brief sojourn in the hospital, and, following this incident, the ward sister's demands for positive action met with a sympathetic response. The meeting to discuss the patient took place the following morning and included three doctors, plus members of the nursing staff. The sister planned to move Mr Donaldson to a side room to try and minimize the disturbance, and commented it might be easier to deal with his problem if they understood the cause. This prompted an unusual suggestion from one of the medical team.

The doctor was a junior, young enough to be receptive to unconventional methods. 'Despite his head injury, there is nothing of concern on the scans to account for his behaviour. If Mr Donaldson can't or won't explain why he screams out, perhaps it might be worth trying hypnosis to get at the truth. Once we know the cause, we might stand a chance of dealing with it, as Sister says.'

After some debate, it was agreed to try, and the doctor was charged with following up his idea. Later that day, in the patient's side room, the psychologist, a licensed hypnotherapist, conducted the session.

Once it was over, the two medical professionals discussed the result. 'As I see it, there's no option,' the psychologist told his colleague. 'We have to call the police.'

'They're going to love that,' the doctor replied. 'They must have been celebrating the fact that they'd seen and heard the last of Harry Donaldson. He's caused them enough bother already. And not only them, but Mountain Rescue, the ambulance service, and a helicopter as well.' He shrugged. 'OK, I'll talk to my boss.'

Before consulting his superior, the medic decided to check the patient's belongings contained in a small rucksack. To the best of his knowledge, nobody had looked inside the bag since Mr Donaldson had been admitted. As he removed various items of waterproof clothing, he noticed another object nestling in a small zip pocket in the front of the bag. The doctor removed a mobile phone and plugged the charger into a nearby socket to enable him to operate the device. Perhaps some of the photos in the gallery might prove useful, he thought.

He opened the first one and stared at the image in horror. Without conscious thought, he flicked his thumb across the screen and stared at the second, then the next. One thing for certain, whatever else might be wrong with his patient, he certainly wasn't hallucinating. Having recovered his composure, the doctor scooped up the mobile. Calling the police had now become a necessity.

'This is Dr Roberts from Netherdale Hospital. Could I speak with Sergeant Meadows, please?'

'This is Sergeant Meadows. How can I help you?'

'You remember Harry Donaldson, the man who was rescued from Layton Woods a week ago?'

The silence that greeted his question spoke volumes, so he hastened to explain, 'He's recovering OK physically, but he's been having some dreadful nightmares that result in him screaming the place down in the middle of the night. The problem was he couldn't, or wouldn't, tell us what was terrifying him, until today, when we put him under hypnosis. We were unsure whether what he revealed was a result of his imagination or false memory, but after I made another discovery, I don't think that's the case. What Mr Donaldson experienced was far, far worse. Let me explain . . .'

Two minutes later, the phone rang in the CID suite upstairs and was picked up by an attractive blonde. 'Clara, it's Steve. I've a Dr Roberts from Netherdale General on the line. He rang to tell us something about the guy who had to be rescued from Layton Woods. I think you ought to hear what he's just told me.'

'OK, Steve, put him through.' Clara waited, then greeted the caller, 'Doctor Roberts, you're speaking to Detective Sergeant Mironova. I understand you have some information for us?'

She listened for a few moments, making several notes before asking the medic, 'Could you send those through to me, please?' After reciting her work mobile phone number, she thanked him and ended the call. A few minutes later, she walked downstairs.

'What do you reckon, Clara?' Meadows asked her.

'I wasn't sure at first,' she replied. 'I thought it was a fantasy resulting from the man's ordeal, but now I'm certain that Donaldson stumbled across something terrible.' She showed him the photos on her mobile, before adding, 'One thing for sure, we can't ignore it, in view of what's on there.'

She glanced out of the window, where the street lights were already glowing, their rays picking up the odd flakes of snow drifting lazily past on the breeze. 'It'll have to wait till morning, though,' she added.

'Isn't Mike due back tomorrow?' Meadows asked.

'He is, and he's going to love having to go out in sub-zero temperatures after spending time in Spain.'

'It seems an odd time of year to take leave. February is hardly peak holiday season.'

'It's Daniel's half-term at boarding school, so they've taken a family break.'

Clara paused and changed the subject back to work matters. 'Can you have a word with Mountain Rescue, Steve? We need someone to guide us to the place they found Mr Donaldson. That will save us lots of fruitless searching. You know how huge an area they had to cover before they located him. We could be there for weeks, unless we get help, and by the sound of it, Mr Donaldson won't be in a fit state to assist.'

* * *

Next morning, Mironova was first to arrive, but she had barely reached the CID suite and was removing her coat, when the DI walked in. The break had obviously been good for him. He looked tanned, happy, and fitter than Clara had seen him for some time. 'I don't have to ask how things went,' she greeted him. 'It's good to see you back, Mike, and looking so well. I take it you had a good holiday.'

Nash's response made her blush. 'And a good morning to you, Mrs Sutton.'

Despite having been married for some while, she still wasn't used to being called by that name.

'Yes,' Nash continued, 'we had a great break. It's the first time Daniel and I have visited the home where Alondra grew up. She was thinking of selling it, but we've decided to keep it as a holiday retreat.'

'But you already have a house in France.'

'That's Daniel's, not mine; his mother left it to him. I'll tell you all about the holiday later — well, almost everything,' he added with a grin. 'Have I missed much? I hope you've been keeping Mexican Pete busy.'

Clara smiled at the pathologist's nickname. Professor Ramirez was Spanish, but the title 'Mexican Pete', which stemmed from the *Ballad of Eskimo Nell*, was a joke throughout the local force. 'Sadly, we haven't troubled him once. That might change, though,' she added, darkly.

'I take it that cryptic remark means there's something brewing. Tell me.'

'It's nothing definite, but it certainly needs investigating. It began when a local man's family contacted us to report him missing. He's fifty-odd years old, and had taken up hiking after his wife's death earlier this year. He hadn't been seen or in contact for almost a week, so the family were getting very anxious. We followed MISPER procedures and issued a photo along with the appeal. A pub landlord spotted it and contacted us. Apparently, the missing man, Harry Donaldson, stopped there for a night and told the landlord he was going walking through Layton Woods. He planned to follow the banks of the River Helm and on up Black Fell, before circling back to pick up his car. That was the last sighting of him. The car was still in the pub car park three days later, so the landlord called us. We had to mount a search and rescue operation.'

'Is the hiker still missing?'

'No, we got Mountain Rescue involved, and they found him wandering about in the forest. He had a bump on the head, was malnourished, suffering from hypothermia, and unable, or unwilling, to tell anyone what had happened to him.'

Nash frowned. 'Why do you say "unwilling"?'

'I'll explain that in a minute. He was taken to Netherdale General, and they assumed he was suffering concussion as a result of a fall. But yesterday afternoon, I got a call from the doctor treating him. Although Donaldson is recovering well physically, he's been suffering horrendous nightmares, causing him to scream out in terror. It got so bad, they decided to hypnotize him. While he was under, he told them what he'd seen.'

'And that was?'

'He told the medics he'd strayed from the track and lost his way. He spotted what he thought was a strange-looking branch on the ground, but when he looked, he claims he'd discovered a skeleton.'

'Really?' Nash looked surprised.

Clara nodded. 'Then he tripped over a root and fell, and doesn't remember much more. That explained the nightmares, but the doctors thought he was hallucinating. When he was found, he had a bad bruise on his temple, and they assumed he must have fallen and probably cracked his head, knocking himself out.'

'His story does sound like the after-effects of concussion. Why do you think we need to investigate it?'

'The doctors thought much the same as you, until one of them checked Mr Donaldson's mobile phone. That's when he called us. On the mobile there were three images of a skeleton. Donaldson must have taken the photos before he got even more lost.'

Nash stared at Mironova for a few seconds. 'That certainly doesn't sound like an hallucination.'

'That's right. The doctor sent me the photos, and I can tell they're genuine. The problem is, the place where they found Mr Donaldson is pretty remote, and there's a large area to cover.'

'I guess you're proposing that we should send a search team to Layton Woods, hunting for a skeleton. That may take months without finding anything. Of course, there's always the chance that they'll stumble across a lake with wild geese on it, and they could chase them to ease the boredom.'

There was a time when Clara would have winced at Nash's sarcasm, but they had worked together for long enough for her to know that he was merely blowing off steam.

'Have you finished?' she asked. 'Because if so, I was about to tell you something else Mr Donaldson revealed during his hypnotic trance. Donaldson said when he found the skeleton, he could hear the sound of running water nearby. Steve phoned Mountain Rescue and asked about this, and their man said, that given where they'd found Donaldson, he believed he must have been near Black Fell Foss during his wanderings.'

'Steve didn't mention the skeleton, did he?' Nash looked alarmed.

'This is Steve Meadows we're talking about,' Clara said with a withering look.

'Yes, sorry. I'm assuming you mean "foss" as in waterfall? I didn't know there was one on Black Fell.'

'It's not very well known. Only a few locals and some hikers are aware of it. The good news is, the Mountain Rescue guy has agreed to act as our guide though the forest. He reckons it's little more than a fifteen-minute drive along the trail once we've left the main road. He also said the ambulance couldn't negotiate the track, and they'd loaded Mr Donaldson in their vehicle to transport him to the road. So it would be better if we had a four-wheel drive.' She paused. 'Like a Range Rover, for example.' She stared pointedly at Nash, who owned such a vehicle.

'I take it we're going, are we?'

Clara nodded, and grinned as Nash told her, 'My first task on returning to work is to act as your chauffeur, right?'

Clara couldn't resist a sly allusion to Nash's recent vacation. 'That's right, and if we *do* find that skeleton, you can have the joy of renewing your little chats with Mexican Pete. That way you'll know the holiday really is over, even if you converse in Spanish.'

'Oh, very funny,' Nash retorted. 'With jokes like that you should be on the stage — sweeping it.'

At that moment the office door opened, and the tall Antiguan detective constable, Viv Pearce, walked in, followed by DC Lisa Andrews. Viv was talking to Lisa about his young son when he saw Clara laughing.

'We missed something?' Viv asked.

'Yes, filling the coffee machine,' Nash told him. 'Clara and I are going for a walk. You two can carry on with whatever has been keeping you busy while I've been away. Just make sure the coffee is hot when we get back. I have a strong suspicion we're going to need it.'

CHAPTER TWO

Nash and Mironova set off on the drive towards Layton Woods. Seeing the twin peaks of Stark Ghyll and Black Fell ahead of them, Nash noticed the summits of both were capped with snow. He was thankful he'd put his waxed jacket with thermal lining, flat cap, and gloves, in the car before leaving Smelt Mill Cottage early that morning. Even without the need to readjust to the Yorkshire winter, he'd definitely need them today.

When they reached the turn-off from the Kirk Bolton road, they joined the Mountain Rescue vehicle waiting at the junction, and followed up the track into the woodland.

Clara stirred in the passenger seat. 'Do we need a search warrant? These woods are on private land.'

Nash pointed to a board containing a sign that had been erected on a fence post. The image was a blue arrow, signifying a bridleway. 'This is a public right of way. I certainly don't think the owners are going to quibble about the legal niceties in the circumstances.'

Although Nash drove slowly and with extreme caution, there were places further along the trail where the Range Rover, and the Land Rover belonging to the Mountain Rescue team leader, struggled, even with the assistance of four-wheel drive. Having negotiated a particularly boggy stretch full of ruts, Nash complained, 'Accounts department are going to have kittens when they get the car-cleaning bill, because I'm certainly not paying it.'

Eventually, the track ended and the vehicle in front pulled to a halt in a small glade. Nash parked alongside. They all donned their wellington boots and warm clothing, and set off through increasingly dense woodland, following a trail made for them by deer, badgers, and other animals. After twenty minutes or so, their guide stopped and gestured to a break in the trees ahead. 'This is the spot where we found Mr Donaldson, sitting on that fallen tree.'

Nash looked round and nodded. 'Thank you, now can you point us to anywhere within the sound of the foss?'

'Easy enough,' the man replied. 'If you look beyond through the trees, you'll just be able to see the light glistening on the water cascading down from Black Fell Foss in the distance. Want me to show you?'

Nash told their guide, 'Protocol demands that we should take it from here, so would you mind waiting, while we have a look?'

'No problem, I'll wait in the car — where it's a damn sight warmer.'

'What if we get lost in the woods?' Clara was feeling unsure.

The man laughed. 'Why do you think I'm carrying these?'

She looked at the wooden spikes with gaily coloured tops he was holding, and shook her head.

'Path markers,' he said, as he stuck one in the ground. 'I don't know what you're looking for, but I thought you might need these.'

'Thank goodness,' Clara said. 'I don't have any crumbs with me to lay a trail.'

The detectives headed forwards, placing markers as they went, until they could just hear the sound of the waterfall and entered a large clearing. By the look of the undergrowth, the trees had been sawn for lumber many years ago. It took them less than fifteen minutes before Clara saw what looked like a set of twigs in a row ahead of her. 'Mike,' she called, 'I think I've found some ribs.'

Nash hurried over, and squinted towards where she was pointing. Together, they walked carefully forwards. As they got nearer, they saw a skull and the rest of the skeleton.

Nash turned to Clara. 'We need Mexican Pete here, plus a CSI crew. I think it's time for us to enlist our mountaineering friend's help again.'

When they reached the cars, their guide was gazing at the screen of his mobile.

'Can you get a signal on that?' Nash asked.

'Unfortunately not, I've been using the reading app. I didn't think to bring the two-way radio along. Why, did you find what you were looking for?'

Nash nodded before asking, 'Would you mind doing us another favour? All I need is for you to return to the main road and then phone Helmsdale police station. Ask for Sergeant Meadows and tell him we need the pathologist and a Forensic team out here, preferably with four-wheel drive vehicles. Then, if it's OK with you, will you wait there to rendezvous and direct them here?'

'I'll do that, no problem. Can I ask what you found over there?'

'It was as we suspected. Let's leave it at that, shall we?'

As they watched him disappear into the distance, Clara asked, 'What next? We could be left kicking our heels here for some time.'

'We could sit in the car, where it's warm and comfortable. Alternatively, we could make a preliminary search of the area surrounding the skeleton. Admittedly, it's extremely unlikely because of the location of the burial site, but we might get lucky and find something.'

'Is there anything in particular you want to look for?'

Nash told her, and Clara's eyes widened with surprise. After giving it some thought, she responded, 'I've no idea how you worked that out. You think the remains were of someone who was stabbed to death, and you want us to look for the murder weapon, right?'

'That's correct.'

'What makes you think the person was murdered, and the weapon was a knife? There's nothing remaining to display stab wounds. So what did you spot that I didn't — or is this more of the famous Nash intuition at work?'

'It's not intuition. But I did notice something. If you'd looked carefully, you'd have seen there are at least three notches on the rib cage, which I reckon were caused by a knife blade. If the killer discarded the weapon, we might get lucky and find it. Alternatively, it might be the other side of Netherdale, heading for the North Sea by now.'

'You think the killer threw the weapon in the river?'

'It's what I would have done. But possibly they weren't thinking rationally at the time.'

The wind, a cold north-easterly, picked up at that point, making Nash shiver. 'On second thoughts,' he told her, 'we'll wait in the car. Let CSI conduct a search. It's what we pay them for, and I've not yet readjusted to North Yorkshire temperatures.'

When they got into the Range Rover, Nash switched the ignition on and turned the heater up to full blast for a few minutes. As they waited, Clara brought up the subject of Nash's altered circumstances. 'How's Alondra doing?' She patted her tummy as she spoke.

'Very well, so far.' Nash smiled slightly, as he added, 'She reckons all the exercise she's been getting has left her fitter than for a long time.'

'I'm not sure I wanted to hear that.'

'I'm referring to the long, daily dog walks she takes with Teal,' Nash told her. 'What did you think I meant?'

Ignoring the leading question, Clara asked, 'When do you intend to tell the others?'

'I thought we'd hold off for a while. Alondra's only four months pregnant. Plenty of time yet.'

Clara thought for a moment before saying, 'With those horrendous injuries she sustained when she was attacked, and the resultant miscarriage, I thought the specialist told her she was unable to have children. Did it come as a shock when you found out she was expecting?'

'It certainly did — for me, for Alondra, and certainly for her specialist. He was delighted, and I reckon quite astonished, when he admitted he'd got that wrong.'

'What are you hoping for, a boy or a girl?'

'I'm not bothered. The specialist asked Alondra if she would want to know the sex of the baby, and she told him no, because I'm a detective and we like mysteries in our house.'

Clara knew the couple had used the visit to Spain to break the news of Alondra's pregnancy to Nash's thirteen-year-old son. 'How did Daniel take the news?'

Nash laughed. 'He's over the moon, and I reckon that's partly because he's been an only child for so long. I also think he's hoping for a younger brother, someone he can play cricket with. That would probably mean the poor child will have to bowl for hours on end while Daniel gets in some batting practice. When we dropped him back at school, I was told emphatically that I was to take good care of her.'

Clara chuckled, but asked, 'Doesn't he feel at all resentful at the new situation? I've heard of cases where older siblings aren't at all happy with new arrivals.'

'There's certainly no sign of that, quite the opposite. He's already started teasing Alondra by calling her "Mummy Dearest", which totally confused her to begin with, but she's now delighted. I think, deep down, she has always retained a scintilla of doubt regarding Daniel's complete acceptance of her. I can't understand why. Especially when you and David helped him to find her in Spain and, as he keeps reminding me, he's responsible for bringing her back. Now, I think all her misgivings have disappeared.'

After a while, Nash suggested they ought to buy a Thermos flask. 'We could top it up from the coffee machine whenever we're called to a crime scene. That way, we'll not risk dehydration or hypothermia, like this morning.'

Their discussion was interrupted at that point by the approach of three vehicles being driven in convoy, signalling the arrival of the pathologist, the mortuary assistants, and the CSI team.

* * *

Professor Ramirez' greeting was predictably sarcastic. 'I was told you were away, but as soon as I received the message summoning me here, I realized you must have returned. Nobody but you would drag me out to the back of beyond to view what I understand is nothing more than a bag of bones.'

Nash smiled at him. 'I value you so highly, Professor, that I thought the fresh air would be beneficial to your health and well-being.'

The reply was in Spanish and made Nash smile. When Clara asked for a translation, he told her, 'Our learned friend said something which is extremely rude. It is also physically impossible, even for a contortionist.'

Having directed Ramirez to the remains, Nash and Clara retired a few paces to allow him to examine the victim. The inspection didn't take long, following which the pathologist told them what he'd deduced, and in the process added one important item to their small fund of knowledge.

'The remains are those of a female. That much is clear by the pelvic bone structure. The unfortunate woman appears to have been stabbed several times.'

'I'd guessed that by the marks on her ribs,' Nash told him.

Ramirez eyed him with mock respect. 'Really? Have you ever thought of a career as a detective?' He continued on more a serious note, 'From the multiple stab wounds, I'd say this was a crime of passion, or at least made to appear that way. But I'll leave you to judge the rights and wrongs of that if, and when, she can be identified. I suppose you'll want DNA?'

Nash nodded. 'How long has she been there? Can you tell?'

Ramirez shrugged and gestured to the scene. 'The post-mortem will give me more of an idea. But it will have to wait as I'm on leave from tonight. There will be a locum available should you have urgent need of one, but I think the post-mortem can wait until I return. When the photographers have finished, I'll get my assistants to take the remains to the mortuary and instruct them to try and obtain a bone marrow sample for DNA analysis.'

He turned to walk towards his car, but stopped when Nash called after him, '*Hasta la vista*, Don Pedro. *Vaya con Dios.*'

Ramirez looked over his shoulder. He was laughing as he replied, '*Muchas gracias*, Don Miguel.' He waved one hand in farewell.

Clara realized with a shock that she'd never seen the professor laugh before. 'What did you say to him?'

'Basically, I wished him well.'

'Oh, I see.' She frowned. This really was an unusual scenario.

Before he and Clara departed, Nash spoke to the CSI team leader, 'I don't think there's much for us to do here. Unless the killer has engraved a confession in stone, the only thing we need is to try and locate the murder weapon. Even that seems highly unlikely. I doubt the murderer would be stupid enough to leave it in situ, especially when there's a fast-flowing river close at hand to drop it in.'

The man looked round at the undergrowth and grimaced. 'We'll give it our best shot.'

As they were getting into the Range Rover, Clara asked, 'What if it's just a body dump and the killing took place elsewhere?'

'We'll have to wait and see if there's anything found here before we take things any further. We've no idea how long the body's been there.'

CHAPTER THREE

Early that evening, as Nash and Alondra were about to sit down for their meal, his mobile rang. Alondra giggled at his rueful expression before he answered it. He listened for a few moments, agreeing a couple of times to what he was being told, before ending the call. 'It's OK,' he reassured her, 'I thought I was going to be needed, but thankfully not.'

'Who was it? Not one of your admiring females, I hope.'

Nash was about to respond when he saw the mischievous twinkle in her eyes. 'There are no admiring females. You're the only woman in my life, and that suits me just fine.'

'You still haven't told me who called you.'

'It was Tom Pratt, and what he said might prove extremely interesting and helpful. I'll have to wait until tomorrow before I get the full story, though.'

Next morning, Nash briefed Clara. 'Tom's on his way over from Netherdale. He phoned me last night. He'd been playing golf yesterday afternoon, and when he was in the clubhouse afterwards, that guy from Mountain Rescue wandered in to attend a meeting. Apparently, when he's not saving people who have got into difficulties on Stark Ghyll or Black Fell, our friend is a keen golfer, and is on the club committee. Knowing Tom's job, he mentioned seeing us yesterday, and told him we were in Layton Woods. Tom asked Steve Meadows what was going on, and as soon as he mentioned the skeleton, Tom got quite agitated. He reckons he knows who the victim is, so he's calling at HQ to collect the file and bring it to us.'

Former Superintendent Tom Pratt, who, before his retirement on health grounds from active duty, had been the head of the area's detective force, was a mine of helpful information. Unable to remain idle at home, he had returned as a civilian support officer, working between HQ and Helmsdale.

Shortly after 10 a.m., Tom joined the team in the CID suite and sat down.

'Morning, Tom,' Clara said. 'I thought you were bringing a file?'

As Tom was about to answer, Clara's phone rang, she picked it up. 'OK, Steve, I'll tell him.' Turning to Tom, she said, 'Sorry, hang on,' and called to Nash, who was in his office. 'Mike, Steve wants you downstairs. Said it was urgent.'

Heading for the door, Nash spotted the look of innocence on Tom's face. When he reached reception, Steve Meadows was watching an officer from HQ offloading several file boxes out of a police van, and stacking them on the floor.

'You could have warned me,' Steve said. 'Where am I supposed to put all these? Tom said they're for you.'

Nash shook his head. 'So much for bringing a file over — I'll deal with it.'

Back in CID, he called Viv over. 'Got a job for you. Nip down and see Steve, he has a file needs bringing up.'

When Viv had left the room, Nash turned to Tom. 'What are you up to?'

'I'll explain when everyone's here.'

After Lisa had sorted out a drink for their visitor, and Viv had finished loading the boxes against the office wall, Nash invited Tom to tell them what he knew.

'I may have an identity for the body in Layton Woods. It was sixteen years ago, before any of you were working here. A woman by the name of Demetra Sinclair was reported missing. When we investigated, suspicion fell on her husband, Nicholas Sinclair. He was twenty-five years old, Demetra a couple of years younger, and they had only been married less than a year. The closer we looked at Sinclair, the more convinced we were that he was responsible for his wife's disappearance, and that the outcome would not be good. Two or three witnesses who came forward alleged Sinclair had a short fuse, and one of them said he was more than a bit handy with his fists.'

'Demetra doesn't sound like an English given name,' Viv Pearce suggested.

'No, it's Romanian. She came over to the UK to work in one of the hotels in Netherdale, which is where she met Sinclair. When we narrowed down the timescale during which she vanished, we got a report from someone who had seen a Mini Cooper, similar to the car Sinclair owned, turning off the main road onto the track that leads through Layton Woods. That sighting was slap bang in the middle of the time frame of her disappearance. Part of the area is open to the public, so there seemed to be nothing suspicious about it, until the witness read our appeal for help and remembered the incident.'

'Did you search the woods at the time?'

'We tried — but have you seen the size of those woods? Unfortunately, this happened in winter, and we had to abandon the search after a heavy snowfall rendered the area out of reach.'

'If they'd only recently got married, what was the motive?' Clara asked.

'That's where it gets interesting,' Pratt told her. 'As we questioned everyone close to the missing woman, we learned that Sinclair only married Demetra because she was in the early stages of pregnancy. But one of the people we spoke to suggested Sinclair wasn't the father. That she had conned him into believing the child was his. By the nature of his job at Netherdale Engineering he was away much of the time, only coming home on occasional weekends. We reckoned that was when she had a fling, leading to her pregnancy before they married. Naturally, Sinclair denied this. But we were convinced he'd got the truth out of her, and was so outraged by the deception, he killed her.'

'That all seems very circumstantial. Was there any solid, physical evidence?' Nash asked.

'There was indeed. When he reported her missing, he said he'd just returned home from a job down south and found the flat in a mess. Our officers went to look. There was considerable damage to the furniture and fittings. So we sent in the Forensics boys, and they discovered bloodstains on the kitchen floor. Although an attempt had been made to clean them up, there was a DNA match to Demetra. They also discovered a large carving knife that had a residual amount of blood close to the handle, which also matched hers. We believe Sinclair smashed the flat in a violent rage at the point when he confronted and killed her.'

Tom paused. 'Although the evidence pointing to Demetra Sinclair being murdered is purely circumstantial, there is absolutely no doubt regarding the other murder Sinclair was convicted of. A few days after Demetra allegedly disappeared, a man's body was found dumped in an alleyway near the village green at Kirk Bolton. He'd been stabbed three times, one blow piercing the carotid artery. We found a Swiss Army knife in a pocket of a gilet at Sinclair's flat, and there were traces of the victim's blood both on the knife and the jacket. Although the dead man has never been identified, we were certain he was Demetra's lover.'

'Why do you think that?' Clara asked.

'Because we found traces of her DNA on the victim's outer clothing. That led us to Sinclair and was sufficient for us to charge him with both murders, even though his wife's body hadn't been recovered. Many of the locals were convinced he was guilty, so much so that they even coined a phrase, *as guilty as Sinclair*, a play on the expression *as guilty as sin*, which was doing the rounds in the pubs and media at the time. It seems the jury was of the same opinion, because they returned a guilty verdict, and he was sentenced to life imprisonment.'

'Did you interview Sinclair personally?' Nash asked. 'If so, what was your opinion of him?'

'I only sat in on one of the interviews. It confirmed much of what we suspected. Although he didn't admit to anything, I was convinced he was not telling us everything. I assumed what he was hiding related to his wife's murder, and how he'd disposed of her remains.' Tom shrugged. 'We'll probably never know, because Sinclair didn't change his story during the trial, in spite of one of the most ferocious cross-examinations I've ever heard from the Crown prosecutor.'

'If this all took place sixteen years ago, won't Sinclair be due for release on parole by now?' Lisa asked.

'That would normally be so,' he agreed. 'But Sinclair hasn't been a model prisoner. He's forfeited his right to parole. In fact, time was added to his sentence. That's due to one of his altercations with another inmate, which resulted in Sinclair spending a good deal of time in isolation, while his unfortunate victim ended up in the prison hospital.' Tom looked up, signalling the end of the briefing.

Nash thanked him and then explained, 'Because of the decomposition of the remains in Layton Woods, there was no immediate means of carrying out identification. The facts appear to fit, though, as the woman whose skeleton was found had suffered stab wounds sufficient to leave notches on her rib cage. Mexican Pete has arranged a sample for DNA analysis. I assume, from what you've already told us, there's a DNA record on file for us to compare the results with?'

'There certainly is, Mike. We collected plenty of samples at Sinclair's flat. Anyway, I've done everything I can, so I'll leave it to you guys from here. I guess when you get the DNA confirmed, this case can finally be put to bed, and hopefully that poor girl can rest in peace.' He indicated the files he had brought from Netherdale. With a sly sideways glance at Viv Pearce, their computer expert, he told them, 'Sorry we only have hard copy. We hadn't gone digital crazy back in the day.' With that, he bade them farewell.

When he had left, Nash told the others, 'Everything Tom told us sounds very convincing, and I've no doubt he'll be proved absolutely correct in his assumptions. But just to be on the safe side, I think we should try and acquaint ourselves with the full facts. We'll have plenty of time to study the paperwork. As things stand, we're not rushed off our feet.'

Clara groaned in mock despair. 'Yes, we've even got time to listen to your dreadful puns. "As things stand, we're not rushed off our feet"— is that really the best you can do?'

* * *

The detectives took it in turns to peruse the documentation within the boxes. Whereas his colleagues concentrated almost exclusively on the evidence presented at Nicholas Sinclair's trial, Nash's interest was caught by details contained in a report from the governor of Frankland prison, following the inmate's violent outburst. When they had all completed their provisional read-through, Nash asked for opinions.

Pearce was the first to react. 'I reckon the jury's decision was correct, and Sinclair is as guilty as sin. Apart from the physical evidence of his wife's bloodstains at the flat and the dead man's on the Swiss Army knife, there's Sinclair's violent reputation. Couple that with the likelihood of him going off the deep end when he found his wife had been having it off with someone else, and was carrying that man's child, there seems to be no other explanation.'

'I agree with Viv,' Lisa told them. 'Although Sinclair had a decent, well-paid job at Netherdale Engineering, even his fellow employees confirmed that he was fiery-tempered. Apart from the forensic evidence Viv's just mentioned, there's all the damage inside the flat.' She looked at the page in the file. 'Broken chairs, smashed coffee table, cracked mirrors, curtains ripped from their rails, and a whacking great hole in the TV screen — all point to a man with an uncontrollable temper.'

'I'm not saying you're wrong, either of you,' Clara responded, 'but Sinclair did give an explanation for the bloodstains on the floor, albeit rather a lame one.'

Viv shook his head. 'Telling the police she cut her hand badly while chopping vegetables sounds more like a convenient excuse than a reasonable explanation. And his tale about the broken furniture is even less credible. He claimed he arrived home, found the place smashed up and his wife gone, taking all her possessions, clothing, shoes and toiletries. I don't think so! That has to be the lamest defence of all time — he dumped them. Besides, whatever the rights and wrongs are about his wife's disappearance, there can be absolutely no doubt regarding her lover's murder.'

Having tried Sinclair and found him guilty by proxy, the trio of detectives looked at Nash, who thought for a moment before responding.

'I'm not for one minute suggesting you're wrong, but something I read in there,' — he pointed to the bulky folder in front of him — 'plus something Tom told us, has raised a contradiction. However, it's probably not significant. Part of it might even be down to a clerical error.'

'Tell us,' Clara urged him.

'I read the report from the prison governor and found it quite intriguing. When he was giving evidence at the hearing into Sinclair's assault on a fellow inmate, part of the wording of his statement caught my attention.'

'Surely that assault is yet more proof of Sinclair's violent temper,' Viv stated to the others, who seemed to agree.

Nash opened the file at the relevant page. 'The governor quoted Sinclair's verbal outburst before he and the other prisoner came to blows. Sinclair shouted, "I love Demetra. I adore her, whatever she's done, and wherever she's gone. I would never harm a hair on her head". That caused me to check Sinclair's other verbal outbursts, and they all occurred after inmates taunted him about Demetra.'

'Why does that intrigue you?' Clara continued her questioning.

'The words Sinclair used were "I love Demetra, I adore her" not, "I loved" or "I adored". Using the present tense like that suggests Sinclair believes his wife is still alive. However, maybe I'm reading too much into it, and like you say, Sinclair is guilty.'

'What was it Tom told you that made you wonder about Sinclair?' Clara asked.

'He told us the weapon used to kill the supposed lover was a Swiss Army knife, while the one with Demetra's blood on was a kitchen utensil. Why change weapons? It seems a bit curious.'

Nash paused, before following another line of thought. 'I just wish there was more insight into Sinclair's character. This file only contains statements from his employers, plus one of his fellow workers, even though they were all questioned. If he's got such a violent temper, how come he never appeared on our radar before his wife's alleged murder? Come to think of it,' he added, 'why is there no mention of the other side of Sinclair's personality?'

'Perhaps there isn't another side. Perhaps that's who he is, nothing more,' Pearce suggested.

'If that's really true, what was it that attracted Demetra to him? I don't think she'd be impressed by someone who was forever blowing a fuse, do you?'

None of Nash's colleagues had an explanation for this apparent anomaly, so he summed their situation up. 'One way or the other, there's nothing we can do at present. We'll have to await Mexican Pete's findings, and if the DNA test results confirm the victim's identity as Demetra Sinclair, we can finally draw the line under this very sad case. Given that the post-mortem and DNA won't be available until next week, we'll have to put this on the back burner. That leaves us free to concentrate on our current caseload.'

Clara summed these up succinctly. 'We've a shoplifting outbreak in Netherdale, a couple of burglaries in Helmsdale and a flasher displaying his tackle in Bishopton.'

'There's a brave man in this cold weather,' Nash commented. 'Any idea who the exhibitionist might be?'

'Not yet. Although we do have a description.' Clara saw Nash's grin, interpreted it correctly, and added hastily, 'I mean a facial description.'

'OK, nothing else?'

'No, his victims tried not to look at his other parts.'

'I didn't mean that. I can understand your fascination with male genitalia, but I was asking if there were any other cases that might be ongoing.'

'Oh . . . er . . . no, I think that's everything.'

Later, when Clara and Nash were alone, she returned to the Sinclair case and asked, 'Do you have reservations about Sinclair's conviction?'

'Not really,' Nash replied. 'It all seems pretty cut and dried, apart from the prison governor's account of what Sinclair shouted at the other inmate. That's a bit of a loose end, and you know I don't like loose ends.' He paused before adding, 'The other item I'm slightly puzzled about is the other man.'

'What other man?'

'If what the gossips suggested is true, why is there no mention of the man Demetra was supposedly having an affair with, the man who supposedly fathered the child she was carrying? Apart from an unidentified male being found dead at Kirk Bolton, and the murder weapon being discovered in Sinclair's flat, we know nothing about him. That seems really strange, because although a couple in an adulterous relationship try to keep the affair secret, there must surely have been occasions where people saw them together. And the headlines this case made would surely cause those witnesses to come forward, don't you think?'

Nash continued his line of thought. 'And there seems to have been no attempt to discover the identity of, or anything about, the dead man in Kirk Bolton. I find that very odd. Surely someone must have known him, or recognized his photograph in the papers and on TV. If he was Demetra's lover and, for example, perhaps a married man, he might have an equally strong motive for killing her — and putting the blame on Sinclair.'

It was all true, Clara acknowledged, and these were points everyone had missed, both in their perusal of the files and during the initial investigation. Mike had raised valid issues, but discovering the mystery man's identity after all this time was likely to prove close to impossible.

CHAPTER FOUR

Although the CSI team, along with a contingent of officers, had returned to Layton Woods that morning, they had little expectation that their renewed search would yield anything positive. They had commenced work at the site of what everyone assumed to be Demetra Sinclair's remains, moving out slowly and carefully. Three sides were surrounded by woodland, areas that had not as yet been thinned out by logging operations. The fourth, most distant border, was the steep, near vertical escarpment alongside Black Fell Foss, where the waterfall tumbled spectacularly over a series of large boulders, making for an impressive sight — and sound.

The task of searching that remote section had been assigned to the CSI team's newest member. Following his qualification, passing his examinations with distinction, Ian Holmes had joined the unit, where he would get his first hands-on, practical experience of forensic work. From his first day in Netherdale, the recruit's surname had inevitably led to him being saddled with the nickname 'Sherlock'.

The team were inching steadily outwards, a task that had taken all morning and into the time slot usually devoted to lunch. Conscious of the limited hours of daylight, their leader had instructed them to complete the task without breaking for refreshment.

Ian Holmes was nearest to the waterfall, and after a prolonged tussle with a dense briar patch that had left him with several superficial wounds, he paused for breath, resting his weight on the thumb-stick he had brought along. As he looked round, the low angle of the sun picked out something half concealed by dead leaves. He used the tip of his stick to move these to one side. Once he had cleared the obstruction, Holmes was able to see the item more clearly.

He bent over to get a closer look. There was a thin ridge, no more than two to three inches in length, underneath which was a small, roughly triangular cavity. Below the cavity he could see several tiny, almost oblong shapes. It took several seconds before the significance of what he was staring at stuck home.

He straightened up, shouting to attract his colleagues' attention. This had no effect, the sound of the gushing waterfall deafening his call for assistance. None of the other officers were facing in his direction, but after a few moments, just as Holmes was considering having to tramp all the way across the site, one of them turned round.

Holmes waved furiously in a desperate attempt to catch the man's gaze. The ploy worked, and the officer shouted to the team leader. 'It looks as if Sherlock's found something. Either that or he's got stuck in a bog. If he's injured himself, we might have to call on Dr Watson.'

All humour vanished rapidly once they crossed the clearing, travelling as quickly as the terrain allowed. They stared at what Holmes had discovered, confirmation of his guess coming once the CSI leader scraped away the surrounding soil and leaves. The thin ridge of a forehead, the triangular nasal cavity, and the teeth from the upper jawbone were distinctive now they were fully exposed.

'Well spotted, Sherlock,' the team leader commended him. 'I'll go back to the main road to summon Nash and his team. The rest of you can mark this location and continue your search. Hopefully we can finish here this afternoon, unless Sherlock or any of you make further discoveries.'

* * *

Nash had just finished his sandwich and was about to head for the coffee machine when his phone rang. Clara glanced round from her desk alongside Nash's office window and saw his expression change. This was obviously not good news. Ending the call, he waved to her to join him. 'I've just had the head of the Forensics team on the phone.'

'Have they finished at Layton Woods already?'

'Not yet, and I've instructed them to continue their search, because they've made a discovery.'

'The murder weapon?'

'No. They've found another skeleton.'

Shock deprived Clara of the ability to speak. Seeing how horrified she was by this news, Nash continued, 'We'll head off out there and supervise things until the pathologist arrives. Better wrap up warm — it could be a long, cold vigil.'

Before setting off, Nash told Clara and the team about an idea that had come to him after learning of the second set of remains. Clara stared at him, her expression a mixture of horror and disbelief, one that Nash noticed she shared with her colleagues.

'Have I got this right, Mike, you think there might be more bodies, so you're going to ask for someone to use ground-penetrating radar to find them?'

'That's pretty much it, yes.'

'Does that also mean you believe this man Sinclair is a serial killer?' Pearce asked.

'That could well be so, but let's not get ahead of our-selves. Jumping to conclusions isn't going to help. There might be an innocent explanation for this body.'

'I don't see how,' Lisa Andrews said.

'It could be another lone hiker who got lost and failed to survive. And unlike the guy who found the first skeleton, nobody sent out a search party.'

'Do you think that's likely?'

'Not really, Clara, but we can't discount any possibilities at this stage, no matter how remote they seem. Going back to Viv's question about Sinclair possibly being a serial killer, if that is the case, we will definitely need GPR. I doubt whether Sinclair will have been satisfied with two victims. That isn't the way serial killers operate. They kill and kill again, time after time, until someone puts a stop to them. However, we're jumping the gun a bit. Until we learn more, all our theorizing is nothing but guesswork.'

* * *

When Nash and Mironova arrived at the end of the track to Layton Woods, they found the glade being used as a convenient car park. The officers were seated in their vehicles drinking coffee. Noticing this, Nash told Clara, 'I said we ought to have bought a Thermos flask.'

The team leader lowered his window and told Nash, 'We've searched the rest of the area and haven't found any more corpses. That doesn't mean there aren't any, but if so, they haven't surfaced. Neither have we found anything resembling a murder weapon.'

If Nash was relieved, it wasn't apparent, either by his expression or his response. 'That's OK as far as it goes, and I'm certainly not decrying your efforts, but I'm not prepared to take any chances. I've asked for someone to be brought in to do a complete sweep of the large clearing using ground-penetrating radar. I'm not discounting the possibility of there being more bodies interred here. In the meantime, if you want to return to base, we'll wait here until the pathologist and his merry men arrive.'

'The GPR equipment sounds a sensible idea to me. If we're not needed, I'd better show you the second set of remains before we go.' He led Nash and Mironova along the track and across the clearing until they were close to the waterfall, and then pointed to the large stake with a strip of cloth attached. 'It was pure luck we found it. Our newest team member stopped for a breather and spotted something odd, which turned out to be part of the skull. Anyway, I'll leave you to it.'

* * *

The Forensics team had only been gone a quarter of an hour when the sound of approaching vehicles signalled the impending arrival of their replacement crew. 'If things continue like this, I might ask the landowners to consider providing toilet facilities here,' Nash said.

The locum pathologist introduced himself. 'Detective Inspector Nash? I'm Doctor Denton. I'm standing in for Professor Ramirez. Will you show me the burial site, please?'

Having viewed what little of the skeleton was visible, Denton issued instructions to the mortuary attendants. 'I want you to uncover the remainder of the bone structure using extreme care. I appreciate that daylight is against us, but we have to ensure every possible part of the skeleton remains intact.'

The attendants had obviously come prepared, Clara thought, unless small garden trowels and paintbrushes were standard issue for mortuary workers. As they watched the team work, Nash explained his theory to Denton, and what he had in mind to test it.

The pathologist looked across to the clearing, before responding. 'That will take a couple of days to complete. Given the terrain, plus the obstacles, and the way those devices work, it will be no easy task.' He paused, before explaining what was behind his insight. 'I've been on a few archaeological digs where GPR machines were at work. It's an interesting, occasionally fascinating process, with a high degree of success, although rarely promising such a gruesome potential outcome as the one you're proposing. However, I can appreciate the necessity, given what has already been discovered.'

As they were nearing the end of their recovery task, Denton told Nash, 'In the light of what you plan to do here, I see little point in conducting a post-mortem on either this or the other skeleton for the moment. That would be pointless if there are further sets of remains to be dealt with.'

'I'm not certain we're going to get much useful information in any event,' Nash said, a trifle despondently.

'There is one fact I can reveal, although I'm not sure if it's of much help,' Denton responded. 'The skeleton in this grave is also that of a female. I'm sure Professor Ramirez will try and extract a sample for DNA analysis, just as he had done with the first set of remains.'

* * *

As they drove back to Helmsdale, Nash and Mironova discussed what the pathologist had told them about the GPR search Nash had planned.

'If the survey is going to take two or more days, we will need someone to remain in attendance throughout, to act as police presence, and to supervise,' Nash said. 'I'm not suggesting the same person stays here all the time. That would be unfair.'

'How do you plan to work it? On a shift basis? I hadn't thought about this before, but it could be tricky if someone was here for too long, with refreshments and toilet breaks to consider.'

'I thought two people to each day would work, that way one does the morning, the other the afternoon, which shouldn't cause too much inconvenience. To help with refreshments, I suggest we call and do some shopping on the way back to the station for Thermos flasks.' Nash paused and grinned. 'As for toilet breaks, there are plenty of trees.'

Back at Helmsdale, there was a message waiting for Nash. It was from Superintendent Fleming and was conveyed by Steve Meadows. 'The Super wanted me to tell you she's engaged the services of an archaeologist based in York who is a specialist in the operation of GPR. The guy's name is Mr Walker, and the good news is that he's prepared to make a start the day after tomorrow, if that's convenient.' Meadows handed Nash a slip of paper. 'Those are his contact details. If you're OK with it, he'll report here first thing and we can direct him to the site.'

'I'll ring him and confirm,' Nash told Clara, as they walked upstairs. 'I'll also ask if his vehicle is a four-wheel drive. There's a fair chance it might be, giving the equipment he needs to carry, and the locations he visits.'

Nash stopped speaking suddenly, causing Clara to glance at him. She saw the brooding expression on his face and remained silent. Something he'd said had obviously sparked an idea. No doubt he would share his train of thought when the time was right.

CHAPTER FIVE

Two days later, Nash and Mironova were in CID early, but they had only just switched the coffee machine on when Meadows rang through to tell them Mr Walker had arrived. Before leaving, Nash told Clara, 'I'll drive back to the main road at one o'clock. If you set off in time, I'll meet you there. You can take the Range Rover back to the clearing and I'll use your car. We can swap vehicles tomorrow. If Mr Walker is OK with the arrangement, I'll get him to meet Lisa at the end of the track in the morning. I'm sure Alan will lend her his Land Rover.'

The first day's search yielded nothing, but midway through the second morning, Lisa phoned Nash to inform him that another skeleton had been revealed by the radar. As Nash walked out of his office, Clara, who had been watching through the window, didn't need his statement to confirm her worst fears. His expression said it all. By the time he told her they were to return to Layton Woods, she was already on her feet, reaching for her coat.

Pausing only to ask DC Pearce to inform the pathologist, and to update Steve Meadows, they set off for the forest. As they approached the turning that marked the end of the track, Clara told Nash, 'I'm beginning to get sick of this road.'

'I agree. Let's hope it's our last visit.'

When they reached Lisa Andrews, she was seated in the Land Rover, staring morosely into the distance. The reason for Lisa's gloomy expression soon became clear.

'Where's the other skeleton?' Nash asked, as she got out of the car.

'I'm sorry to say it isn't just one. Mr Walker has located two. After I phoned you, I went straight back to the clearing, and by the time I arrived he'd already found another. Now we've got four skeletons in total.'

When they reached the clearing and looked across the open area, Clara could see four stakes with strips of cloth attached, marking the locations of the graves. 'Oh dear Lord, this is truly evil,' she muttered.

Nobody disputed her statement, and after inspecting the two new burial sites, the detectives waited in gloomy silence for the pathologist and his team to arrive.

Eventually, having given the matter much thought, Nash spoke. 'I'm going to talk to Jackie about visiting Sinclair in prison,' he told Clara.

The arrival of the pathology unit coincided with Walker's completion of the survey for that day. 'I have to leave,' he told Nash and Mironova. 'I have a lecture to attend this evening in Leeds.'

'Couldn't you give it a miss on this occasion, given what you've found here?' Clara asked.

'That's not possible,' Walker told her, adding, 'the reason is I'm giving the lecture. I also have other work to attend to, so I won't be able to return until later next week, I'm afraid, but I will be able to complete the survey then.'

'Lisa, will you show Dr Denton the new sites while I help Mr Walker with his equipment?' Nash asked. 'And when you've done that, get yourself off home. Make sure Alan pampers you tonight, makes you a nice meal, and opens a good bottle of wine.'

'Drinking wine and getting someone else to cook a meal, that's Mike's favourite therapy,' Clara commented.

The work of uncovering the skeletons was protracted, the team scraping carefully at the wet ground, removing the soil with extreme care. Eventually, both skeletal remains were revealed. After examining them, Denton told Nash, 'I think the post-mortems on all four should be carried out simultaneously. That way, any similarities or anomalies will be more likely to emerge.' He smiled fleetingly. 'I'm afraid that means Professor Ramirez is going to be kept fairly busy on his return from holiday.'

Nash winced. 'If he's unhappy about it, I'm sure he'll make his feelings known — to me, probably in Spanish, and undoubtedly rudely. If there's nothing more we can do here, we'll leave you to it. Thanks for your help, Dr Denton.'

'There is one more thing you should know. The final set of remains is different to the others, which might make your job easier — or harder.'

'In what way?'

'The last one we uncovered is male — and he was shot.'

* * *

As they reached the end of the track and turned onto the main road, Nash said they should go to HQ rather than returning to Helmsdale. 'We need to update Jackie Fleming and the chief on the situation back there, and also get them onside with the plan to interview Sinclair.'

When they reached Netherdale their luck was in. Superintendent Fleming had just ended a meeting with Ruth Edwards, the chief constable. One glance at the visitors' expressions as they entered her office told the chief and Jackie that they weren't the bearers of good news.

'I hope you're not here to tell us your GPR man has found another set of remains,' Jackie commented.

'No, not exactly — he's actually located two more skeletons. The pathology crew is removing them as we speak,' Nash responded.

Clara reckoned Nash could have detonated a stun grenade within the confines of the chief constable's office with less effect. It was a long, protracted silence before anyone spoke.

'Where is this all going to end?' Edwards asked, rhetorically.

'Unfortunately, the archaeologist doing the GPR survey had to leave early today, so he hasn't completely covered the ground. He will be back next week. So at the moment we can't be sure there are no more bodies buried there.'

'What's all this GPR costing us, Mike? You know what the budget is like.' Jackie was concerned.

Nash quoted some figures, causing the chief a sharp intake of breath before she said, 'Sorry, Mike. Without knowing how long this exercise is going to take, I can't sanction that. It was a good idea. But no — use the cadaver dogs.'

'As you wish, ma'am. I'll sort that out.'

'Were the remains he's found in the same state as the others?' the chief asked.

'If you mean are they all completely skeletal, the answer is yes, but with one huge difference. Doctor Denton informed us that one of the skeletons is that of a male.'

'And are you thinking along the same lines as me?' the chief continued, when she'd recovered from this further shock. 'Do you believe that far from simply having murdered his wife and her lover in a fit of jealous rage, Sinclair is actually a psychopathic serial killer? If that's the case, perhaps having him imprisoned when we did has prevented him continuing his killing spree. It's terribly tragic for his victims, but maybe we should pray that the body count doesn't go even higher.'

'If the first body is that of his wife, then I think Sinclair being a serial killer seems the logical conclusion to draw,' Nash agreed. 'And part of the reason for our visit is to ask you to arrange a production order for Clara and me to visit Frankland Prison in order to question him, and to confront him with what we've found. It would have to be a formal recorded interview, so Sinclair should be advised to have a solicitor present. That might delay our visit, but it can't be helped. I'd also like to speak with the prison governor while we're there.'

'That sounds reasonable.' She turned to the superintendent. 'Jackie, will you set to work making the arrangements immediately? Any problems, refer them to me.' Jackie nodded and the chief turned back to Nash. 'Have you anything else to tell us? Did the new discoveries yield any usable evidence, or is that hoping for too much?'

'All we know from what Dr Denton told us is that he believes them to be reasonably young, but he can't swear to that. He's suggested the post-mortems should be carried out in tandem when Mexican Pete returns, which I think is the sensible course of action. We'll only know the extent of what we're facing when the entire site has been checked.'

'I think four is plenty — in fact, I reckon it's more than enough,' Ruth Edwards muttered.

Before they left, Jackie Fleming asked, 'Should we involve the media now the situation has changed?'

Nash responded immediately, 'I'd advise against that for several reasons. I certainly wouldn't want the news to get out until after we've interviewed Sinclair. Even then, I don't think it would be wise for them to get hold of the story until the search of that crime scene, plus the PMs and DNA tests have been completed. I don't know much about the area, but for all we know, Layton Woods might have been a Saxon burial ground, or the place where Druid extremists made human sacrifice to the gods. Alternatively, having fled London, Jack the Ripper could have moved to Helmsdale and continued his killing spree in this area.'

'Mike, I don't think you're taking this seriously enough.' Although Ruth Edwards reprimanded him, her censure was accompanied by a smile.

'I'm merely pointing out that those graves might have nothing to do with Sinclair. So it would be unwise to condemn him out of hand.'

'OK, we'll hold off from informing the media for the time being. Let's just see what Sinclair has to say.'

Nash's decision to involve the chief constable had obviously proved effective, because late on Friday afternoon he received the news he'd been hoping for, much earlier than expected. He strolled into the main office. 'Viv, you and Lisa are in charge on Monday. Clara and I have been sent to prison.'

There was a moment's stunned silence before Clara twigged. 'You've had the go-ahead to visit Sinclair, haven't you? That's come through quickly.'

'Yes, and it's bad news for you, because you'll have to drag yourself out of bed early. It's quite a drive to Durham and we have to be there, conduct the interview, and leave before lunchtime. We're also going to talk to the prison governor.'

'What's the purpose of speaking to the governor?'

'I want him to confirm the accuracy of his account of what Sinclair shouted during his clash with the other inmate. Plus, a bit of background into Sinclair's demeanour during his time there.'

'Why do you have to do it in the morning?' Lisa asked.

'To avoid being seen during visiting hours. If other inmates or their visitors recognize us, they might get the wrong impression, believing the person we're speaking to is a snitch. That could have very unfortunate consequences. I must admit I didn't expect things to come through so quickly, and before the PMs. But Sinclair waived his right to a solicitor, which no doubt speeded the process up no end. One thing we will need is to record the interview. Viv, give Frankland a call and see if they have one in their interview room. If not, get permission for us to take one in. There's probably one at HQ.'

'We don't need one, Mike,' Clara told him. 'I have a recording facility on my mobile phone.'

'That won't do, Clara. We must let Sinclair have a copy. Otherwise, he could claim we've distorted the facts.'

CHAPTER SIX

On Monday morning, as they were driving to Durham, Clara posed the question that had been troubling her all weekend. 'Do you think Sinclair will reverse his decision not to have a legal representative in attendance when he hears what we want to speak to him about?'

'I certainly hope not. I also don't want him to adopt the "no comment" routine. Some people are too dense to realize that if we aren't certain whether they're innocent or guilty, offering "no comment" simply convinces us we've got the right person. If either of those scenarios happens with Sinclair, we'll have had a wasted journey, except to confirm what we already suspect, that he could be a serial killer.'

Clara stared at the prison walls as Nash manoeuvred the Range Rover into a parking spot. If the stark, drab stone walls had been designed specifically to deter inmates from reoffending, she thought, the architect had certainly earned his money.

After presenting their documentation and passing through security checks, they were taken to the governor's office. There they found him, along with another man he introduced as the prison doctor, who, in addition to his medical qualifications, the governor explained, was also a practicing psychologist.

Nash informed them a body had been found which they believed might be Sinclair's missing wife. Having ascertained the accuracy of the governor's account of Sinclair's verbal and physical encounter with the other prisoner, Nash asked him his opinion of Sinclair and his overall behaviour.

'I have to admit to being puzzled by him. He is normally quiet, unobtrusive, and causes little bother. The only times he's flared up are when someone provokes him by mentioning what he did, or refers to his wife. I was convinced his silence was down to guilt, but now I'm not sure. I've had to deal with several psychopaths and a couple of serial killers during my time here, and he is nothing like them. However, I'm not the expert, so I'll let my colleague have his say.'

The doctor's assessment tallied with that of the governor, and he added, 'Sinclair is difficult, because he won't allow anyone near him. I'm speaking figuratively. It's as if he's resolutely keeping his personal life private. I also think he's determined to keep his wife's memory alive, even if she's dead. I got reports from several officers who had witnessed Sinclair reading a bundle of old letters he keeps in his cell. When I challenged him about them, trying to get a reaction, he clammed up and refused to say a word.'

Nash looked from the doctor to the governor, before asking, 'What would your reaction be if I was to tell you we've found more bodies buried in the same location, which we strongly believe to be the victims of the same killer?'

Their reactions were obvious, by the shock and disbelief in their expressions. 'I assume you think Sinclair is responsible for all the murders?' the governor asked. 'That hardly tallies with what we've just told you. And he hasn't been convicted as a serial killer. Had that been the case, he would be bragging, telling anyone who would listen. Maybe that's why he keeps quiet, to avoid discovery.'

Nash nodded in response to the governor's question, telling him, 'I wanted your opinion of Sinclair before you were aware of the new situation, thereby avoiding any bias. Thank you for your input, but I think we ought now to see what he has to say when faced with further potential murder charges.'

'One more thing.' The governor smiled at Clara as he explained. 'In light of what you've just told me, I want one of my officers in the room with you — just for your protection.'

* * *

Nash and Mironova were escorted into a private room, where they were able to set up the in-house recorder in preparation for the interview. A few minutes later, a prison officer ushered the inmate into the room. Despite the passage of time since he'd posed for the mugshot on his file, Clara had no problem in recognizing Nicholas Sinclair.

Clara's task, as Nash outlined beforehand, was to act as an observer. This was a routine they had adopted over the years with great success.

The first thing Clara noticed was the wary, apprehensive expression on Sinclair's face. Was this because he'd already guessed what Nash was about to reveal, she wondered?

Nash signalled her to make the opening announcement, and was about to question Sinclair, when the prisoner forestalled him. 'Do you know you're the first visitors I've had since I entered this place fifteen years ago? That hasn't worried me, but I hope you're here to bring me good news. I assume this is about Demi? Have you found her? Is she safe and well? If that's so, can the murder charge be dropped?'

'That isn't exactly why we're here. Before I explain, I understand you waived the right to have a legal representative present at this interview. Is that still the case?'

'Yes, I don't need a lawyer. They were no good to me back then, and I doubt they'd be any better now. Besides, I can't afford one.'

'Very well. In that case, I must inform you we have found skeletal remains in Layton Woods. We believe they may belong to your wife, and that you buried her there after you stabbed her to death.'

Clara saw the colour drain from Sinclair's florid complexion, and was shocked to see tears in his eyes as he said, 'No, no, no.' It was several moments before he spoke again. 'Demi's dead? Are you sure? Is it definitely her?'

'Now that is a very interesting question, Mr Sinclair. Why do you think a set of remains discovered in that particular location might not be those of your wife?' After a fractional pause, Nash continued, 'Did you think they might belong to one of the other murder victims you buried there?'

The silence this time was even longer, before Sinclair said, 'I don't understand. I haven't buried anyone — in Layton Woods or anywhere. And I didn't kill that man found at Kirk Bolton. I said all that sixteen years ago, but nobody believed me, so I'll say it again now.' Sinclair raised his voice, his tone matching his complexion, which was now burning with anger, 'I didn't kill Demi. I didn't kill that man they said was her lover, which is all rubbish. I didn't kill anyone. Is that clear?'

'The evidence would tend to contradict that statement.' Nash's voice, by comparison was gentle, relaxed and encouraging. 'What we really need from you is to give us the identities of the other three people you killed and buried in Layton Woods, where they've been rotting and uncared for all these years.'

Clara took a sideways glance at the prison officer who had been looking bored by the whole procedure until that point, but was now staring in astonished disbelief at Nash.

The long, agonized silence was broken eventually by Sinclair. The anger had left his voice, to be replaced by infinite sadness as he told the detectives, 'I have nothing further to say. It's clear I would be wasting my breath, because whatever I say, you won't believe me. Nobody believes me. They never have, right from the start of this unholy mess.'

Despite Nash pressing him, using various tactics from gentle coaxing to hectoring demands, Sinclair remained silent. At the end of the interview, Nash told Sinclair, possibly in a final attempt to goad him, 'Why don't you tell us what we need to know? The worst that can happen to you is a whole-of-life sentence. We don't hand out sentences of nine hundred and ninety-nine years, like they do in America. It might even go easier on you if you cooperate. If you tell us, it would let the relatives of those people you slaughtered get closure.'

That hadn't worked, because Sinclair had the last word, and what he said merely caused Clara bewilderment. 'You told me the worst I would face is a whole-of-life sentence,' he told Nash. 'But I think you're wrong. If DNA proves one of those skeletons is Demi's, then I already have a whole-of-life sentence. Without Demi, my existence is totally without meaning.'

Again, Clara saw the glint of tears in Sinclair's eyes.

As they left the prison, she was still unsure whether Sinclair's obvious surprise on learning of the other skeletons was due to him being unaware of their existence, or because he hadn't expected them to be discovered.

'What do you make of everything that went on in there?' Clara asked, when they were back on the road.

'I'm not sure what to make of it, to be honest,' Nash responded. 'I went there convinced I was about to come face to face with an evil, psychopathic serial killer. But now I'm beginning to wonder if Nicholas Sinclair is the victim of a huge miscarriage of justice.'

'Why do you say that?'

'There were a few small indications, which, when you string them together might be meaningful — or might be misleading. There was the way he spoke about his wife, for one thing, plus his reaction when we told him we'd found a body that might be hers. Added to that, there was his shock when I mentioned the other corpses. Now Sinclair might be a damned good actor and liar, but I don't believe he was making it up. And finally, what he said when we were leaving seemed to come straight from the heart.'

'You mean that bit about life without her being mean-ingless? That aside, what did you mean when you mentioned the way he spoke about her?'

'He referred to her throughout as "Demi", which is clearly his pet name for her. It's obvious that's a term of endearment, of continuing affection, which contradicts everything we've been told about their relationship. What he said when we were leaving seemed to show he was distraught at the idea he might never see her again.'

'I noticed a couple of times that he was holding back tears, which shocked me, I admit. And it conflicts with what we've been told. Such as rumours about Sinclair being enraged by his wife's affair, and her expecting another man's child.'

They continued in silence for a few moments before Nash exclaimed, 'I'm a blithering idiot.'

'I certainly won't argue with the description.'

'It was something you said that sparked an idea, which might prove pivotal in deciding whether Demetra Sinclair was buried in Layton Woods, or whether her body is somewhere else. I'm sorry, but we might have to revisit the woods. So will Mexican Pete and a CSI team, and we might be there for quite a while.'

'Why would we have to go back?'

'To search for something we didn't find first time round.'

'Sorry, Mike, you've lost me. Not for the first time, let me say.'

'OK, let's assume one of those skeletons is that of Sinclair's wife.'

'That's pretty much what we've believed all along, so what of it?'

'If that proves to be correct, what didn't we find? Think about it.'

Clara pondered the question without success. 'OK, I give in, tell me.'

'Go back to the information we were given at the start of all this. To what we know for certain about Demetra Sinclair at the time of her disappearance.'

'Only that her husband was angry with her because she was pregnant with this other man's child. Why is that important?'

'It's crucial if her body proves to be one of those found in the woods. Surely, if everything transpired as we supposed from Sinclair's trial, there would have been foetal bones among the remains, wouldn't there?'

'Oh, I never thought of that.'

'There are three reasons I can think for them not being present. One, she suffered a miscarriage. Two, she had an abortion. The third, and the scariest possibility, is that none of those skeletons is Demetra's, which tallies with what Sinclair said as we were ending the interview. He's convinced his wife isn't among the victims, or he knows there's another burial site elsewhere we don't know about.' Nash paused before adding a grim postscript, 'And if Demetra Sinclair is buried in another location, she might well not be alone.'

Clara shivered, a reflex reaction to Nash's macabre idea, before asking, 'Is that everything? Or are you about to have another flash of gruesome inspiration? And what did you mean when you said we might have to return to Layton Woods with Mexican Pete and CSI?'

'Depending on the results of the DNA, if one of the females is Demetra Sinclair, we may need to sift through the site where her skeleton was found. To examine every morsel of soil where she lay, in order to ensure we haven't missed some tiny fragments of foetal bone. That would probably be the best indicator of who the child's father is.'

* * *

Back at Helmsdale, Nash's first task was to phone and update Superintendent Fleming on the outcome of their interview with Sinclair. Having reported their frustrated efforts to discover any fresh information, he broached the theory that had come to him during the return journey.

His opening remark left her temporarily speechless with surprise. 'You think we might need to return to Layton Woods? Is this to do with the possibility of there being more bodies?'

'We will be needed when we go in with the dogs, but this is something different, dependent on the DNA results. If, as we suspect, one of those skeletons is Demetra Sinclair, there would be tiny foetal bones that might have been missed. CSI should be able to find them.'

Nash didn't think this was the appropriate time to mention his alternative suggestion, that the lack of foetal bones might suggest Demetra Sinclair had been buried elsewhere.

'But surely if we have confirmation from DNA, that won't be necessary?'

'Not specifically, but it would confirm if Sinclair actually was the father. Alternatively, it could prove to be the dead man at Kirk Bolton who was her supposed lover.'

Jackie Fleming agreed with Nash's rationale, her only negative comment being, 'I'm OK with your idea, but getting Ruth to sign off the additional expenditure might be a bit of a problem.'

Later that afternoon, having been advised the chief would sanction the expense if the DNA results were positive, Nash phoned the pathologist to inform them of the possible plan of action.

Having enquired about Ramirez' holiday, Nash told him, 'I believe one of the female skeletons might not be complete.'

For once, Ramirez didn't indulge his sarcastic trait. 'Why do you think that?'

'When Demetra Sinclair vanished, she was pregnant. Her husband's jealousy over her alleged affair and its outcome provided the motive for her murder. However, now we have three more sets of remains, the new theory gaining popularity in this office is that Sinclair is a deranged, psychopathic serial killer who went off the rails, murdered his wife and her lover, then set about slaughtering other unfortunate victims.'

Something in Nash's tone and the way he phrased the last part of his statement caused the pathologist to suggest, 'I take it you don't hold with the general opinion about this man Sinclair?'

'No, because Clara and I interviewed him in prison this morning, and his attitude and demeanour are a world away from anything so abnormal. Clara swears she saw tears in his eyes when he spoke about his wife, which is hardly typical serial killer behaviour.'

'And I take it you want me to chase the DNA results. Do we have a record on file?'

'Yes, taken from the house at the time of her disappearance.'

'And I understand you believe there could be foetal bones still remaining within one of those burial sites?'

'That's correct, Professor, and I want to ensure that any such evidence is found. If not, we could be faced with an even more ghastly prospect, that there might be another burial site we haven't as yet discovered, and that site could contain yet more corpses.'

'*Madre de Dios*, you don't do things by halves, do you, Mike?'

'Don't blame me, Don Pedro, blame Nicholas Sinclair.'

Nash put down the phone and went into the general office where Clara was talking to Viv and Lisa, telling them, 'Unless we find something in Layton Woods, there might be another site we don't know of yet. What concerns me is how many more victims may be lying in that place, and we've no identity for those already in the mortuary. It makes me wonder . . .' she stopped speaking abruptly, causing her colleagues to stare at her. After a few seconds mulling over the idea that had dawned on her, Clara turned to Viv.

'Viv, get on the computer and bring up a list of all missing persons from our area between sixteen and twenty-one years ago. I can't believe none of us thought of this before now.'

'That could be a lot,' he pointed out.

'Stick within a five-mile area of Netherdale, that's most central, and see what you can find.'

Nash heard the conversation and said, 'That's sound thinking, Clara. And I'll be interested to see that list. I'd issue a word of caution, though. I wouldn't want us to approach any relatives with questions in case we give them false hope. It could cause immense disappointment if the victims don't turn out to be their kinfolk. On a separate subject,' he added, 'I won't be in the office on Monday. Mexican Pete has scheduled the PMs for then, and they'll probably take all day, so I'll go prepared with a flask and sandwiches.'

'I don't know how you can think of food while you're inside a mortuary,' Lisa said.

'I won't. I'll go sit in my car and eat there.'

CHAPTER SEVEN

When Mironova pulled into the station car park on Monday morning, she was surprised to see Nash's Range Rover in situ. Having greeted Steve Meadows, she headed upstairs. Nash was sitting in his office reading a file, a mug of coffee on the desk close by.

'I thought this was mortuary day?' Clara asked. 'Has something else happened?'

'Good morning, Clara. I was supposed to be there, but I got a call yesterday afternoon from Mexican Pete, changing the schedule.'

'Why did he do that?'

'Yesterday he had to go to examine a corpse. It was a home death, and it turned out there was nothing suspicious about the incident. However, while he was waiting at the mortuary for his attendants to bring the body in, he whiled away his time by looking at the skeletons recovered from Layton Woods, and in the process he noticed something he wasn't happy about.'

'What?'

'I don't know. He didn't go into details. All he said was, "There are certain anomalies that concern me, so I'm deferring the PMs until such time as I've sought and obtained a second opinion, and that could take a while." As a result, the case will have to be put on hold, unless there are further developments. Even that list you got Viv to produce will be of little value until the post-mortems have been completed.'

'What were you studying so intensely when I arrived, if it wasn't connected to the Layton Woods murders?'

Nash grinned. 'It was the latest chapter in the adventures of Free Willy.'

Clara was baffled, trying to picture a killer whale in Helmsdale, without success. 'Free Willy? What are you talking about?'

'That's Viv's nickname for the Bishopton flasher. The report was compiled by Lisa. According to her, he made three guest appearances before the weekend, shifting his exploits between the Mitre Hotel car park, the entrance to Good Buys supermarket, and near the ATM at Shires Bank. Given the cold weather, I hope he doesn't get frostbite in his extremity.'

'Is that all you're concerned about, the state of his member?'

'No, I was pondering an idea when you came in, one that might enable us to identify him.'

Clara eyed him dubiously. 'What was the idea, or shouldn't I ask?'

'He chose to display his manhood to a woman who had been using the ATM, and apparently, as she turned round, he was standing directly behind her, letting it all hang out. At first she thought he was another person waiting to use the machine, but then she noticed that he was improperly dressed.'

'That was politely put — for you. But I still don't see how it helps us identify him.'

'If we're lucky, the ATM security camera might have captured an image of his face.'

'Let's hope you're right, and the camera was pointing at head height, not lower down.'

'Get Lisa to contact the bank, or the company that operates the ATM, and see if she can obtain a usable image. Viv might be able to work his computer magic, making use of that fancy facial recognition software that was installed a couple of years ago. If we're unable to obtain a match that way, we might have to show his photo around Bishopton, and if all else fails, we might get the *Netherdale Gazette* to print it. Between all three we should be able to nail the suspect.'

* * *

Although the detectives didn't expect anything to happen until after the pathologist had conducted the post-mortems, there was a sensational and worrying development on Wednesday morning.

When Nash returned from walking Teal, their black Labrador, Alondra greeted him with the news that he had missed two phone calls. 'Maybe you ought to take your mobile with you when you take madam on her morning constitutional.'

Nash shook his head. 'No way am I going to develop bad habits like that. Who rang me this early?'

'One call was Viv, the other was the chief constable, and they both wanted you to ring back as a matter of urgency. They didn't explain why.'

'Only one way to find out, I suppose.' Nash picked up his mobile, pressed the short code for the chief's direct line, and waited.

When Ruth Edwards answered, she didn't waste time on pleasantries. 'I assume you haven't seen a paper, or had the TV or radio on this morning, Mike?'

'No, that's not part of the routine in this house. I guess something has happened.'

'To put it politely, the excreta has collided with the ventilator, big time.'

Nash grinned at Ruth's euphemism. 'In what way?'

'The media has somehow discovered the body count from Layton Woods and are having a field day with it. Almost every newspaper, TV channel, and radio station is using it as their lead story. They're speculating, and have got Sinclair down as a serial killer. I'm already being pestered for comments by our press officer. I've put him off so far, but it's clearly not going to work for long. I'm open to suggestions as to how to handle it, including taking the next available flight to Papua New Guinea or the Australian outback.'

Nash smiled. 'Are you able to leave contacting a travel agent until I've had chance to give it some thought? I'll phone you as soon as I reach the office, always providing I can get through the door.'

'Please do, Mike. I'll have Jackie with me. We need a strategy that will keep the bloodhounds off our backs.'

During the journey to Helmsdale, Nash touched base with Viv Pearce, who wanted to know if he'd heard the news.

On arrival, aware of the potential for the media massing at the front of the building, Nash parked at the adjoining fire station, and accessed the police station via the linked corridor and went straight to his office. When Pearce arrived shortly afterwards, having battled through the press at the main entrance, he saw Nash was on the phone, and raised his hand in greeting. In return, he received a signal indicating the need for coffee. Pearce grinned and headed for the rest room and the coffee machine.

As Nash spoke to the chief constable he heard his voice echoing. Clearly the call was on speakerphone so Jackie Fleming could hear both sides of the conversation.

Ruth Edwards told him, 'I think we should get the press officer to inform the media that we have recovered bodies in Layton Woods. That's merely confirming what someone has already told them. I think he should also tell them until such time as we've received post-mortem results, we refuse to speculate as to how long those bodies have been there, and what the cause of death was.'

'I don't believe they'll be satisfied with that,' Nash said.

'It isn't our business to feed the media's ghoulish appetite. If they don't like it, they'll have to lump it. I don't think we should join in with what is clearly a witch hunt against Sinclair.'

'I agree, ma'am. OK, there is a possibility he *is* a serial killer, but the more chance I've had to think about it, the less convinced I am of that.'

'What led you to that line of thought?' Jackie Fleming asked.

'Several factors strung together, really, number one among them being the lack of evidence.' Nash grinned as he heard a spluttering sound at the other end of the line.

'What on earth do you mean, lack of evidence? I'd have thought there was a mountain of it, or isn't four bodies sufficient for you?'

Ignoring the chief's snide remark, Nash told them, 'First of all, we don't yet know if Demetra Sinclair *is* one of those bodies. Until we do, we can't put Sinclair in the frame for anything. At his trial, part of the prosecution's case centred on his car, or one identical, seen driving into Layton Woods at the time she disappeared. The assumption is clearly that one of the bodies in the clearing is Demetra Sinclair, but until we have the DNA results back we can't be certain. She might be buried elsewhere, and unless we get confirmation, she might not have been in Layton Woods for the past sixteen years. So, if Sinclair didn't bury her there, how can we be certain the four skeletons are *his* victims? Alternatively, could they be something else entirely, like people who died during the Great Plague, and were buried in a remote place because people at the time believed they still carried infection, even after death? I Understand it's quite difficult to gauge the age of a skeleton after years in the ground.'

'What other lack of evidence are you referring to, or is that all?' Ruth Edwards responded.

'No, it isn't everything. There is one more item that has concerned me ever since I read Sinclair's original case file. It didn't mean much at the time, but with the discovery of four bodies it has now become far more significant.'

'And that is?'

'Where was the blood? Where was the DNA? And for that matter, where was the shovel?'

'Sorry, Mike, you've got both of us baffled — not for the first time.' Nash heard the acid edge to Edwards' voice.

Nash continued, 'It was alleged that Sinclair stabbed his wife's lover found at Kirk Bolton. There can be little doubt of that, given the knife found at his flat. However, he was also convicted of killing his wife, putting her in his car, driving her to Layton Woods, where he dug a grave in that clearing and left her there. The new allegations have him doing the same thing to three other people. If that's true, there should have been gallons of blood in his flat, or inside his car, plus bucketsful of DNA, a knife to kill them with, and a shovel to dig the graves. None of that was found. The only evidence found was the Swiss Army knife used to kill the alleged lover, plus some blood in the kitchen. Blood that belonged to Demetra, and could have been from an accident, as Sinclair claimed. The only DNA of Demetra's was on the car passenger seat, where you would expect it to be, along with strands of her hair. Sinclair and his wife lived in a second-storey flat, without even a window box, so they didn't find any gardening equipment, even a trowel, let alone anything bigger. Why would they? The couple didn't have a garden, so what use would he have for a shovel?'

There was a prolonged silence as Edwards and Fleming assessed what Nash had told them, essentially driving a massive hole through their theory of Sinclair's guilt.

'You said the lack of evidence was number one in your list of doubts. What was number two?' Ruth asked, eventually.

'This is based on Sinclair's attitude, the things he said about his wife, the way he spoke when he mentioned her name, and what he shouted in the heat of the moment during that prison brawl. All those, plus his reaction when we interviewed him, lead me to believe he either knows, or hopes, Demetra is still alive, as did his final statement before Clara and I left the prison. That alone damned near convinced me we'd got it all wrong.'

'Why, what did he say?'

'I'd been goading him. Telling him the worst that could happen, even if he confessed to all four murders, would be a whole-of-life sentence. He replied that if Demetra, who he referred to throughout as Demi, was dead, he was already serving a whole-of-life sentence, because without her, his existence was meaningless. That shows me how much he loves her, whether she's alive or dead.'

After another long silence, Ruth Edwards replied, 'What you've told us hasn't convinced me one way or the other. I still hold to the theory that Sinclair could be a serial killer, but I'm prepared to accept that I could be wrong.'

'Bear in mind the two advantages I have over you in this instance,' Nash cautioned her.

'What advantages?'

'I've met Sinclair, accused him of dreadful crimes, and looked into his eyes as he answered me. That's another reason I don't believe him to be guilty.'

The chief constable mulled this over. 'In view of what you've said, and the doubts you've cast, I'll go along with your idea as to how to handle the media, at least until we get the DNA and PM results on all four victims. Have you any thoughts as to how you can make progress in the meantime?'

'I believe we should go back over the original investigation, look at questioning witnesses again, and also digging into Sinclair's background.'

'That sounds like a sensible course of action.'

Before Ruth ended the call, Jackie Fleming asked Nash, 'You said there were two advantages you have over us that cause you to doubt Sinclair's guilt. What was the second one?'

'The advantage is I've been to Layton Woods. In the original investigation, someone mentioned a car identical to Sinclair's spotted heading into the woods. That might have been a courting couple seeking privacy off the main road, but I don't think it was Sinclair driving to that clearing. The track is OK for the first half mile or so, but beyond there you need a four-wheel drive vehicle, not a Mini Cooper like Sinclair's.

If he did kill those people and bury them there, he certainly didn't use his own car.'

'Is that track the only way to reach the clearing?'

'I believe so — unless you own a helicopter, or erect a bridge to cross Black Fell Foss.'

CHAPTER EIGHT

In CID, the main topic of conversation was speculation as to how the media had latched onto there being four bodies recovered from Layton Woods. And, from there, had branded Sinclair as a serial killer.

It was Nash who came up with the most logical explanation. 'Accepting the fact that, despite their many undoubted talents, our friends in the media are not blessed with the gift of clairvoyance, I think the answer has to be a combination of gossip and greed.'

Clara groaned. 'Would you care to explain that, Mike, and preferably in simple terms?'

'There is a chance that the leak came from a member of the mortuary crew, but I think it's far more likely to have been from the prison.'

Pearce frowned. 'How could that have happened? I thought your interview with Sinclair was conducted in private.'

'The governor insisted there was an officer in the room. Discounting the possibility that the governor or prison doctor let the cat out of the bag, one of the things Clara noticed was that the officer seemed bored with the proceedings throughout the interview. That was until I mentioned the number of bodies we'd recovered. Apparently, after that he was all ears, listening intently to every word.'

Nash furthered his line of thought. 'The way it got transmitted might have started out innocently enough. Let's say the officer and one of his colleagues were standing around, watching an inmate mopping the corridor. If there wasn't any football on TV that night they might have been short of something to talk about, so our friend could have told his mate about our visit. Something along the lines of, "You'll never guess what I heard this morning. We have Sinclair in here for murdering his wife and her lover, but it turns out he's done at least three more. The coppers who were talking to him said they've dug up four skeletons in some forest or other. I never had Sinclair down as a serial killer, but we're going to have to watch him carefully now we know what he's capable of".' Nash shrugged. 'While they're busy gossiping, the inmate wielding the mop is listening to every word.'

'I get the gossip bit, but where does greed come into your theory?' Clara asked.

'Again this is all down to supposition, but what if the mop wielder's wife visited him the following day, and moaned about how hard it is to make ends meet with the main breadwinner locked away, unable to provide for her and their eleven children. That gives him an idea, so he tells her to go home, phone one of the tabloids, and get them to shell out as much as possible for an exclusive, then ring the other newspapers, plus the main TV channels, anyone prepared to pay big money for the story.'

'That sounds feasible enough,' Lisa commented, 'apart from the eleven children bit.'

'Of course, it doesn't have to be Mr Mop who gave the media the heads-up. Either he or one of the warders could have mentioned it elsewhere. When word got around, someone with an eye to the main chance might have jumped on the bandwagon, seen the opportunity to earn big money and snatched it. That sort of tasty titbit would have spread like wildfire. Prisons are notorious gossip shops.'

'I bow to your superior knowledge of life behind bars,' Clara told him. Once the amusement died down, she asked, 'Why are you discounting the governor or the doctor as the source of these revelations?'

'Because we didn't tell them how many bodies had been found, and the media reports are quite specific, numbering them as four.'

'This speculation is all very well, but it doesn't get us anywhere, so my question is, what are we to do? How do we go about finding justice for Sinclair's victims?'

'Always assuming they *are* Sinclair's victims,' Nash replied.

The two detective constables, who had not been party to either Nash's conversations with Mironova or his phone call to the chief constable, stared at him in astonishment. It was a while before Pearce spoke, the incredulity apparent in his voice, 'You surely don't believe Sinclair to be innocent, in spite of all the evidence, do you?'

'I'm certainly not discounting the possibility, Viv. To be honest, I'm not convinced one way or the other. To begin with I was absolutely certain of his guilt, but the more familiar I've become with the case, and having met Sinclair, the greater my doubts have become.'

Nash outlined his thinking, but at the end, realizing he'd failed to convince either Viv or Lisa, he asked, 'If you're still certain Sinclair committed at least five murders, would you care to produce incontestable evidence of his guilt for the four in the woods?'

The long silence that followed told Nash that he'd proved his point. 'From now on,' he told his colleagues, 'I think it would be better for us to approach this with open minds, rather than being swayed by the original convictions — or the flights of fancy conjured up by the media.'

'OK, Mike, accepting that, I return to my original question, which was, where do we go from here?' Clara asked.

'We go back to the beginning and work from there. We ignore all pre-conceived notions and start from scratch.

Having read Sinclair's file, I still know little or nothing about the man, his early life, parents, siblings, other relations, friends, academic record, or other aspects of his personality. Let's put that enormous lack of information right, and at the same time do exactly the same with his wife, although that won't be easy, as she was Romanian.'

Nash looked across at Pearce. 'Much of that is going to be down to you and your computer skills, Viv. But there is also going to be some legwork involved, such as conducting interviews. Clara and I will handle that side of things, which will leave Lisa free to collate the information from all sources.' He grinned at DC Andrews. 'When she can spare the time from trying to arrange a date with Free Willy, that is.'

The gesture Lisa Andrews gave in response was both vulgar and highly insubordinate.

Nash's plan to research Sinclair's background had to be put on hold, however, when further information caused them to rethink their opinion on Sinclair, and to return to Layton Woods. As Nash was heading for his office, his phone rang. He answered it, and Clara could tell he was shocked by the caller's comments as he ended the call, before picking up the handset again. He rang off and returned to his colleagues.

'The call was from Mexican Pete,' he told them. 'He's received the DNA results. None of the skeletons is a match for Demetra Sinclair. In fact, there is no match on file for any of the victims. I've informed the chief and she said it places great importance on getting back on site, because if we fail to find any more corpses in that clearing, we're going to have to search all of Layton Woods.'

'That could take forever, surely?'

'It could have done, but the burial site would have to be in open ground, and there aren't too many such places. However, the chief has already refused to allow bringing in Mr Walker and his GPR, citing the cost, and said to call in the cadaver dogs. The DNA results have merely strengthened both hers and Jackie Fleming's conviction that Nicholas

Sinclair was a psychopathic serial killer who had buried not only his wife, but an untold number of victims in Layton Woods. They are basing this solely on the alleged sighting of his car. There again, he *has* been found guilty of killing her supposed lover. Our priority now is to find Demetra's body, if it is there. I'm leaving you in charge tomorrow, and probably the day after, as I'm going to watch the dogs.'

'Why don't we take it in turns, like we did before?'

'This time it shouldn't take as long, unless of course there's been foliage growing over the site. Besides which, I wouldn't want you to miss out on the chance to meet up with Free Willy.'

* * *

It was almost lunchtime on the first day of Nash's forest vigil when Clara's mobile rang. She glanced at the screen, then answered the call. 'Mike, does this mean what I think?'

Her forebodings were proved correct by Nash's reply. 'I'm afraid so, Clara. Will you phone Mexican Pete? We need him and his crew out here. We've two more skeletons for his mortuary drawers, both from within the first clearing. We've marked the position, and we're now moving on.'

After supervising the removal of the remains, Nash returned to Helmsdale, and his colleagues were relieved to see his cheerful expression. 'We've finished all the sites without finding any more,' he told them. 'Now all we have to do is prove whether those six people were killed by Sinclair — or by someone else.'

He headed for his office and sat down wearily, thanked Viv for the much-needed coffee, and phoned HQ. The chief constable was unavailable, so he told Superintendent Fleming what the new search had revealed. 'There are two more victims, both female, and we've almost finished in the other pieces of open ground. Hopefully, that's the final body count.'

'Are you only searching the open ground? What if there are more elsewhere?'

'Apparently, digging between the trees would be impossible due to the roots meshing beneath. The only other potential site was covered in dense forest until twelve months ago. I took the precaution of walking across that area, and there is no sign of the ground having been disturbed. There's a carpet of fallen leaves which would have been shifted when someone dug there, but the dogs are going to cross it just in case.'

'I think that will be a wasted effort, unless you needed the exercise,' Fleming responded. 'Sinclair couldn't have visited Layton Woods twelve months ago — he's in prison.'

'I take it you're still assuming Sinclair must be the killer.'

'I am, despite your reservations. Will you be attending the post-mortems soon?'

'No, they won't be taking place yet. After Mexican Pete examined the ones we found today he's even more concerned about something, but wouldn't tell me what. He's already deferred the PMs on the first four, because he wants a second opinion from a forensic anthropologist, and the person he's asked won't be available until sometime next week. In the meantime, he'll be sending DNA samples from today's skeletons for testing. I'm on standby this weekend, but I'm giving the others time off. We've a lot of digging to do, figuratively speaking, so I want them all at their best on Monday.'

CHAPTER NINE

As there was nothing further to be achieved until they had
the PM and the remaining DNA results, Nash instructed the
team to return to the task he had set them before the latest
series of interruptions.

'Let's dig out all we can about Sinclair, his wife and their
backgrounds. Despite what Ruth and Jackie think, I still have
some doubts over Sinclair's guilt. We need as much info as
possible to determine whether I'm right or wrong.'

'I don't see how there can be any doubt regarding the murder of his wife's lover,' Lisa Andrews objected. 'The Swiss Army
knife and bloodstains on Sinclair's gilet prove that, surely.'

'I accept that. I was referring to the bodies in Layton
Woods.'

Viv Pearce headed for his computer and began work.
Clara and Lisa, who had studied the files previously, headed
to Sinclair's apartment block to see if they could find any
neighbours who knew him at the time. It was a wasted effort.
Speaking to the only resident available, they found that all
the current occupants had moved in at a later date. Reporting
back, Clara told them, 'It seems those who lived there sixteen years ago no longer wished to be associated with the
building.'

Viv's first discovery regarding Sinclair's background came the following day, and it provided something of a surprise to his colleagues. He began his report by telling them, 'Sinclair's parents were reasonably well off, but they both died before he was five years old. His mother died of cancer within eighteen months of giving birth. Two and a half years later, his father also died. The cause listed on the death certificate is something called cirrhosis of the liver, whatever that is.'

'It's liver disease. Overconsumption of fortified wine such as port, sherry, or any alcohol can be a factor, although there are many causes,' Nash explained.

'And do you know what happened to Sinclair afterwards?'

'There's a note on the original case file which indicates one of the detectives investigating Sinclair had been instructed to contact Social Services. Interestingly, there is no record of the outcome of that call. I was able to get hold of the case worker who handled Sinclair when he was placed in care, and she was adamant no such conversation took place. Which seems to verify what happened — or in this case, didn't happen. She told me how shocked she was when she read about Sinclair's arrest and trial.'

'And you've no idea who the detective was?' Nash asked.

'No I haven't, Mike, but I'm glad to tell you it definitely wasn't Tom Pratt. The note on the file was handwritten and bears no resemblance to Tom's neat script.'

'I didn't for one minute think it could have been Tom. He wouldn't countenance such sloppy police work. If I had to guess, I reckon the guy was convinced Sinclair was guilty, and wasn't about to waste time on something he considered to be irrelevant.'

'Did you ask the social worker if there were any other relatives who might have taken care of Sinclair?' Clara asked.

'I did, and she told me there was nobody close to him. There were no living relatives. Neither of his parents had siblings, and his grandparents were long gone by then.'

Pearce glanced down at his notes. 'Sinclair went into an orphanage as a temporary measure, and from there into a series of foster homes, all on a short-term basis. I asked if there was a particular reason for there not being a long-term home, and she cited a number of examples, such as couples dropping out of the foster care system, moving house to another district, illness, and in one case pregnancy. She stressed that none of the terminations of care were down to Sinclair's misbehaviour, just that he was unlucky. She said this sort of thing happens more often than people think.'

'I wondered if that might have given an indication of his violent temper, but instead it seems to contradict what we know, which puzzles me,' Lisa stated.

Pearce ended his report by telling them, 'Sinclair dropped off Social Services' radar when he turned eighteen and ceased to qualify for foster care.'

'You mentioned his parents were well off. What happened to the money from their estates?'

'Sinclair's father made a will shortly before he died, leaving everything in trust for the boy. The solicitor he used was made sole trustee, and when Sinclair reached majority and left care, he received the capital sum plus accumulated interest. From what I've been able to learn, it seems Sinclair invested some of the money in the apartment he bought in Netherdale, the one he lived in with Demetra, leaving the remainder in several building societies. I guess that's all gone now, being used to pay his legal fees — much good that did him.'

'That's excellent work, Viv, as far as it goes, but there's an aspect of Sinclair's early life and upbringing you haven't touched on, and it's one that might be a useful source of background information. Do you know where Sinclair was educated?'

'Sorry, Mike, I forgot to mention that. He went to Helmside Primary School and from there to Netherdale Grammar, and later attended Netherdale Technical College, where he studied electrical and mechanical engineering, as an accompaniment to his apprenticeship.'

'That's excellent, and with luck it might provide us with a valuable insight into Sinclair's character and behavioural development, in contrast to the information we've got so far. That's down to you and me, Clara. Having been to prison, we're now going back to school.'

'I assume that means you want me to phone and make appointments?'

'Yes, although I don't think you need to bother with the primary school. While you're about it, try and find the names of any teachers who were particularly involved with him, plus the engineering tutor at the tech.'

As Clara moved to her desk to begin her task, Pearce told Nash, 'Meanwhile, I'll see if I can unearth something about Demetra Sinclair, née Zamfir. Apparently that's Romanian for sapphire, and there are a lot of people with that surname, many of them actually involved in the jewellery trade. Because it's so common a name, I'm not holding my breath for positive results.'

Once he was alone, Nash pondered the recent revelations. Something Pearce had told them ought to have rung a bell with Nash, but at the time he had accepted the statement at face value. It was a while before he recalled Pearce's statement about legal fees. Nash lifted the folder containing Sinclair's original prosecution notes and began to read it. At the top of page two he saw the name he'd been looking for. He reached for the telephone and punched in the number listed alongside the name he'd found.

* * *

Half an hour later, Clara reported to Nash, 'I've managed to arrange an appointment with the headmaster of Netherdale Grammar for tomorrow afternoon at 4.30 p.m. The head told me there had been quite a change in their teaching staff since Sinclair was a pupil, with the result that he's the only active teacher who remembers him. He did supply the name of one retired master who we could contact if we desperately need to, although he's believed to have moved to live in Spain.'

66

'That could make it tricky. What about the tech?'

'We're seeing the principal of Netherdale Tech an hour and a half later. We're in luck there, because the principal is also the engineering tutor, and he recalls Sinclair well.'

'Did you get the impression they were surprised to know we wanted to ask about Sinclair?'

'I did, and also that they were keen to give us their input, although I could be mistaken. It's a bit difficult to gauge someone's expression over the phone, unless you're using one of those video calling apps.'

Nash then said, 'I've also arranged an appointment for us, but that's not until next Monday.'

'Who are we going to see?'

'James Anderson. That's James Anderson, the senior partner in Anderson and Holden, solicitors in Netherdale, not the world-famous England cricketer with the identical name.'

'Why are we going to see him?'

'I want to ask his opinion of Nicholas Sinclair. I noticed Anderson represented Sinclair sixteen years ago, so I rang Paul Holden — you remember him? He's helped us before.'

Clara nodded.

'Paul hadn't joined the firm back then; he was too young. But he's been talking to Anderson about it since the story broke in the media, and Paul knows he's far from happy about the revelations. Whether we'll get him to overlook his client privilege is another question.'

* * *

Whatever reaction Nash and Mironova expected from the grammar school headmaster, it certainly wasn't such a vehement espousal of Sinclair's case. 'I assume you want to know my impression of Nick Sinclair's character,' the teacher said, after the introductions.

'Yes, but also any incidents he was involved in that might provide useful background,' Nash replied.

'What I'm about to tell you might not be what you're either hoping or expecting to hear. I followed the trial closely, having a personal interest, and some of the so-called evidence of Nick's character left me totally confused. And, I will admit, by the end of the proceedings, very much annoyed. I was beginning to believe they were describing someone else with the same name.'

'Can we assume from what you've just said that Sinclair wasn't badly behaved while he was a pupil here?'

'Certainly not — quite the opposite. Nick was a quiet, studious, and intelligent boy. He got on well with his fellow pupils and didn't get into fights, or any other sort of trouble, during the six years he was here.'

'What did you think when he was found guilty of murdering his wife and her lover?'

'I didn't believe Nick was capable of committing such a wicked act, no matter what the provocation was. Now, having read the garbage in the press, and heard some of the comments on TV, I'm more convinced that the person you locked away in Frankland Prison has been the victim of a grave miscarriage of justice.'

Having thanked the headmaster, Nash and Mironova took their leave — his testimonial, and the accompanying rebuke for the processes of law, ringing in their ears. As they drove the short distance to Netherdale Tech, Clara asked Nash what he thought about the recent conversation.

'It's certainly created a bit more doubt in my mind,' Nash replied. 'What about you?'

'Although it's an interesting insight, I suppose there's every chance that Sinclair might have changed as he moved from being a schoolboy into an adult. Our next interview might give us a better glimpse of Sinclair's developing personality, given the closer relationship with the person who tutored him, rather than the more remote position of the headmaster.'

If Clara hoped their conversation with the college principal might clear up the contradictory message of the headmaster's statement, she came away from the second interview bitterly disappointed, and not a little confused.

The principal's defence of Sinclair was just as strong as the teacher's had been. In the midst of his remarks, he cast further doubt on the character assessment delivered during the trial, providing a possible motive for some of the scurrilous comments.

'I read something about him being fiery-tempered at work. I knew for a fact that was a load of rubbish. Sinclair was a level-headed, highly intelligent young man with a bright future ahead of him. He was without doubt one of the best students I've ever taught. I believe those derogatory remarks were made with malice in mind. Nicholas was working at Netherdale Engineering, and at that time the company was struggling, facing intense competition. Much of that came from overseas, mainly from China and America. I also know that in the year before Sinclair got into trouble they had lost two big, lucrative contracts. Rumours were rife that if they were to stand a chance of survival they would have to make a load of redundancies, both from on the shop floor and within management. When that sort of thing happens, employers tend to retain their best workers and discard the rest. If the workers could eliminate one of their strongest competitors, it would increase their own chance of survival.'

'Were there many redundancies?' Clara asked.

'There certainly were. From memory, I think almost forty per cent of the workforce got the chop. Most of those were from the shop floor, because managers were more concerned with saving their own skins. I firmly believe Sinclair was victimized, possibly from the boardroom down, making one less problem they had to deal with.'

The tutor paused, before continuing, 'I guess the reason you're here is to ask me if I believe he killed his wife and her lover. The answer to that is categorically no, and as for this latest sensation-seeking rubbish being peddled by the media, that is pure fiction — fantasy fiction at that. The young man I spent many hours tutoring didn't, in my opinion, have it in him to harm a fly.'

CHAPTER TEN

Next morning, Nash and Mironova filled their colleagues in with the gist of their twin conversations with Sinclair's tutors, which left them, as Pearce observed, totally confused.

'Join the club,' Clara agreed. 'But although it contradicts what we already knew, like much of the evidence gathered sixteen years ago during the initial investigation, this is mostly hearsay and opinion.'

'It certainly doesn't do anything to support the ruthless, cold-blooded serial killer theory,' Nash commented, before asking Pearce, 'Did you get anywhere with your research into Demetra Sinclair's background?'

'Unfortunately not, Mike, because most of the records are unavailable to us, even if we had a fluent Romanian speaker in our ranks. Added to that difficulty, both her Christian name and surname are fairly common. I'm not saying they're as widespread as Jane Smith, for example, but not far off. Having had no luck with where Demetra originated, I had another idea, along the lines of what you and Clara did yesterday, that might prove fruitful.'

'What was that?'

'I thought it might be worth having a word with the manager and some of the staff at The Golden Bear in

Netherdale, the hotel where Demetra worked. I made a call and the manager is the same person as sixteen years ago. He, or some of the others who work there, might be able to give us some insight into how happy, or otherwise, Demetra was. They might even be able to reveal what she thought about her husband, and perhaps give us a clue as to the bloke she was having an affair with.'

'*Allegedly* having an affair — again, that's mostly hearsay. But that's an excellent suggestion, Viv. Clara, get on the phone and arrange for us to visit, will you? This afternoon, if we can.'

As Clara moved across to her desk, Viv said, 'I have more news for you, Mike, on quite a different subject. Lisa obtained an image of Free Willy via the company operating the ATM where he displayed his wares. I ran it through facial recognition but failed to come up with a match, which suggests he isn't in our system. I think the only course open to us is to show the photo around Bishopton.'

'That's good work from both of you,' Nash told the detective constables. 'But unfortunately, I think you've just talked yourselves into a job.'

* * *

Having explained the reason for their visit to the hotel manager during her phone call, Clara and Nash drove to Netherdale and walked into The Golden Bear, where they only had to wait a few minutes before being ushered into an office to the rear of reception. The detectives were surprised to find a group of four waiting inside, and Clara noticed that their expressions were guarded, almost hostile.

The manager introduced his three colleagues, the house-keeping chief of staff, the senior barman, and the head waiter. He then explained the reason for their presence. 'Demetra worked in all three departments. She started as a chamber-maid, but we soon realized how doing that alone undervalued her talents. Seeing how well she interacted with customers, she was given additional duties as a barmaid and waitress.'

His three colleagues all confirmed how diligent an employee Demetra had been, and how popular she was with other members of staff and customers. Having heard their glowing testimonials, Nash asked the leading question, 'Can any of you tell us what her relationship with her husband was like? The detectives investigating her disappearance were told she'd been seeing someone else, and was expecting his child. Evidence collected at the time points to a man who was killed in Kirk Bolton being her lover. Have you any idea who he was?'

The housekeeper spoke up, 'I can answer that.'

Clara looked at the middle-aged, stiffly built, rather matronly woman and noticed her cheeks were suffused with colour, her eyes flashing with anger.

'All that stuff about Demetra having an affair, is a load of bull . . . er . . . hogwash. Demetra adored Nick, and would never even give another man a sideways glance. She and I used to talk regularly' — she glanced at the manager, smiling as she added — 'during our rest breaks, I hasten to add. Demetra confided in me, because she was a long way from her home country, and her parents were dead. I think I became a sort of substitute for them. From the moment she met Nick, Demetra fell for him in a big way, and when I saw them together I could tell he was absolutely head over heels in love with her.'

'How did they meet? A hotel employee and an engineer don't normally move in the same circles.'

'Nick had been attending evening classes at the tech just down the road, and he called in here for a drink. It was mid-week, during that dead time of the year, late January or early February, as I recall, so the bar was almost empty. Perhaps that's as well, because Andy' — she gestured towards the barman — 'was off sick, leaving Demetra to run the bar. At one point in the evening she was collecting glasses and collided with a customer. The tray and glasses went flying, and Demetra sustained a bad gash to her wrist. Nick, who apparently had some first-aid training, attended to Demetra's injury, told the customer off for being clumsy, and then swept up all the broken pieces of glass. That was only a small act of kindness, but it was enough for Demetra to fall for Nick. Before long, I guessed where their relationship was going. The expression on Demetra's face when she spoke about Nick, or as she called him, Nico, was a real giveaway.'

The housekeeper paused and smiled, a rather sad expression, Clara thought, before she picked up the tale. 'They dated on and off for a long time before they became lovers. From what Demetra inferred, once they started, they were unable to stop themselves, so it was no surprise when she announced that she was pregnant.'

'Why did they only date on and off to begin with?' Nash asked. 'Surely if they were so much in love, they'd want to spend as much time together as possible?'

'They did, but there were times when they couldn't see one another. That was down to Nick's job. The firm he worked for had a large installation to complete, somewhere down south. It took several months, during which he was away quite a lot.'

'That's true,' the barman said. 'I was serving him, and Nick told me about the contract and how he would miss coming into the bar to see Demetra.'

The housekeeper added, 'That didn't mean they lost touch, though. Demetra used to read Nick's letters to her over and over again. She even told me what was in them — or at least part of it,' she ended with a grin. 'It was clear from that they were intended to be together for life.'

'How did Sinclair take the news of the pregnancy?' Clara beat Nash to the question by a split second.

'He was over the moon, and insisted they move the wedding day forward.' Noticing the detectives' surprise, she told them, 'Oh yes, they were already planning to get married, well before the baby was conceived.' She paused before adding, 'If you want a measure of how strongly Nick felt for Demetra, I can give you a prime example. Demetra was studying English and the lessons were at the tech in an evening. Nick used to escort her there and then wait in a nearby café reading a book until she finished. That's true devotion, I'd say.'

When the housekeeper had ended her story, Nash said, 'OK, now for the big question. Do you believe he killed her and this unknown man?'

All four of the hotel staff shook their heads, and the manager summed up their feelings. 'We didn't think so at the time, partly because we didn't want to believe something so horrible. But now that other nonsense has come to light, we're all convinced that Nick Sinclair didn't kill Demetra — or anyone else.'

'Did you ever see Demetra with injuries that might have been inflicted at home? Cuts or bruises, that sort of thing?' Clara asked.

Once again, it was the housekeeper who replied. 'The only one I saw was when she cut her hand, but that certainly wasn't caused by Nick.'

'How can you be certain?'

'Demetra told me about it when she brought me a portion of boureki next day.'

'What's boureki?' Clara asked.

The housekeeper smiled. 'Apparently it's a Greek dish made with potatoes and zucchini. Demetra learned the recipe from a relative of hers who worked in Crete. She and Nick loved it, so she used to make batches of it for freezing. When she told me, I said it sounded delicious, so she brought me a portion to try. She was right, it is extremely tasty. But when she handed it to me her hand was bandaged and she explained the zucchini fought back while she was slicing it, and she gashed her hand so badly it had bled heavily. Nick attended to the wound for her, and she was lucky it hadn't needed stitches.'

Nash and Mironova looked at one another, both aware that this anecdote tallied with Sinclair's account of the bloodstains in his kitchen. There was a long silence, before Nash asked a question that baffled everyone, including Clara. 'How was Demetra paid?'

'All our employees are paid by bank transfer,' the manager replied.

'I don't suppose after all this time you can recall the details of the account it was paid into, can you? It might be useful to know if it was her account, or a joint one with her husband.'

'I suppose I could look through our records. Some of our employees work on a seasonal basis, so we retain their bank details to avoid unnecessary admin work. Is it important?'

'I'm not sure, it might be crucial, or then again, it might be insignificant, but our work is like that. We have to check out every minute fact.'

'In that case, I'll look out the details and let you know once I have them.'

After handing the manager his card, Nash thanked all four staff members, telling them they should contact him if they recall anything they think of importance.

The minute they got back into his car, Mironova couldn't wait to ask the question that was puzzling her. 'Why did you ask about the way Demetra got paid, and why do you want to know her bank account details?'

'It's a bit of a wild idea, I suppose, but what if Demetra Sinclair wasn't murdered sixteen years ago, by her husband or anyone else? What if she simply vanished? She would have needed money, so it would be interesting to know if she had a separate bank account, and if so, what happened to it, and the money that was in it.'

'What on earth makes you think Demetra ran away? You've just been listening to four people who knew her well. And they stated categorically that she was absolutely devoted to her husband, wasn't the least bit interested in anyone else, and was relishing the prospect of becoming a mother. If those four people are right, what possible reason could Demetra have for leaving everything and everyone she cared about? Particularly her husband, who, as I now believe, was also the father of her baby.'

'That's the trouble, Clara, I have absolutely no basis for thinking she ran away, but then I did tell you it was a wild idea. I thought the boureki story was interesting, though, didn't you?'

'I did, Mike, and I have to admit I'm starting to wonder if you're right, and the original conviction was a mistake.'

'The only problem I have is the evidence regarding the unidentified man killed with the Swiss Army knife. That seems cast-iron to me. I certainly can't think of an innocent explanation, can you?'

Clara agreed this was a major stumbling block.

Only time would make the truth come out — time, plus a fifteen-year-old girl.

* * *

The following day, the hotel manager rang Nash. He recited Demetra's bank account details, and as Nash scribbled them down, the manager added that the account was in her name only.

Having thanked the man for his assistance, Nash ended the call and stared at his notepad for a few minutes, before picking up his mobile and dialling a number from his contacts list.

What followed was a long, sometimes difficult discussion, before he was able to obtain the information he was seeking. Afterwards, Nash stared at the figures he'd written on his jotter, then opened the file alongside it. He compared the two sets of details and whistled with surprise.

Clara, who was the only other person in CID, wandered into his office. 'Is something wrong?' she asked.

'Do you remember that wild idea of mine — and don't say which one. I've just got the details of Demetra's bank account from the hotel manager. It appears Demetra Sinclair did have a separate one to her husband. Fortunately, the bank concerned is the one Alondra and I use, which, with the money her paintings fetch, makes us extremely good clients. After a great deal of effort, I persuaded the bank manager to release some details.' Nash handed Clara the sheet of paper on which he'd scribbled his notes. He saw her eyes widen with surprise.

'That's impossible,' she said after a while.

'Exactly what I thought.'

Over the weekend, with little else to occupy his mind, Nash kept returning to the Sinclair files, reading them time and again. Try as he might, he could not dismiss the doubts raised by Sinclair's verbal outburst in prison, spoken in the heat of the moment. His misgivings were now reinforced by the several testimonials to Sinclair's good character. No matter how he tried to dismiss them as irrelevant, the twin doubts kept returning. He knew that only forensic results would end his concerns once and for all. What they eventually revealed, however, would turn everyone's thinking about the Sinclair case on its head. Before then, however, Nash learned more about Sinclair, and that knowledge, allied to what he'd read in the file, left him even more uncertain about the man's original conviction.

CHAPTER ELEVEN

On Monday morning, the solicitor, James Anderson, greeted Nash and Mironova and took them through into his office. 'My partner told me you wanted to speak to me about Nicholas Sinclair. Normally, I wouldn't even contemplate discussing a client with the police who seem bent on pinning more crimes on him. But Paul said that wasn't the reason for this meeting, so will you explain why you are here?'

'We have serious reservations concerning the original conviction, and since we reopened Sinclair's file, those doubts have increased, fuelled partly by our assessment of him when we interviewed him, plus the opinion of many people who knew him and his wife before she disappeared. What I hoped you'd be able to do is set our minds at rest one way or the other. To put you completely in the picture, though this isn't public knowledge, we have conducted DNA tests on victims found in Layton Woods, and so far there is no match to Demetra Sinclair.'

There was a short silence as Anderson pondered Nash's remarks. 'I wasn't certain about Sinclair when I agreed to represent him, especially with the strength of the evidence about the unidentified man found at Kirk Bolton. That doubt strengthened during the trial, when Sinclair refused to open up, even when prosecuting counsel cross-examined him, trying to goad him into making a damaging admission. Sinclair remained tight-lipped, and I felt sure there was something he was hiding.' He held up a hand. 'Before you ask, no, he never told me what he was withholding, which made me suspect the worst. Then, after his conviction, I began to have second thoughts.'

'What prompted those?'

'The trial had been a long, expensive one, causing Sinclair to run up huge legal bills.' Anderson smiled as he commented, 'Mainly for the barrister and his assistants, I hasten to add. In order to settle them, he had to sell his flat, but before placing it on the market, he asked me to arrange retrieval of two items from inside the apartment. He told me they were the only things he wanted to keep. The first of these was a photograph of him and Demetra, taken on their wedding day.'

'And the second?' Nash asked.

'It was a collection of letters, written by Demetra to Nicholas during the time he was working away, plus those he wrote to her. I took the liberty of reading them before I visited Nicholas to hand them over. They demonstrated the love between the couple clearly enough to have me worried there had been a miscarriage of justice, but with Demetra having vanished and no fresh evidence, there were no grounds for an appeal. That's how things have remained all this time, and I admit I have agonized over Sinclair's situation again and again. Now this latest revelation, the one that has him down as a serial killer, convinces me that sixteen years ago we condemned an innocent man to life imprisonment for a crime he didn't commit. I agree part of the evidence seems irrefutable, but that doesn't allay my doubts one iota.'

Before leaving, Nash returned to one of the pieces of evidence that had helped the jury return a guilty verdict, addressing the issue with a seemingly innocuous question, 'Tell me something, Mr Anderson, did Sinclair ever mention boureki to you?'

Clara saw the look of astonishment on the solicitor's face, and knew the answer before he replied.

'Yes, he told me Demetra was making it when she gashed her hand, causing those bloodstains the prosecution made a meal of. Sorry,' he added, 'bad pun. But how did you know about the boureki?'

Nash explained, causing Anderson to wince. 'I wish we'd thought to interview the housekeeper at the time. That evidence might have instilled sufficient doubt in the jurors' minds regarding Demetra's murder.'

* * *

Nash had been concerned by the delay in conducting the PMs on the skeletons, until he received a phone call from the pathologist. After apologizing for the hold-up, he'd told Nash, 'As you know, there are certain indicators that have led me to request a second opinion. The forensic anthropologist who will give me that opinion is one of the leading experts in this country. But that means their schedule is very crowded. However, I've managed to arrange for the post-mortems to begin tomorrow morning at eight o'clock, and I think it would be sensible for you to be the officer in attendance. I wouldn't suggest this if I didn't consider your presence to be important. But be aware, this may take more than one day.'

Nash had confirmed, 'Of course I will, Professor. Can you give me some indication of what your concerns are?'

'I prefer to leave that for tomorrow, if you don't mind. Otherwise, I might give you a misleading impression.'

That left Nash more mystified than before. He'd relayed the conversation to DS Mironova, adding, 'What that's all about, I have absolutely no idea. I could be unavailable unless there's an emergency, so you're in charge.'

Clara had given a mock salute. 'Yes, sir.'

As soon as Nash arrived at the mortuary, Professor Ramirez came to greet him.

Looking beyond the pathologist, Nash saw an attractive-looking woman, suitably gowned, inspecting a set of skeletal remains on one of the mortuary slabs. Ramirez gestured to the inner room. 'That's the first of the skeletons. We've a few hours work ahead of us, so I think you should get comfortable in the viewing room. Have you brought a book to read? A detective story, for example?'

'No, but I've made other arrangements.' Nash held up the Thermos flask.

Once the long session was over, Ramirez and his colleague joined Nash in the viewing area. Ramirez introduced her, 'This is Professor Amy Foxton, one of Britain's leading forensic anthropologists.' He turned and indicated the detective. 'And this is DI Mike Nash, one of the country's best investigators.'

Nash noticed she was still wearing surgical gloves. 'Pleased to meet you, Professor,' he said, 'but forgive me for not shaking hands.'

Amy Foxton, it seemed, possessed a good sense of humour. As she peeled off her gloves, she said, 'If you're squeamish about shaking hands with a pathologist, I'd steer well clear of gynaecologists.' She indicated Ramirez as she told Nash, 'You'll be pleased to know that, so far, I agree completely with your pathologist's assessment of the remains.'

'Would one of you mind enlightening me?' Nash pleaded.

'Sorry, Mike, this will take time, so you'll have to be patient,' Ramirez told him. 'But I can tell you we have now received the DNA test results on the more recent victims, none of which match that of Demetra Sinclair.'

With that, Nash had to wait. He returned to the mortuary the following day, hopeful he would glean more information. It was lunchtime when Professor Ramirez removed his gloves and asked him to join them in his office.

'Is that everything?' Nash asked.

'Far from it.' Ramirez glanced at his colleague, who explained to Nash what they had both deduced from their inspection of the remains, adding it would take a few days before she could confirm her suspicions. Ramirez added there was no need for him to attend the following day while Professor Foxton continued her examination.

Fifteen minutes later, having requested a hard copy of their report as a matter of urgency, Nash walked out of the mortuary, his head spinning with the shock revelation. He plucked his mobile from his pocket and pressed Clara's short code.

'Clara, get in your car and come through to HQ. Bring Viv and Lisa with you. We need a meeting with the chief constable, Superintendent Fleming, and Tom Pratt. Get here as quick as you can.'

Before Clara could respond, or ask why, she heard the dialling tone.

* * *

Half an hour later, Nash, Mironova, Andrews, and Pearce, along with Superintendent Fleming and Tom Pratt, filed into the chief constable's office.

Ruth Edwards blinked in surprise. 'What's this about?' she asked Nash. 'You said you wished to see me. I didn't expect a delegation.'

'I've just come from the mortuary, having received the initial report and DNA results on all the skeletons found in Layton Woods. The post-mortems were carried out by Professor Ramirez, with Professor Amy Foxton in attendance.'

Clara noticed he'd used the pathologist's real name instead of his nickname, which, to her, seemed to emphasize the severity of what Nash was about to reveal.

'It doesn't need the whole of my detective force to tell me the results of post-mortems, surely,' Ruth Edwards complained, then paused. 'Did you say Professor Foxton, as in the forensic anthropologist?'

'That's correct.' Nash paused slightly before delivering his bombshell. 'Professor Ramirez called on her to give a second opinion, because he was concerned by the state of the skeletons, and his initial findings seemed rather disturbing. Both he and Foxton are convinced that all the female victims were stabbed to death in the same manner. And they confirmed none of them was a DNA match to Demetra Sinclair. The PM also revealed that none of them had ever given birth — they were adamant on that point. Even without the DNA evidence, we'd have known Demetra Sinclair wasn't one of the victims, because we know for a fact she was pregnant at the time she disappeared.'

Ruth Edwards looked horrified. 'I take it that means Sinclair has yet another burial site somewhere else.'

'No, it doesn't. Ramirez called Professor Foxton in because of her expertise in her field. Having examined the skeletal remains she has given a provisional opinion, subject to confirmation in a few days. And if it proves correct, I'm now absolutely certain Sinclair didn't kill any of the people who were buried in Layton Woods, and it's very unlikely he killed his wife.'

'Why?' Tom Pratt interrupted angrily. 'All the evidence proved he did away with his wife and her lover, the man whose baby she was expecting.'

'I don't believe that's true, but it's immaterial, because Nicholas Sinclair has a cast-iron alibi for the time some of those murders took place. According to Professor Foxton's initial findings, at least three of the five women found in Layton Woods were killed less than ten years ago. Probably much more recently, when Sinclair was locked away in prison. As alibis go, I reckon that has to be pretty near watertight, don't you?'

'What about the others?' Jackie Fleming asked.

'She is sure the male, and one of the females, were earlier.'

Everyone in the room looked horrified by Nash's revelation, and his follow-up remarks almost failed to register, so great was their shock.

'So far, what the laboratory tests did reveal was mainly geographical information. The gene pool of the male and the female I just mentioned suggests they hailed from somewhere in Eastern Europe. Familial indicators suggest they are siblings, brother and sister. They have definitely been buried longer than the rest. And they are unrelated to any of the other four — all of whom are women from this country. Professor Foxton's examination of the bone degeneration — or in this case, lack of it — indicates all the victims were somewhere between twenty and thirty years old when they were killed.'

'I thought it was difficult to establish how long ago a skeleton was buried?' the chief asked.

'That's correct, as far as most pathologists are concerned, but a forensic anthropologist is certainly capable of gauging the timeline. Part of this is relevant with regard to some of the victims. Two of them had dental work carried out. The relative lack of wear, plus the procedures involved, suggests to Dr Foxton that the work was carried out recently.' He paused, and looked directly at Ruth Edwards.

'Professor Ramirez is hoping to get our go-ahead to enlist the help of a forensic odontologist.' He could see the chief wince at the thought of more expense, and explained, 'Apparently, they will be able estimate the age of the victims to within twelve months or so. Once we have the approximate age, plus the length of time they have been buried from Professor Foxton, we can compare this with our missing persons list. Any potential candidates can be passed back to the odontologist. They will contact dental practices in their last known location, and obtain dental records to compare with the teeth of the skeletons. With a confirmed match, our task will be to visit the next of kin and, if practicable, obtain a sample for familial DNA comparison. This is a mammoth undertaking for everyone concerned. Only if we can discover who the victims were, can we stand even the remotest chance of discovering who slaughtered them and left them to rot.'

Nash's impassioned final statement left everyone convinced by his obvious determination to seek some form of justice for the deceased. He allowed them to assimilate this information, before adding, 'The post-mortem on one of the bodies was finalized this morning. The male victim had a bullet still lodged in the skull, and the professor retrieved it. That is the only item of solid evidence as to who committed at least six murders we know of — possibly more.'

There was another prolonged silence as Nash's audience attempted to grasp the series of revelations, each more surprising than its predecessor. Eventually, the chief constable asked what Clara thought was an inevitable question.

'Is Professor Foxton absolutely certain the brother and sister were killed earlier?'

'She's conducting more tests to confirm, but believes there is no likelihood of error. I can't remember all the scientific terms she used, but if you're desperate to learn them, they'll be in her written report once that's available. Her opinion, which she stressed more than once, is she believed fifteen years is the absolute minimum those two victims have been in the ground.'

Superintendent Fleming responded, 'It certainly sounds as if she's sure of her facts, but I'm afraid I'm far from convinced. You said it yourself, this is only her opinion. And we all know how often scientific theories are proved incorrect. I still believe Sinclair is a serial killer, and he is where he belongs, behind bars.'

'I think you're wrong. And I believe the evidence, or rather lack of evidence, proves it.' Nash saw Tom Pratt was about to interrupt and raised a warning hand before continuing. 'When I say evidence, I'm referring to the bloodstains on the floor and kitchen knife, and the smashed furniture in Sinclair's flat. Take those items away, and the rest is purely hearsay and gossip, with a possible sighting of a car similar to Sinclair's turning off the road into Layton Woods. If we look at that statement, I'll explain why Sinclair could not have killed his wife and buried her along with the others.'

'You seem very sure of this,' Ruth Edwards interposed. 'I'll be interested to hear your alternative theory. But before we do, I suggest we have some refreshment while we try and digest what you've told us so far.'

* * *

Some forty miles away, a man was awaiting the return of his boss. The news he had to impart wasn't exactly what someone would want to hear on their first day back from holiday. He braced himself for the meeting.

The moment the man entered the office, the boss could tell something was wrong. His deputy's opening words merely proved it. 'Dean's gone AWOL.'

'What do you mean, AWOL? Where the hell is he?'

'That's just the problem. I've no idea.'

'When did this happen?'

'I spoke to him a week ago. He told me he was somewhere in North Yorkshire, checking out a potential target, and that's the last I've heard of him.'

'Have you tried his mobile?'

'Yes, time and time again, but it goes straight to voicemail.'

'Was he in one of our cars?'

'That's what really worries me. He was in the big one.'

'Oh shit! Do you reckon he's done a runner, or is he spaced out on coke, or just screwing some bird he's picked up? Those are his favourite hobbies.'

'I only wish I knew.'

'Rather than chance it, we'd better play safe. Report the car as stolen, and tell the fuzz I only discovered the theft when I came back from Spain this morning.' The boss grimaced slightly as he added, 'at least that bit's true enough.' He thought for a moment, before changing what he required from his assistant. 'I've had a better idea. First off, go to my place and force open the garage doors. You don't have to be subtle about it. In fact, it would be better if you cause a bit of damage. Then I can tell the pigs I'd left the keys inside the garage, thinking it would be safe to do so, with it being such a quiet neighbourhood.'

CHAPTER TWELVE

The chief constable replaced her cup and saucer on the tray, thanked her secretary, and looked directly at Nash. 'OK, Inspector Nash, can we hear your alternative theory now?'

Nash smiled. 'Certainly, ma'am. Point one, Sinclair's car was subjected to minute forensic examination, which yielded no results, apart from some of Demetra's DNA. And where was that? On the passenger seat, exactly where you'd expect to find it. Secondly, if Sinclair drove his Mini Cooper to that clearing, how did he do it? I appreciate that some of you haven't been to Layton Woods, but those of us who have, will tell you the upper reaches of that track are all but impassable, even in a four-wheel drive vehicle. In a Mini Cooper, you'd stand no chance.'

'Perhaps Sinclair used a different vehicle, or took a different track to reach the burial site.' Clearly Jackie Fleming was unwilling to change her opinion.

'There's no evidence to support that,' Nash told her. 'For one thing, there is no other way to get there. So maybe you can find out where he got a four-wheel drive, and at the same time, discover where he got the gun.'

'Gun? What gun?'

'I told you the male victim had been shot in the head, but there is no evidence that Sinclair ever owned, or had access to, a gun of any description. Another point we should take into consideration is that Sinclair had been working down south until the day before he reported his wife missing. I think it's expecting a lot for him to have returned home, killed her, and disposed of the remains, plus all her possessions, within twenty-four hours, don't you? Finally, if Professor Foxton's findings are proved correct, and we accept her expert opinion as to the length of time some of those women have been dead, I'd love to know how he sneaked out of prison, killed them, and then returned to his cell without anyone noticing he'd been out.'

Clara bit her bottom lip as she watched the interplay, aware that Nash was becoming exasperated, very unusual for him.

The chief constable interrupted hastily, 'I think you're right, Mike. Jackie might still have doubts, but I'm convinced. I'm still puzzled by those rumours, though. Might he have killed his wife and disposed of her elsewhere?'

'I think that's unlikely, unless he had a ready-made site. As to the rumours, Clara and I have spoken to his former headmaster, the principal of the technical college, and the staff at the hotel where Demetra worked. As a result, I think we should take the gossip with a pinch of salt, to put it mildly. The housekeeper at The Golden Bear was a confidante of Demetra's and she told us quite emphatically that Demetra was devoted to Sinclair, and wouldn't have been interested in anyone else. She also said how thrilled they both were at the prospect of having a child.'

'If that's true, how did those rumours of an affair and Sinclair's anger come about?' Fleming asked. 'And what about the dead man at Kirk Bolton? Wasn't Demetra Sinclair's DNA found on him?'

'It was,' Nash agreed. 'I went over the forensic report again and the DNA was only on his outer clothing. If this man had been Demetra's lover, wouldn't her DNA have been elsewhere, on his underwear, or on his body parts? Sorry, that's as politely put as I can make it. I'm not sure there ever was an affair. It might have been nothing more than idle gossip, spawned by the fact that Sinclair worked away. Alternatively, it might have been far more malicious, giving rise to the possibility that Sinclair was being set up to take the rap for this man's murder, plus that of his own wife — a murder I am now convinced never happened. There is one other fact I believe we should take into consideration regarding this alleged affair. According to the original post-mortem carried out on Demetra's so-called paramour, the man was aged between forty and forty-five years old. How likely do you think it is for a twenty-one-year-old, newly married woman to enter a relationship with a man old enough to be her father?'

'I think we should accept what Mike says. He's a leading expert on love affairs,' Clara pointed out.

The chief constable smiled at Clara's humorous intervention, but asked Nash, 'If we accept your line of thinking, which I think needs a little more to back it up, what do you think happened to Demetra Sinclair?'

Nash paused, before answering. 'That's the jackpot question. I believe she ran away. I've no idea why she did so, but I'm fairly certain that's what happened.'

'Have you any evidence?'

'Yes, and it was enough to convince me Sinclair could not have killed her. I obtained details of the bank account that Demetra's hotel salary was paid into. Fortunately it's the same branch Alondra and I use. I was able to persuade the manager to release information not normally available. Prior to her disappearance, Demetra had a credit balance slightly in excess of two thousand five hundred pounds. A single withdrawal was made from the account, leaving less than fifty pounds. That suggests Demetra was in urgent need of money, but left a small sum, which would seem to indicate her intention to return.'

'Might Sinclair have withdrawn the money and then killed her?'

'That's not possible. The withdrawal took place almost a week after he reported her missing. On that day, Sinclair was being interviewed inside this building.'

'It's far too large an amount to be taken from an ATM. I assume she used the local branch?'

'No, she didn't. And that's even stronger evidence, both of Sinclair's innocence, and of Demetra being alive at that point in time. The branch was in London. To do that, she would have to present her passport or other photo ID, together with her debit card. Obviously, the bank would ensure the person making the withdrawal was the account holder, and it was not a scam.'

Fleming had apparently bowed to the inevitable and accepted Nash's reasoning. 'Where do we go from here?' she asked.

'That's a simple question to ask, but a difficult one to answer. I do have a couple of ideas on the subject, but I'm open to suggestions.'

The chief constable thought for a moment before saying, 'If we have sufficient evidence from the PM reports, verifying all you have told us, then I think the first step ought to be to inform the Home Office. We need to try to set the wheels in motion for Sinclair's appeal, in the belief that the original conviction was unsafe. An appeal, where CPS could offer no evidence to refute his original plea of not guilty,' she added. 'However, there *was* sufficient evidence to convict him of killing the unknown man in Kirk Bolton, for which I assume by now he has served his time. If the Home Office agree to an appeal, he may be eligible for release.'

'I'm not sure release would be a wise move, ma'am, although that was my original reaction,' Nash responded. 'I'm beginning to wonder if Sinclair was being targeted, both before his conviction, and later in prison. Public acknowledgement of his innocence in the Layton Woods murders might trigger an adverse, possibly dangerous reaction. Prisons are not exactly the safest place if someone is determined to harm an inmate. And there have already been instances of

Sinclair being provoked. Besides, we still need an explanation for the John Doe murder in Kirk Bolton, because I, for one, am totally ruling out the idea he was Demetra's lover. Apart from the comments made by her work colleagues, there's that huge age gap. I think the only person who could provide us with a viable explanation is Nicholas Sinclair, but he won't talk about it. In fact, he won't talk about anything that went on back then, apart from his repeated denials that he killed anyone, and how much he loves his wife.'

'Have you got an alternative suggestion as to how to proceed?'

'Yes, ma'am. I think we should give serious consideration to the professor's idea about getting a dentistry specialist to examine the skeletons. But from what he told me, their services don't come cheap. I do have another, much less costly idea, albeit a rather unorthodox one. I think we should bring Sinclair here to Netherdale, under protective custody, but before we remove him from prison, we should feed a titbit of misleading gossip to the warders, and thence to the other inmates.'

'What sort of gossip?'

'If we hinted that we now believe Sinclair *is* a serial killer, as alleged in the press, and we are going to interrogate him with a view to charging him with six more murders, that should satisfy anyone who wishes to harm him.'

'How will we know if the gossip has done the trick?' Pearce asked.

Nash smiled. 'I feel sure the media will do that for us. Once we see the gory headlines, we'll know it's safe to bring Sinclair here. Of course, we'll probably need extra officers on duty to keep the press bloodhounds at bay.'

'That sounds like a good plan, but we still have no idea who actually committed the murders, excepting the man found at Kirk Bolton, and you're even casting doubts on that, in spite of the overwhelming evidence,' the chief constable pointed out.

'True enough, so we must go through the original prosecution again, but this time in the knowledge of Sinclair's probable innocence. We must look at every aspect of the case, no matter how irrelevant it seems. We will have one enormous advantage over the previous investigators,' — he glanced at Tom Pratt — 'no disrespect, Tom, in that we might be able to get Nicholas Sinclair to cooperate with our inquiries. I could be wrong, because this is pure guesswork, but I have an idea Sinclair might be able to point us in the right direction, even if he's unaware of the significance of what he knows.'

'I'm happy to go along with that idea, and I'll have a think about the odontologist,' Ruth Edwards said after a while. 'Is that everything, Mike?'

'There is one snippet of information from the DNA analysis that slipped my mind. With the gene pool of the brother and sister suggesting they are of Eastern European origin, it might have some significance, given that Demetra Sinclair is from Romania, which is within that area.'

'When I have the full PM report, and if it proves everything you've told us, I'd better get hold of someone from the Home Office and see if I can stir up some action.' The chief grimaced. 'And won't that be fun.'

Nash smiled. 'If we can also refute the allegation for the man in Kirk Bolton, it might help if you remind them that Sinclair might now have a sixteen-year claim for wrongful imprisonment, and that every day he spends in prison will add to that bill. If that doesn't work, point out that once a defence lawyer learns Sinclair's being held despite his possible innocence, the cost will skyrocket.'

'How would a defence lawyer get to know that?' Tom Pratt asked.

'I feel sure someone will tell them.' He shrugged. 'If not, I'll do the job myself.'

* * *

They were leaving the chief constable's office when her secretary detained Nash. 'I've a message for you from Inspector Grant. He asks if you can spare a minute to pop in his office.'

'OK,' Nash agreed, wondering what their recently appointed head of Traffic Division might want with him. He winked at the secretary and told her, 'I hope I haven't got a speeding ticket.'

He'd liked the look of Paul Grant on the previous occasion they'd met, and hoped he would be easier to deal with than his predecessor.

It was almost half an hour after his colleagues returned to Helmsdale that Nash joined them, and was greeted by Viv, 'Everything OK? Got a ticket? Speeding? Parking?'

'For that comment, I'd like a coffee,' Nash said, and when supplied, told the team about his conversation with Paul Grant. 'Traffic division has been dealing with several incidents of what they consider to be "arranged" accidents. These RTAs can be anything from shunts to direct crashes caused by the scammer, and laying the blame on the innocent driver. Paul had word that the insurance companies are not at all happy.'

'So why did he involve you?' Lisa wanted to know.

'No particular reason, just sharing information, as we all should do.'

With that he took his coffee to his office, sat down, and stared into space. Throughout the journey back he'd been plagued by a comment he'd heard at some point during the investigation, but not picked up on at the time. He couldn't for the life of him remember what it was. The information passed to him by Inspector Grant hadn't helped, and although his news had been important, it had side-tracked Nash sufficiently for it to be a while until the memory returned to him. Only when that recollection came would Nash and his colleagues get the first small clue to the identity of the serial killer they were seeking.

In the meantime, they now had an additional series of crimes to investigate, albeit ones he didn't believe would involve fatalities.

In this, for once, Nash was proved totally wrong.

CHAPTER THIRTEEN

The storms of early spring were now only an unhappy memory, but the harm they had caused around the county was still evident — and, in many cases, as yet unrepaired. One place that had suffered badly was the old packhorse crossing of the River Helm at Winter Bridge. Although this route was little used by vehicular traffic, the carriageway being far too narrow for anything but small cars, the importance of the Grade II listed structure meant regular maintenance was vitally important. The route was highly popular for hikers, ramblers, cyclists, and horse riders, so the crossing had to be kept in good condition. Therefore, after inspection, it was deemed necessary to rectify the damage caused by the adverse weather to the mortar binding the stonework of the bridge supports.

The technician charged with carrying out the repair had arrived on site that morning at 7.45, soon after first light. Having removed the tools and materials from his van, he donned his waders and commenced work, his intention being to complete the task by that evening, so he could take his son to Leeds to watch football the following day. Midweek soccer matches played in the evening were a great chance to allow the boy to indulge his love of the game.

He had been at work for just less than an hour and had returned to the riverbank to mix another load of mortar. The break would also allow some feeling to return to his toes and fingers, by now numb with cold. As he climbed ashore, the contractor glanced back, a reflex action to check what progress he'd made. It was only then he saw the body floating towards him.

His break forgotten, the lack of feeling in his extremities a distant memory, he waded back into the river and grasped the inert figure by the shirt collar. He hauled the body onto the riverbank and stared down at the man he'd rescued. It was only then he realized this was no rescue. It was the recovery of a corpse.

The workman's hands trembled with shock, not cold, as he pulled his mobile phone from his pocket to dial 999. He interrupted the emergency operator as she was asking which service he required. 'Police,' he gasped. 'I need the police. I'm at Winter Bridge. It's much too late for an ambulance.'

Nash had only been in his office a few minutes when his phone rang. He listened to Steve Meadows, who relayed what the Netherdale emergency operator had told him.

'OK, Steve, as Clara's the only one here, I'll take her along. Get the others to hold the fort here once they've managed to stagger out of their pits.'

He signalled to Mironova. 'We've to go to Winter Bridge. A guy repairing last winter's storm damage has pulled a body out of the river. There's no saying it's a crime, but we can't afford to take any chances. Steve is contacting Mexican Pete, so at least we've got a bit of time to brace ourselves for the inevitable bout of sarcasm.'

* * *

When the detectives arrived there were only two vehicles in sight. The name and logo on the first of these proclaimed it to be that of the contractor who had found the body. The other vehicle, a gaudily painted saloon car, was even more recognizable as that of a police patrol car.

'I think that's a bit unnecessary.' Clara pointed to the blue and white incident tape the uniformed officers were unrolling to seal off the area alongside the river. 'For one thing, the body is alleged to have floated downstream. In addition to that, there aren't exactly hordes of people milling around to gawp at the remains.'

'You might have a point, Clara, but I expect that sort of thing gets to be a habit. Let's go see what the workman has to tell us. Who knows, he might be able to provide us with some concrete evidence.'

Clara's groan of disapproval at Nash's pun was only partially masked by the sound of the Range Rover door closing.

Having chatted briefly to their two colleagues, Nash and Clara approached the contractor, who was seated in his van, morosely nursing a mug of coffee from the flask on the passenger seat. The workman had little to add to their existing, sparse fund of knowledge. 'Did you hear any sounds before the body floated downstream?' Nash asked him. 'A vehicle, or perhaps a loud splash?'

The contractor, already visibly distressed, was appalled by the obvious implication that this had been a body dump. He shook his head. 'No, there was no noise whatsoever. It's been as quiet as the . . . er . . . quiet as anything. The only sound I've heard since I got here was a randy cock pheasant after a spot of leg-over. There's been absolutely no traffic. No vehicles, horses, bikes, or people on foot.'

'OK, I've no doubt our officers have taken your details, so I suggest you go home. We'll attend to things here.'

The contractor's look of relief emphasized the trauma he'd suffered from his discovery. They watched him drive away, and once he'd departed, Nash and Mironova walked over to the riverbank.

'What do you think, Clara?' Nash asked.

'Male, approximately thirty years of age, I guess, and he isn't either a hiker or a biker.'

'Why do you say that?'

'He's not wearing the right footwear for walking, and if he was a serious cyclist, he'd have been dressed differently, in Lycra shorts and top, say. And where's his helmet? He's dressed more like a motorist.'

Clara gestured to the short-sleeve polo shirt the dead man was wearing. 'The weather is not exactly ideal to be outdoors in a shirt like that. I've got a top coat on, and even with that protection I'm only just warm enough.'

'That's extremely observant, Clara. Let's see what Mexican Pete can tell us.' Nash gestured to his left, where two vehicles had just pulled to a halt.

Nash's previous prediction about sarcasm was proved incorrect. The pathologist was in strictly business mode. Having greeted them, he said, 'Professor Foxton is working with one of my capable technicians and was happy to continue without me.'

He waited for the photographer to finish, before he concentrated on examining the body. 'There appear to be no visible signs of foul play,' he reported, 'but I will know better once we have him back in the mortuary.' Ramirez glanced at his surroundings before adding, 'If I had to hazard a guess, I'd say this man probably drowned, but whether he was assisted or not is a different matter. I will conduct the PM tomorrow. I should have a slab free by then.' With a brief flash of humour, he told Nash, 'I hope that won't spoil your appetite.' With that, he nodded farewell, signalling to his waiting assistants to collect the corpse.

Nash turned to Clara and suggested they go back to Helmsdale. 'I don't think there's anything more we can do here, and I'm beginning to get caffeine withdrawal symptoms.'

* * *

The post-mortem revealed facets of the deceased's case neither the detectives nor the pathologist had been able to identify at the scene. As he delivered his preliminary findings, Ramirez told Nash, 'My initial suggestion was correct. The man did drown, but there are two anomalies. One of those is bruising stretching from his right shoulder across his chest to the left-hand side of his waist, consistent with a seatbelt.

'In addition, when I examined his scalp, I noticed several particles of grit in his hair. After I shaved that section, there was some discolouration that suggests bruising. That opens up two possibilities. Either he fell and banged his head, or someone hit him with a rock. Of the two, I think the first alternative is far more likely, because a deliberate blow would have left a much bigger wound, and would almost certainly have penetrated the skin, or caused a fracture. At present, I'm unable to explain the relevance of the bruising across the chest in these circumstances.'

Nash recalled Mironova's summary as she viewed the corpse. He suggested to Ramirez, 'If the dead man was driving a vehicle and there was a collision, the force of the impact would have activated the safety belt.'

'That is a very plausible explanation for the chest bruises, but it doesn't account for the head injury.'

'At present, all we have is supposition. One other question, how long do you think this man has been dead?'

'That isn't easy to say, given the immersion in water, but I'd say at least a week.'

'Our next priority is to identify him, and then we might learn why he ended up in the River Helm.'

'One thing I can tell you, there is no fingerprint match in the system. I've sent a sample for DNA analysis, and a second one for a toxicology report. I will let you know the results as soon as I have them.'

* * *

Owning a dog is a rewarding experience, but there are downsides, such as the need for the animal to have regular exercise, even if the weather conditions are inclement. However, on this particular morning, the day dawned bright and sunny, with little breeze. Having been away for the weekend, visiting family, the cocker spaniel and his companion emerged from the cottage they shared in the village of Winter Bridge, envisaging an enjoyable walk. Their chosen route, a favourite of both man and dog, was the path leading from their village along the western bank of the River Helm.

One of the reasons the dog looked forward to this particular path was that perhaps there would be pheasants or mallards to scare into flight, or rabbits to chase. All these events had occurred on previous outings, giving the spaniel immense satisfaction. The dog's daydreaming came to an abrupt halt only halfway along the path. As he roamed ahead, the spaniel glanced back occasionally, ensuring his companion was keeping up, not idling, or playing with the toy that he invariably carried and sometimes spoke to.

He'd looked back three times, but on the fourth he stopped. Something was obviously wrong. The man was staring fixedly towards the river. Oblivious of the barking, designed to capture his attention, he remained motionless, still gazing at something. The dog turned and ran back, eager to see what had captured his master's interest.

The man whistled his dog, and gestured towards the village, curtailing their walk. He needed to return home. It was typical, he thought, on the one morning he needed his mobile phone, he'd left it in the house. He'd seen it as they were leaving, but ignored it. That had been a huge mistake.

* * *

Nash and Clara were discussing the weekend calls and the post-mortem results on the Winter Bridge body when Nash's phone rang.

'Good morning, Paul,' he said, then listened for a moment. 'How do we get there? OK, we're on our way.'

Nash ended the brief conversation and told Clara, 'That was Paul Grant from Traffic. I hope you've got your hiking boots to hand. A man walking his dog at Winter Bridge has found a car in the river. Paul thinks it might be connected to the body we were just talking about. He's also making a possible link to those arranged road accidents he mentioned.'

Clara puzzled over Nash's final statement. It made sense to connect the vehicle to the body, but she failed to understand why Inspector Grant thought it might have something to do with the RTA frauds. She voiced her doubts, but listened with increasing surprise as Nash explained.

'Paul told me the make and model of the car are far away from your run-of-the-mill vehicle. It's an almost brand new Mercedes S580 4matic. Buying one of them would set you back somewhere in the region of £180,000, if not more.'

Clara whistled. 'I can't wait to see that. It must be some hunk of metal. It's certainly not something a police officer could afford, not unless their wife happens to be a highly sought-after landscape artist whose paintings command six-figure sums.'

Nash grinned. 'I'm not sure I'd want to shell out that sort of money for a car, even if I won the lottery.'

'There speaks a true Yorkshireman.'

Having reached Winter Bridge, Nash followed Grant's directions to head along the main road to where he would find the inspector's and two other police vehicles. He did so, and pulled into a lay-by, where an officer indicated the path they should take. Having changed into more appropriate footwear, the detectives set off to walk down to the river. As they neared the scene, Clara could see a car roof and windows above the fast-flowing waters of the Helm. A member of the diving team was leaving the river, having checked to ensure there was no one inside, hidden from view. A trio of uniformed officers, led by Inspector Grant, were examining the riverbank.

Nash gestured, indicating the crushed undergrowth. 'I can see how the car ended up imitating a submarine. If the driver lost control on that hairpin bend, there would be nothing to stop it until it hit the water.'

Clara looked at the spot he'd indicated. 'That could be the reason. But what if the driver was forced off the road, rather than simply making an error of judgement?'

Paul Grant greeted them, having heard Clara's comment. 'I think that's a bit unlikely. That road isn't used much, even at the best of times. Two vehicles would constitute a traffic jam on there. Thank God there's no one inside. I've requested a tow truck to get it out of the water, once my lot have finished the photography.'

Even though Clara was no fan of what she classed as 'boys' toys', she could not help but admire the sleek lines of the vehicle as it was hauled from the water, the grey metallic paint gleaming in the sunshine. The classic appearance ended, however, as she surveyed the front end of the car. Even viewed from her acute angle, she could see that the bonnet and driver's wing were crumpled beyond recognition. 'That car must have been travelling at a heck of a rate of knots to get smashed up so badly,' she said, almost without thinking.

Nash grinned. 'You've accused me of some bad jokes from time to time, but saying "a rate of knots" is pretty awful given the car finished up in the river.'

'At least my pun was unintentional. You inflict them on people regularly, and in your case they're premeditated.'

Nash asked Paul what he and his team had found, if anything.

'I'm afraid there's nothing here to give us a clue as to the identity of the driver. That means we can't tell if it was the man fished out of the river lower down or not, although that seems the likeliest explanation. There is one possible reason for the lack of documentation. The car's leased to a company in Leeds, but was reported stolen earlier this week.'

'The bloke found in the river's been dead much longer than that. If he was the car thief, why was there a delay in reporting the theft? At that sort of money, I doubt you'd think you mislaid it,' Nash pointed out.

'Apparently the Managing Director of the company only discovered the car was missing when he returned from holiday. We'll take the car to our garage, and, with a bit of luck, the boffins will be able to lift some prints from the parts of the vehicle that weren't submerged. Then we might be able to rule your corpse out — or rule him in.'

As Grant was speaking, Nash's mobile rang. He listened for a moment before telling the caller, 'Thanks for that. My colleague, Inspector Grant, hopes to have some fingerprints from a crashed car for comparison, but we won't know for certain until Forensics have checked it over.'

Nash told Grant, 'That was Mexican Pete. He's got the toxicology results back on our drowning victim. If the dead man was behind the wheel of this car, I'm now fairly certain we can establish the cause of the accident. According to the report, the man was high on cocaine. To such a degree that Mexican Pete reckons he probably had a seizure and passed out.'

Nash pointed to the area alongside the site of the driver's door. 'As the car door's open, I'm wondering, if that was the case. Perhaps he came round, tried to get out, fell, and hit his head on one of those rocks in the river.'

'That seems logical enough. I'll get someone to check the site over, see if they can retrieve any hair or skin.'

Nash glanced at Clara before continuing, 'I think the combination of drugs and the location are the contributory factors, and the massive amount of coke would explain why the driver became a diver.'

Clara snorted with disgust. 'And you have the nerve to criticize my puns.'

CHAPTER FOURTEEN

Paul Grant phoned next morning to confirm what they already suspected. The man pulled from the river at Winter Bridge had been driving the crashed Mercedes. He also confirmed that CSI had retrieved a minute skin sample off one of the rocks. Although these factors confirmed Nash's theory regarding the crash, they were still no nearer to identifying the victim, apart from the knowledge that he was a suspected car thief.

As Nash told Mironova, somewhat despairingly, 'We've now got an accumulation of eight dead bodies, without a clue as to who any of them are. Beyond identifying cause of death, we know absolutely nothing about the victims.'

Clara frowned, wondering if Nash's arithmetic was incorrect. 'I can only think of seven bodies, six found in Layton Woods, plus the new case from Winter Bridge.'

'I've included the man who was suspected of being Demetra Sinclair's lover, found stabbed in Kirk Bolton. He has to have some connection to the Sinclair case, even if he wasn't having an affair with Sinclair's wife — but what that connection is, I've no idea.'

'How do you know he's linked to it?' Clara said, before she remembered. 'Oh, yes, her DNA was found on his clothing, wasn't it?'

'That's right, and I just wish we could work out what his connection to Demetra Sinclair actually was. I've all but discounted him as being her lover. And, from what we were told by her friends and fellow workers, I don't believe there ever was another man in her life, despite the gossip. I don't know why, but I have this vague feeling that might be at the root of her sudden disappearance. More to the point, I hope and pray the dentistry expert can help us to identify at least one of the victims, hopefully more. Only then might we stand a chance of making progress.'

Clara dwelt on what Nash had said but didn't contradict him. She knew from experience that his 'vague feeling' might well develop into a workable theory, one which more often than not had proved correct in the past. As things stood, her input should be to encourage such feelings if, and when, Nash shared these with her, rather than discount them.

Fortunately, for Nash's peace of mind, the situation he had mentally categorized as an impasse would soon change, but it would involve a lot of work, plus a combination of several differing skill sets. Whether it would give them any clue as to the serial killer's identity was a vastly different question.

* * *

'I've had an idea,' Nash announced half an hour later, as Clara brought him a mug of coffee.

She looked round, giving the impression of being panic-stricken. 'Damn, Lisa's borrowed my car. I need to escape, quickly.'

Nash smiled. 'Don't worry, Clara, it doesn't involve you doing any work. You can continue to act as my personal barista. Now, would you like to hear my idea or not?'

'Go on, if you must.' Clara folded her arms and feigned boredom.

'I think we should ask Mexican Pete to review the original PM findings on Kirk Bolton man.'

'You mean Demetra's lover — or non-lover, as the case might be? Why do you want Mexican Pete to look at it?'

He tapped the John Doe file on his desk. 'I read something that I couldn't equate to what we know, so I'd like our worthy pathologist to give us a second opinion.'

'What did you read?'

'It was to do with the stab wounds. After we've got a second opinion, I need to know a couple of facts. One of those we can get from Sinclair's file. To get an idea of the other one, either you or I ought to have a word with the head of housekeeping at The Golden Bear.'

Nash explained his theory, which, as Clara later acknowledged, had to be the foundation for one of his more brilliant pieces of detective work. Not that she was going to tell him that.

Nash's conversation with Ramirez involved a great deal of diplomacy, as he explained the reasons for his request to review the original file. 'I'm not attempting to discredit your colleague's report on the unidentified male found stabbed in Kirk Bolton. With the facts available to him at the time he conducted the post-mortem, he came to the only reasonable conclusion.'

He paused, aware of the diplomacy needed to ensure the pathologist appreciated why he was being asked to review the initial findings. 'Certain facts have come to light since then, ones that might cast a totally different light on the murder.'

Nash explained what he had in mind and waited tensely for the response. He was vastly relieved when Ramirez told him, 'I appreciate where you're coming from, and will do my best to assist. If the information is complete, which I feel sure will be the case, I should have news for you tomorrow.'

* * *

Nash had only just removed his outer coat and hung it up in the CID room when his phone rang. He hurried to his office to answer it. Having listened for several minutes, scribbling

105

notes on his jotter, he thanked the caller and replaced the receiver. After staring at the details he'd been given, he picked up his mobile.

When the other detectives arrived a few minutes later, Nash called them into his office. As Clara entered, she recognized the folder he was studying as the one containing the Sinclair case notes. He looked up and told them, 'There has been an important development with regard to the Kirk Bolton stabbing.'

'Has the victim been identified?' Pearce asked.

'No, but I believe I know who killed him. And I'm certain it wasn't Nicholas Sinclair.'

'How can you be sure of that?' Lisa Andrews beat Pearce to the question by a short head.

'I already had my doubts, but when I read the file again, something in the nature of the wounds didn't seem right, so I asked Mexican Pete to review the original PM reports. His findings confirm my suspicions. The dead man was five feet, eleven inches tall. The person who stabbed him was standing in front of him, not behind — that's important to remember. The angle of the wounds, in particular the fatal blow, which slashed his throat, suggests he was stabbed by someone shorter than him. According to Mexican Pete's estimation, they would have been no taller than five feet two or three at most. According to this file, Nicholas Sinclair is six feet three and a half inches tall.'

Nash paused to allow them to digest this sensational news, before adding, 'After Mexican Pete told me that, I had a word with the housekeeper at The Golden Bear. She couldn't be absolutely certain, but she's confident that Demetra Sinclair is only an inch or two over five feet tall. I believe that is the reason her DNA is on the dead man's clothing. I think that also provides an explanation as to why she ran away. I think Demetra was scared that if she remained here, she would be arrested, and charged with murder.'

After the others had left his office, Clara stayed behind and asked him what he intended to do with this information.

'I'll have to pass it on to the chief constable and Jackie Fleming. On file, this is the only murder containing what appeared to be cast-iron evidence of Sinclair's guilt, and now even that's been blown clean out of the water. I bet I'm going to be really popular when this hits the fan.'

As the chief constable was away at a conference, Nash explained the pathologist's conclusions to Superintendent Fleming. 'I think this makes talking to Nicholas Sinclair even more important,' he told her. 'If anyone knows what really happened back then, it has to be him. Going from what Demetra's friends and co-workers said about their relationship, I think Sinclair would go to any lengths to protect her. That makes me wonder if he knew what she'd done, and kept quiet for her sake, even though it resulted in him spending a potential lifetime in jail.'

Although nearly every detail of Nash's summary was spot-on, one detail was incorrect, and that was to have an immense bearing on the outcome of the case.

* * *

Next morning, Paul Grant phoned Nash to relay an update on the Winter Bridge case, as they now referred to the road traffic accident. 'I phoned the managing director of that firm in Leeds who leased the Mercedes. He seemed more upset about the car than the dead thief, but I suppose that's a natural reaction. There was something in the guy's tone of voice I didn't warm to, so I had a word with West Yorkshire CID. The guys there handling the supposed car theft told me they couldn't be certain, because there's insufficient evidence one way or the other, but they're more than a bit suspicious about it. They think the garage break-in might be a setup.'

'How so?'

'The incident report states the MD of the firm who leased the Merc left the car in his garage at home while he was away on holiday — said he thought it would be safe enough. He also claims to have been so confident the place was secure he left the car keys inside the garage on a work-bench. The comment from the lead detective was something along the lines of "nobody in their right mind would leave such an expensive, high-end, virtually brand new luxury car without taking basic precautions". That's a précis of what he said, without the swear words.'

'I agree, it all sounds more than a bit dodgy. The problem as I see it, from what you've told me, is that without something in the way of solid evidence, we're at a dead end.'

'West Yorkshire are of the same mind, but they're not taking any chances, so they're running a background check on the company that leased the Merc, the managing director, and any known associates. If they unearth anything out of line I'll be sure to keep you posted.'

While Nash was on the phone, Clara had been studying the files on the Sinclair case, which had recently been updated to include accounts of the interviews she and Nash had conducted with people who knew Nicholas and Demetra Sinclair. Something the housekeeper from The Golden Bear had told them caused her to stop reading. She pondered the sentence for several minutes, and after much thought, she walked through into Nash's office just as he was replacing the receiver.

'Mike, do you remember when we decided to talk to everyone who knew Demetra Sinclair?'

Nash nodded.

'Well, I think there was one person we missed.'

'I thought we'd covered everybody?'

'So did I, but just now, when I read the report of the interview with the housekeeper at the hotel, she told us Demetra had been taking evening classes to improve her English. She cited it as an example of Sinclair's devotion, by sitting for hours in a café drinking coffee and reading a book as he waited for Demetra's lessons to end.'

'Yes, I remember that. What of it?'

'Perhaps it would be useful to have a word with her old tutor.'

'That's an extremely good idea. It shows the value of teamwork. I'd probably have missed that, no matter how many times I read those reports. First of all, though, we need to try and locate the tutor, unless they still work at the tech, which I believe is where most evening classes were held.'

Mironova glanced at Nash's desk and saw the surface was empty, apart from a morning paper. 'I'll get on with trying to find them, shall I, as you're obviously snowed under with work?'

She started by contacting the college principal. He was as helpful as possible, first by confirming it to be the venue for the tutorials. However, when Clara ended the call, she had only gained two salient points. The first was the English tutor's name, Arthur Barrett. Having told her that, the principal added, 'Arthur resigned about the time Demetra disappeared. He'd been offered a job with a recording company in Manchester. However, I was told later that he'd died, but that was only hearsay.'

Clara thanked him, rang off, and reported the news to Nash, who said, 'See what Viv can find out about this Barrett chap, using his computer magic.'

'Of course.' Clara gestured to the desk, now completely empty. 'You're clearly busier than ever.'

It didn't take Pearce long to come back with the information. The news left Nash and Mironova open-mouthed with surprise. 'Arthur Barrett is certainly dead, like the college principal said,' Viv began. 'But when he said he'd died, the guy was either being extremely tactful, or he was unaware of what had actually happened. He took up the post in Manchester, where he was recording a series of CDs and downloads to aid translation from a host of different languages into English. They were to be offered for sale to students worldwide.'

Pearce paused before delivering the appalling news. 'Barrett had only been working there six weeks or so when he was mugged in a multi-storey car park. The assailant stole his wallet, briefcase, and laptop, having first stabbed him to death. None of the missing items has ever been recovered, nor has anyone been charged with theft, receiving stolen property, or murder. Barrett's widow even went to the trouble of offering a reward for information leading to an arrest, but nobody came forward with anything useful.'

'Do you know what became of Mrs Barrett? Does she live in the Manchester area?'

'She never left Netherdale. The couple put their house on the market when her husband got the new job, and a sale had been agreed. After Arthur was killed she withdrew it, and according to the voter's roll, she still lives in Daleside Avenue.'

'Thanks, Viv, that's good work.'

Clara waited until Pearce had left the office and asked Nash whether they should contact Mrs Barrett.

'I'm not sure,' Nash replied, after giving it a moment's thought. 'She might not be able to tell us anything useful. And asking questions about her husband could evoke some extremely painful memories. On the other hand, I'm more than a little concerned about the way Mr Barrett died. Admittedly, on the face of it, the attack seems to have been a random act in the course of a robbery, but the fact that he was stabbed in a similar manner to the other victims worries me, as does the timing.'

Clara frowned. 'What do you mean about the timing?'

'According to what Viv discovered, Barrett was killed only a matter of weeks after Demetra Sinclair vanished. Tie that in to the similar method of killing of the Layton Wood victims and it begins to appear suspicious.'

'Hang on though, Mike, Barrett's murder was in Manchester,' Clara protested. 'That's more than a hundred miles from here. I don't see how it can be connected to the other murders.' She paused and smiled slightly. 'I was going to say it was pure coincidence, but I know you think coincidences don't exist.'

'The distance wouldn't present a problem if the killer was determined, or desperate enough. As for the travelling element, there are these new-fangled gadgets known as motor cars and trains. They're much faster than using a horse and cart.'

Clara muttered something that sounded like 'sarcastic sod' then asked, 'OK, accepting the travel isn't a problem, what motive could the killer have?'

'I can think of a connection, albeit a tenuous one, that might have been behind it. Barrett came from Netherdale. What if he knew or suspected something, and started asking questions? If the killer thought he represented a potential threat, it would be an ideal opportunity to silence him without the murder being linked to anything happening in or around here.' Nash paused. 'Having taken all that into account, I think we ought to risk upsetting Mrs Barrett by paying her a visit. If her husband did suspect something, he might have taken her into his confidence.'

'Wouldn't she have come forward with such information after her husband was murdered?'

'She might not have thought his murder was anything apart from what it was made to appear like — a mugging gone wrong. It's only people with devious minds like mine who think the worst.'

'OK, you deviant, I'll phone her and ask if she's prepared to see us.'

'Yes, and ask if tomorrow's convenient.'

CHAPTER FIFTEEN

Contrary to any preconceived notions the detectives might have formed about her, Gemma Barrett was an attractive, smartly dressed woman, with a pretty face and slim figure. Her good looks were framed by a mane of auburn hair. Clara estimated her age as being between the late forties and early fifties. I hope I look as good as that when I'm her age, she thought.

'You told me over the phone you wanted to discuss Arthur's death,' Gemma said, as she ushered them into her sitting room. 'Does that mean you have some news for me, at long last? Have you some idea who murdered my husband?'

There was never a greater need for tact, Clara thought, as she wondered how Nash would respond.

'We're not certain one way or the other,' he began. 'I know that sounds awfully vague and not at all what you were hoping to hear, but at present that's all I can give you. Let me explain exactly why we're here. We're investigating those bodies you've probably read about or seen on TV, the ones found in Layton Woods. During the course of our enquiries we looked into the disappearance of Demetra Sinclair, and also looked further into her background. Amongst many things, we learned that she had been taking English lessons at evening classes, and her tutor was your husband.'

Nash paused momentarily. 'There is no certainty that your husband's murder is connected to those other deaths, but I find it curious he was killed within a matter of weeks after Demetra vanished. What we're keen to discover is if Arthur mentioned anything at the time. Anything, no matter how irrelevant it may seem, might help us move our investigation forward. I appreciate it's asking a lot after such a long time, and with the trauma you must have suffered since then, but anything, no matter how trivial, could prove vitally important.'

'I need to think about this,' Gemma told them. 'How about I make a drink of tea or coffee? While I'm preparing it, I'll try and cast my mind back and see what I can recall.' With a glint of humour, she added, 'And perhaps the caffeine will stimulate the thought process. I'm not promising, because I've tended to try and blot everything that happened back then from my mind.' She smiled a trifle sadly. 'Occasionally, I actually succeed in erasing some of the memories, usually with the help of a large gin and tonic.'

After delivering their drinks, Gemma asked Clara if she would mind moving from the settee to one of the armchairs. Although at first puzzled by the request, Clara did so. When Gemma sat down in Clara's former position and asked if they had a photo of Demetra, the reason soon became clear.

Clara produced a photo and passed it to Gemma. She held it up at arm's length, positioning it so that it covered the TV screen opposite the settee. Obviously, she was using the image to stimulate her memory of having seen the photo on the television.

After a long silence, she lowered the photo and told them, 'I remember when this girl vanished. Arthur was very upset about it, and I remember him saying something. I didn't pay much attention at the time, because my mind was full of surveyors and solicitors and searching for property, plus packing boxes ready for the move. When that man Sinclair was arrested, it all seemed to make sense. But you've now raised some enormous doubts in my mind.'

'Can you recall what Arthur said?'

'When he saw the photo, he told me, "This is really weird. In fact, it's way beyond weird. That's the second pupil from my English classes at the tech who has vanished suddenly, without warning, or telling anyone they were going. What makes it even stranger is both girls hail from Romania". Like I said, he was upset when Demetra vanished, but later, when Sinclair was arrested, we thought it was nothing more than coincidence, and the other girl had gone elsewhere.'

'Why did you say we've raised doubts over Sinclair's conviction?' Nash asked.

'There are two reasons, really. One is that if you're right, and there is a connection to Arthur's murder, Sinclair could not have done it. He was already in custody awaiting trial, as I remember. When you mentioned a possible link, it reminded me of something else Arthur said. He told me, "I'd never have believed it of Sinclair. I thought he was devoted to Demetra. He used to sit and wait for her to finish classes". Now I'm totally confused.'

Nash thanked her and promised to keep her up to date when, or if, they found anything relevant to her husband's murder.

As the detectives drove back to Helmsdale, Clara asked, 'Are you thinking what I'm thinking?'

Nash kept his face straight as he replied, 'That depends on what you're thinking, but if you mean do I think the other girl from Romania that Arthur Barrett taught is one of the Layton Woods victims, then I think you're right.'

'I'll try and make sense of that later,' Clara said, tartly.

'Actually, I'll go even further. I reckon the killer believed Arthur Barrett either knew, or suspected, what had happened, and might have been ready to share that knowledge or suspicion with the police. From what Mrs Barratt told us, that might have been an overreaction, but with her husband silenced and Sinclair in prison, two potential threats had been eliminated. If that is how it played out, I'd say the killer was remarkably successful, wouldn't you?'

* * *

There was an unexpected development in the Winter Bridge case. News came later that day via a phone call from Paul Grant. 'When Forensics brought the Mercedes back to our workshops, they gave it a thorough going over and got a welcome surprise.'

'I was about to ask if you'd found another body in the boot, but that would hardly class as a welcome surprise.'

Grant chuckled. 'It might do for you detectives, but not for us. It wasn't anything so dramatic, but it could prove extremely useful. When we opened the boot, we found a hold-all. It contained clothing, plus a wallet and mobile phone.'

'I assume they belong to the dead man?'

'Yes, the photo ID on the driving licence is a match. The deceased is called Dean Stokes, and his address is on the outskirts of Huddersfield.'

'Huddersfield? That's at the far side of the West Riding, about as far as you can get from here without venturing into Lancashire. I wonder what brought him to this neck of the woods?'

'That remains a mystery. Obviously, after such a long time, the mobile was dead. But we've managed to get it up and running. We've one more problem to overcome. The device is password-protected, so we've handed it over to our IT guys. They've promised to tackle it as soon as the opportunity arises, but they warned me they're extremely busy, so it could be a while before we can gain access, and even then, it might not give us anything useful. When we do get a result, I'll keep you posted.'

Later, Nash received another phone call, one which gave the promise of an equally important development, this time in relation to the Layton Woods murders. It came with a stipulation, however, which tempered any excitement Nash might have felt.

The caller was Ramirez, who told Nash he had received a call from Dr Foxton. She had suggested a possible solution, to help identify the remains, but warned it wasn't exactly foolproof. 'She also said that given the number of victims, it might prove quite expensive, so I thought you should be aware of that before I ask for the go-ahead.'

'What is it she's referring to?'

'The process is called facial reconstruction.'

'I've seen that on TV, but I wasn't sure if it was practicable, accurate, or even if it was merely fiction.'

'No, it's far more than that. It's been tried and tested in real life, via subjects with either a photograph or painting to compare the results with, and it's quite accurate. Up to press, it has mainly been used for archaeological purposes. Professor Foxton is very enthusiastic about it. She said if we brought her the head of Julius Caesar, the experts could show you what he looked like before Brutus and his cronies dealt with him. The decision as to whether to go ahead rests with you.'

'Actually, I think I'll have to pass it up the line. Someone with a higher pay grade than mine can have that responsibility. No doubt the cost element will weigh heavily in the balance, but if it proves instrumental in bringing justice for those victims and putting their killer behind bars, I'm all for it, no matter what the cost.'

'If I was you, I'd stress the two most effective weapons at our disposal are forensic odontology and facial reconstruction. I say that because between them, they should give us the means to put the correct names to the victims, and avoid potential errors. I can't imagine a more distressing outcome than approaching the next of kin, only to find you are causing unnecessary suffering to the wrong people.'

'That is an extremely valid point, Professor, and I will put your views across as strongly as possible.'

Nash contacted the chief constable without delay, and the strength of his argument, including the pathologist's outline of the need to avoid potential mistakes, must have been persuasive enough, because within forty-eight hours, Nash was able to call Professor Ramirez back and ask him to arrange for the experts to proceed with both procedures.

* * *

With the prospect of a considerable delay before they received any results from the scientists, Superintendent Fleming suggested she, along with the Helmsdale team, should re-examine what they knew so far, and conduct a brainstorming session to attempt to find alternative ways forward.

'I'm concerned we might be in danger of placing too much reliance on the forensic side of things,' she told Nash. 'There is no guarantee they'll come up with anything positive. Even if they are successful, those results might not yield any clues as to the identity of the person who killed them. Our focus has to be on putting this evil monster behind bars, and science alone isn't going to make that happen.'

Nash agreed, as Jackie's words echoed his own reservations, and they agreed to call a meeting for the following day.

When Jackie arrived, and with the team assembled, they began the painstaking process of reviewing every aspect of the original prosecution files from which Sinclair had been sentenced to life imprisonment. Before they began their assessment, Nash, with Jackie Fleming's approval, cautioned them to take a different approach to the normal method of working.

'It is standard procedure for detectives to examine evidence in order to establish a person's guilt or innocence, but in this instance, we must all read the facts bearing in mind that Nicholas Sinclair is innocent. We must also forget any preconceived notions we might have absorbed from our previous reading of what's in this paperwork, much of which we should discount. Part of what we will read has now been shown to be factually incorrect, but there is another aspect I feel is equally important. I'm referring to the gossip and hearsay, much of which seems malignant. But that helped convince the original team of detectives they had the right culprit. Having reached that conclusion, they failed to look for alternative explanations.'

He paused and gathered his thoughts before continuing, 'What I find intriguing, and not a little disturbing, is how those rumours were allowed to gather momentum. Was it a single source? If so, it might be beyond our reach to identify that person, but it has to be at the back of our minds. And, that being the case, what has thus far been written off as a collection of errors, combined with a misinterpretation of facts, might turn out to be something far more sinister. In other words, Nicholas Sinclair might have been the subject of an elaborate and cleverly executed frame-up. So let's get to it, and as we study the documents, feel free to give voice to any thoughts that occur to you, no matter how irrelevant they might seem.'

As she listened, Clara realized this was probably the most comprehensive briefing she'd ever heard Nash deliver. She guessed it was intended to spur the team to their best efforts, and if so, it proved about as successful as they could have hoped for.

CHAPTER SIXTEEN

The first of the files involved the murder of the man found at Kirk Bolton, who was referred to throughout as John Doe. Having already examined the file more than once, Clara asked a question designed to remove the last shadow of doubt from her colleagues, knowing that both Viv Pearce and Lisa Andrews were still sceptical about Sinclair.

'Apart from Mexican Pete having established Sinclair's innocence, what do we know that wasn't apparent when the first investigation assembled the evidence?'

'Is that now beyond doubt, though?' Jackie asked. 'We seem to be placing a lot of reliance on a very minute section of evidence.'

'I take it you haven't read Mexican Pete's summary,' Nash replied. 'He said, from the angle of the wounds, the only way Sinclair would have had the strength to deliver the blows was if he'd been lower than the victim.'

'What if the victim was lying down?' Lisa suggested.

'If he'd been in a horizontal position, the blood splatter from the severing of the jugular vein would not have reached the victim's trousers and shoes. The conclusion Mexican Pete came to, which he says is unquestionable, is that John Doe was standing up when he was stabbed, and his assailant was approximately twelve inches shorter than Sinclair, which puts them at little over five feet tall. The prime suspect for that is Demetra Sinclair, who has conveniently vanished without trace. Her involvement in the murder would also explain her DNA being found on the victim's outer clothing, but nowhere else on the body.'

Nash paused and smiled at Clara's audible sigh of relief at his euphemistic final phrase. He waited for a few seconds to allow the detective constables time to digest what he'd said, and was about to continue when Viv interrupted.

'Hang on a minute, boss. If Demetra Sinclair killed him, where did she do it? And how did she get him to Kirk Bolton? She doesn't have a car. And how could she move a bloke bigger than her?'

'I've no idea, Viv. But no doubt we'll find out, eventually. Now, in regard to Clara's question about new information, there is one assumption I think it's safe to make, and that is, the killer must be a local or have in-depth local knowledge. This is reminiscent of another recent case where we searched in vain for someone, although in that instance they were the innocent party.'

'How can you state so emphatically that the killer must be local?' Lisa asked.

'OK, let's assume you're in the centre of Harrogate or Leeds, for example. If you were to stop a couple of dozen people in the street and ask them if they'd ever heard of Layton Woods, how many of them would say yes? Even if you got one or two to confirm they knew of it, do you think they could give you directions to get there, and then reach a clearing near to Black Fell Foss?'

The silence that followed Nash's question indicated that he had convinced his audience. Happy with this, he continued to press the point. 'One of the other reasons we can discount Sinclair is his lack of access to a four-wheel drive vehicle or a handgun. Those would both have been needed, to access the site, and to shoot the male victim. However, a depraved digger driver, or a twisted tractor operator, would definitely be worthy of consideration.'

With this at the forefront of his mind, Pearce suggested they should re-examine the reported sighting of Sinclair's Mini Cooper being driven up the track into the woods. 'Would it be worth talking to the man who came forward in response to the appeal for information that appeared in the *Netherdale Gazette*?'

'That's a good idea,' Nash told him. 'Make a note of it, and when we've finished climbing this paperwork mountain, you can go online and find out if he's still living locally.'

A few minutes later, Clara looked up from the document she had been studying. 'I wonder if we ought to go to Netherdale Engineering and ask a few questions there? I know we've pretty much established Sinclair's innocence, but I was wondering why one or two of his co-workers were so keen to tell the detectives about the fiery temper they said he had, which we know to be a tissue of lies. OK, the college principal gave us one possible motive for their slander, but could there be a more sinister reason?'

'What sort of reason, Clara?' Jackie asked.

'I wondered if they might have been offered an inducement to lie about Sinclair. A cash payment, perhaps, or the promise of a better job. Either would have been difficult to resist, given the uncertain future of the company.'

'It might not yield anything, but like the eyewitness Viv mentioned, it's certainly worth a try,' Jackie agreed.

Once they'd reached the end of their review of the documentation, which, as Jackie commented, had been like the curate's egg — good in parts, Pearce turned to his computer. His intention, to track down the person who had mentioned Sinclair's car being seen in Layton Woods. Having entered the man's name and address, he looked at the result on screen with dismay. He called through to Nash's office, signalling for him and Jackie to come through.

'What's the problem, Viv?' Jackie asked.

'I checked out the guy who claimed to have witnessed Sinclair's car, but I'm afraid it's a dead end.' He winced. 'Sorry, that was a very bad pun.'

'I should warn you Mike's in charge of bad puns,' Clara called across from her desk.

'The man lived in Kirk Bolton, close to the boundary between the Winfield and Layton estates.'

'Why was it a bad pun?' Jackie wanted to know.

'Less than two months after making that statement, the guy was killed in a road accident. He was alone in the car when the brakes failed as he was approaching a ninety-degree bend on the descent from Black Fell. The car hit a dry stone wall, overturned, and burst into flames.'

'That's extremely unfortunate,' Jackie responded. 'But do you know if he had any family, anybody he might have talked to about his sighting of the car?'

'He was married, but I can't find any trace of his widow,' Pearce replied.

As they were talking, Nash glanced across at Clara, who was staring back at him. He raised his eyebrows and saw her nod, as if in agreement with something he'd said.

'You referred to it as being unfortunate, Jackie,' he told the superintendent, 'but I think it might be far more sinister than that.'

'Are you thinking this might not have been an accident? That his car was tampered with?'

'I find it highly suspicious that this man died only a short time after making his statement. Add that to the murder of Demetra's English teacher. According to his widow, a few weeks before he was stabbed to death in Manchester, the teacher mentioned another Romanian girl from his class who had disappeared, shortly before Demetra. I think it might be worth taking a trip to Kirk Bolton, which seems to have been the centre of activity back then. Not only was the eyewitness living there, but it's also where John Doe's body was found.'

'What would a visit achieve?' Jackie asked.

'If the witness's widow moved away, perhaps the people who bought the house or one of the neighbours might know where she is now, and then we could speak to her. As it was your idea, Viv, would you follow up on it tomorrow, please?' Nash turned to Lisa Andrews. 'That'll leave you to mind the shop, because Clara and I are going to Netherdale Engineering to follow up on her bright idea.'

* * *

The following afternoon, Lisa Andrews reported a nearly entire lack of activity. 'There was a reported sighting of someone who the caller said resembled our flasher. But when a couple of uniformed officers talked to the suspect, not only did this guy have the wrong colour hair, but he's only just arrived back from a three-week holiday abroad. I think that rules him out.'

'It sounds as if you've had as much luck as we did, or rather as little,' Nash told her. 'Netherdale Engineering is quite a small concern, with a workforce of only fifteen men, less than a quarter of the size it was in its heyday. The managing director took over from his predecessor six years ago, and everybody on the shop floor had been recruited during his tenure, with one exception. He joined the firm twenty years ago, and although he's a bit hazy on names, he recalled a couple of his fellow workers who seemed to have a bit of a downer on Sinclair for some reason. Speaking for himself, he'd always thought Sinclair was a decent bloke, until the trial. He told us one thing we found curious, though. He said when he and the others gossiped about Sinclair during the trial, those two never joined in. He said it was almost as if they didn't want to know. Soon afterwards, they both resigned and went to work abroad. He can't be certain, but he believes they'd gone to India.'

'You think they're the ones who spread the lies?' Lisa asked.

'I do, and what I find most disturbing is that almost everyone who might have had something to tell us either died, or went out of reach. Perhaps I'm being a bit fanciful, though.'

'Like that's never happened before,' Clara said, smiling sweetly at Nash.

Nash ignored Clara's insinuation. 'Anyway, how did you get on, Viv?'

'By the sound of it, you had about as much success as me. I went to the house in Kirk Bolton, but the people who live there only moved in a couple of years ago, and they certainly don't know anything from before then. Having hit that brick wall, I went to talk to other people in the village, and luckily I went into the shop, which also acts as a sub-post office. I talked to the woman who works there.' Pearce grinned. 'Or rather, I listened while she talked. I'd class her as being your typical nosy neighbour. She told me the widow sold up soon after her husband's death and moved to live abroad —in Spain, she believes, or possibly Italy. I thought she might remember if the widow had her post redirected, but she couldn't. She was far more interested in telling me about the fancy man she'd gone with. I wasn't quite certain what "fancy man" meant.'

'It's an old-fashioned expression for a married woman's bit on the side,' Nash explained. 'So that's yet another person who might have proved useful, conveniently vanishing before we can talk to them.' Nash glanced at Clara. 'So maybe I'm not as fanciful as people round here seem to think.'

* * *

Although Nash was still plagued by an errant memory, on this occasion he wasn't the only member of the team to suffer from a recollection failure. Clara remarked to her husband David, as they were eating their evening meal, 'What concerns me is, I might be starting to think matters through the same way Mike does, and suffer the same memory lapses.'

'Adopting Mike's line of thinking is no bad thing, though,' David pointed out. 'Mike's a bloody good detective. So are you, for that matter. The biggest difference is you're far prettier than he is.'

Although she revelled in the compliment, Clara was keen to change the subject. 'Did I tell you Mike has decided not to tell the others about the baby until we've solved this case? I keep having to watch what I say — it would be so easy to let things slip. I know they'll all be delighted at the news.' She smiled at the prospect.

David laughed. 'Not feeling broody are we, *Mrs Sutton*?'

'No, I am not!' she responded. 'I'm just so happy for them. Anyway, what have you got planned for tomorrow?'

David grimaced. 'Not one of my favourite jobs. I'm speaking at a seminar where a collection of medics and other professionals are being tutored on how to deal with soldiers who have a range of physical and mental issues stemming from their active service. My input will involve me baring my soul about life on the front line, and working in enemy territory. Plus the physical and psychological effects of being wounded.'

Clara put her hand on his and squeezed it gently. 'You'll be fine, David. If anyone can get the message across, you'll do it. As a bonus, I have to thank you, because you've just solved a mystery that has been puzzling me about the case we're investigating, which might prove useful.'

Sutton grinned. 'In that case, I'll claim my reward later.'

Clara paused in the act of refilling their wine glasses. 'Does that mean we're in for an early night?'

His grin was answered with a loving smile.

* * *

When Nash reached the station the next day, he saw Clara was poring over the files they had examined a couple of days earlier. She looked up and smiled. 'Thanks to you, I think I've just identified something that's been bugging me for a while, but I need to talk to that housekeeper again.'

'The woman from the Golden Bear? What do you think she can tell us we don't already know, and why is it thanks to me?'

'Yesterday, when you told me you'd be late in because you were going with Alondra for her routine check-up, it didn't ring any bells. But later, I realized something we'd missed regarding Demetra, something I'd been trying to recall for ages. I thought the housekeeper might be able to give us a clue as to how far gone Demetra was in her pregnancy.'

'Why would that be helpful?'

'I'm not certain it will, but as it was her first child, I feel sure she would have consulted a doctor, a midwife, or even attended antenatal classes, if the pregnancy was sufficiently advanced. If she did talk to medical professionals they might have some information or background, providing we can persuade them to share it with us.'

'That's a good idea, Clara. I just wish my errant memory would return as easily as yours did. I've been puzzling over something for weeks now, and try as I might, it won't come back to me. It was a fragment of conversation I had with someone, and I know there was something relevant within the discussion, but so far I haven't the faintest idea what it was about.'

'Give it time,' Clara said, as she picked up the phone.

Her conversation with the housekeeper proved disappointing, ending in yet another blind alley. As she told Nash, who was busy filling the coffee machine, 'Apparently Demetra hadn't seen anyone in the medical profession. She was planning to make an appointment, but she disappeared before she had chance to do so.'

'That's a shame, but it's about on a par with all aspects of this case. We seem to be thwarted at every step, no matter what we try. I'm beginning to despair of ever moving this investigation forward. Let's hope Mexican Pete's boffins can provide us with something. Other than that, I reckon we're up the creek without a paddle.'

Although Clara smiled at Nash's euphemism, she recognized the frustration behind it. There were times when even an optimist like Nash needed encouragement. 'It does seem like that at present, but we've been at this stage before and we've usually found a solution — either that, or something happened we hadn't anticipated, and it provided the inspiration we needed. That could happen again, with or without the forensic specialists' input.'

Clara had never regarded herself as a prophet, but in this case her words of support would later prove unerringly accurate.

CHAPTER SEVENTEEN

Aware of the potential hiatus before progress on the iden-tification of the victims was possible, Nash had an idea he needed to run past DC Pearce. 'Viv, when the boffins have completed a facial reconstruction, will it be possible to elim-inate or reduce the number of candidates by matching their image to ones from MISPER using your computer?'

Pearce looked surprised by the question. 'Yes, of course it will, Mike. It will be done digitally. Although I should warn you, I don't think you will get infallible likenesses. However, the software we have should reduce the margin of error considerably.'

'I suppose that's the best we can expect. Let's hope it doesn't take too long for the boffins to come up with the goods.'

Nash turned to go back into his office, then stopped in his tracks. He glanced sideways and signalled for Mironova to follow him. When they were inside, he told her, 'I've just had a thought. Why I didn't have it ages ago beats me.'

'Is this the elusive memory you mentioned?'

'No, that's still elusive. This is something else. We tried to talk to the English tutor, but found he'd been murdered. What we didn't think of was attempting to trace the other students who attended the same classes. They are as likely to tell us something relevant about Demetra and this other Romanian girl as Mr Barrett. In fact, I'd say they probably knew more about them than their tutor. I think we ought to investigate the possibility of tracing those students, because there could be an additional benefit. Once we have the facial recognition results, we could show them a likeness of the one we know comes from Eastern Europe, and maybe get confirmation or otherwise as to whether it's Demetra's fellow student.'

'That's a really good idea, Mike.'

'I only have one reservation, or perhaps two. First, will the college have a record of their names after all this time? Second, even if the college comes up trumps, will we be able to trace them?'

'Do you want me to phone the principal and find out if those records are available, and if they are, to get the ball rolling?'

'Please do.' Nash smiled. 'Although, the number of times you've phoned him, he probably thinks you fancy him.'

Half an hour later, Clara reported back. 'I had to wait until he'd finished a lecture, but it was worth the delay. He told me we're in luck, because they only started keeping records on their computer a couple of years before Demetra's disappearance. It will take a while to locate the relevant file, but he's promised to get his secretary onto it immediately. It's quite detailed apparently, giving every student's date and place of birth, nationality, and their home address in the UK at the time. With luck, we should have the information sent by email tomorrow.'

'Pass it to Viv and Lisa as soon as it arrives, and they can make a start trying to locate as many of the students as possible.'

* * *

On Monday morning a list containing twelve names arrived from the technical college. One of those was Demetra, who had enrolled, prior to her marriage, using her maiden name, Zamfir. The only other Romanian national was a girl called Felicia Baciu. Clara knew this must be the girl Arthur Barrett had been referring to when he was telling his wife of a student's disappearance.

Clara handed the list to Viv and Lisa, who got to work on it immediately. She left them poring over their computer screens and told Nash what she'd received. 'If the other Romanian student turns up alive and well, at least we can rule her out. But if she is one of the skeletons, we'll also be able to put a name to the male victims.'

'I take it you're referring to her brother?'

'That's right, so we've made a little progress already.'

'Let's hope the name isn't an alias,' Nash responded. 'It's been known before, particularly in respect of illegal immigrants wishing to hide their true identity for fear of being deported.'

Twenty-four hours later, Pearce was able to advise the team of his findings — or, in several instances, lack of findings. 'One of the more mature students died five years ago.' Seeing the look of speculation on Nash and Mironova's faces, he added, 'The death was from natural causes. Five of the others have returned to their home countries — Brazil, Finland, Latvia, Thailand, and Uganda. Of the remaining five, I could find no trace of three of them, including Felicia Baciu, which leaves only two I've been able to track down.'

Pearce paused and glanced down at the paper in his hand. 'I'll willingly volunteer to go interview one of them, because she married a chef, and they now run a hotel in Shetland.'

'You can join the queue for that job, Viv,' Lisa told him.

'What about the other one?' Clara asked.

He laughed. 'That's not quite as long a journey. In fact, if you look out of the window you should be able to see her shop window. Her name is Elsa Franks, née Schaffer, from Germany originally. Her husband is Joe Franks, the baker and confectioner where we usually go for our sandwiches.

His wife's shop is next door to his, alongside the sweet shop that was one of Jack Binns' favourite haunts.'

They smiled at Viv's reference to their retired uniform sergeant, but listened as he continued, 'Elsa is a seamstress, selling clothing, knitting wool, and all sorts of haberdashery.'

'I'll volunteer to interview Elsa,' Lisa Andrews told the others. 'I need a new outfit for summer, and I've got Alan's credit card in my purse.' She grinned.

'If you're going to talk to Elsa, you can combine the trip and bring our sarnies back with you,' Nash told her.

When she returned, Lisa brought some news. 'I spoke with Elsa Franks, and I must say her English is excellent. She remembers Demetra and Felicia, and was shocked at the situation, but would be more than happy to assist with identification if the need arises. I asked her about events back then, and she told me the students didn't think much about Felicia disappearing, but when Demetra also vanished, they talked about it quite a lot. It was near the end of term, so by the time the students returned the following year, everything had changed. By then, they'd all read the headlines and knew Sinclair had been arrested for killing his wife and her lover. There was a new tutor in place who had no interest in what had gone on previously, so in amongst all this, Felicia's disappearance was more or less forgotten. She told me Demetra was extremely concerned when her fellow countrywoman went missing. She'd asked everyone in the class if they had seen Felicia since their previous lesson, but nobody had. Elsa told me she's sure there was something else Demetra said at the time. She's promised to let me know if she remembers.'

'Did Elsa say anything about Demetra's personality or her character?' Nash asked.

'She told me she was surprised to learn that she had a lover. She seemed devoted to her husband, and the marriage was a happy one. This more or less confirms what others have said.'

What they'd learned from Elsa was at least a step forward, as Nash told Clara, albeit a very small one — more of a shuffle than a giant stride. They returned to the files and kept digging.

* * *

On the following Monday, Nash had only been in Helmsdale a couple of minutes when he was surprised to get a phone call from their pathologist. 'I have sent an email to DC Pearce containing attachments which are the facial images of all the victims, as you requested,' Ramirez told him. 'If you are able to find a close likeness from your missing persons' files, send me the relevant details, and I can alert the forensic odontologist. He, in turn, will contact dental practices in the relevant parts of the country.'

'That was very quick, Professor, I thought such a complicated procedure would take far longer.'

'Science has moved on considerably since the time of Sherlock Holmes. I would advise obtaining DNA from potential next of kin before proceeding with confirmation of identity. That would avoid causing further unnecessary distress. I'll leave you to work on it.'

'One thing before you go, Professor. We have found someone who could confirm the identity of the Eastern European female whose skeleton was recovered. Have you marked that facial image?'

'No, but I can tell you it is labelled number four.'

When Viv Pearce walked into the CID suite, he found a deputation comprising his three colleagues awaiting him. Having greeted him, Nash told him, 'There will be an email in your inbox from Mexican Pete.' Nash explained what the message contained, before adding, 'We need the images printing off, but priority must go to number four, which is the Eastern European female. We need that to show to Elsa Franks. If she confirms it to be Felicia, we'll also have identified the male skeleton — Felicia's brother.'

Twenty minutes later, Lisa returned from another trip across the market place, and her colleagues knew immediately from her expression that the walk had been successful.

'Elsa agrees this could be Felicia Baciu. Looking at this stirred Elsa's memory about Demetra. Apparently, Demetra told Elsa she'd been to the flat Felicia shared with her brother, thinking she might be ill, but the place was deserted. Apparently, Felicia and her brother were orphaned when she was about twelve years old, so when her brother came to England looking for work, Felicia naturally accompanied him. Although Elsa can't be certain about this, she believes Demetra or Felicia might have mentioned that he worked on a building site.'

'OK, get her address off your student list and go and have a word with her landlord, show him the picture, and see what he can tell you. Take Viv with you.'

Reflecting on these developments gave Nash an idea, which he put to Clara later that morning. 'Now we've got those images, I thought it might be worth releasing them to the media. So far, we've only got one potential positive.' He shook his head. 'We need more confirmation.'

'Putting all six out at once might cause more confusion than positive feedback, and it might also cause distress to relatives of people reported missing.'

'Sorry, I didn't make myself clear. I wasn't suggesting all six. Just the two we know won't cause distress. If they yield positive results, we could consider releasing the others later. We could add a little speculative information, along the lines of, "This man is believed to have worked on one or more building sites approximately fifteen years ago, and his surname is thought to be Baciu." If we do that, one or more of the people he worked alongside might come forward with some information. In the meantime, when Viv and Lisa return, we should get them working on those images and comparing them with any potential matches from the MISPER list.'

'I don't envy them that job. It could take forever and a day.'

'There are ways of streamlining the process. If they limit the parameters to those reported missing between the relevant dates, as Professor Foxton suggested, it should reduce the numbers considerably. Meanwhile, I think you and I should go to Netherdale.'

'Any particular reason?'

'There are actually three reasons. I want to find out if the chief's had any success in getting Sinclair brought to Netherdale for questioning. I also want to show her and Jackie Fleming those images and seek their approval for the media approach. Then, if they give the OK for that, we can visit the *Netherdale Gazette.*'

Clara whistled. 'Is that wise, visiting your old flame Becky Pollard?'

Nash smiled. 'I don't think that's going to be a problem. Alondra told me she bumped into Becky in town a week or so ago and they got chatting. Becky invited her to go for a coffee, and it was all very amicable.'

Clara grinned. 'They were probably comparing notes. Is that part of your secret agenda, trying to gauge your rating?'

'Absolutely not. I merely want to get Becks onside to print those photos and the backstory to accompany them.'

'That's a relief. If it had been anything else, I'm not sure I'd have wanted to witness it.'

Having checked that the chief constable and the detective superintendent would both be available, Nash and Mironova set off for Netherdale.

* * *

Their meeting with the two senior officers had mixed results. Both gave approval for the plan to approach the *Netherdale Gazette* and approved Nash's secondary idea, to release further facial recognition images at a later stage in the investigation. When Nash asked what progress had been made in moving Sinclair to Netherdale, however, the response was not as positive as he'd hoped.

'It isn't because the powers that be are against the idea,' Ruth Edwards told them with a grimace. 'But there seem to be reams and reams of red tape to be cut through. And to cap it all, the person with overall responsibility for signing off the movement order is away on holiday. Hopefully, when they return, we'll be able to organize the transfer.'

'I think there's a way of bypassing the red tape,' Nash responded. 'It might be pure bluff, or not, but it's definitely worth a try.'

'Go on.' Ruth Edwards eyed him suspiciously.

'You'd have to begin by pointing out that Sinclair has been attacked on more than one occasion. Every day he spends in prison his life could be in danger, and now the media have labelled him a sadistic psychopath, that danger has increased dramatically. If anything bad did happen to him, and his next of kin were to find out it was avoidable, they would have every right to sue for punitive damages, to add to the possible wrongful imprisonment claim already on the table.'

'Hang on there, Mike. I thought the file stated Sinclair was an orphan, with no living relatives?' Jackie Fleming interposed.

'Yes, I agree he is an orphan, but he does have at least one, hopefully two living relatives that I'm aware of.'

'Who are they?'

'There is his wife Demetra, and — if her pregnancy went full-term — a fifteen-year-old son or daughter. That's assuming nothing bad happened to Demetra after she ran away.'

'I hadn't thought of that,' the chief admitted. 'And you're right, Mike, it's definitely worth a shot. I'll get on it straight away.' She smiled rather cynically as she added, 'I'll tell them the payout could run into millions. That'll focus their minds.'

As Nash and Mironova were leaving headquarters they were intercepted by Paul Grant. The Traffic division inspector had news for them, and it contained the prospect of positive results. 'The IT boys have managed to unlock the mobile belonging to Dean Stokes.'

Nash looked confused.

'Dean Stokes, the bloke pulled out of the river at Winter Bridge.'

'Sorry, Paul, I'd almost forgotten about him.'

Paul nodded. 'I'm not surprised, with all those skeletons. Anyway, it gave us a load of very useful information, via SMS, voicemail, and his contacts list. We're still going through them all, along with our colleagues from West Yorkshire, but with luck, we might soon be in a position to make a number of arrests. The offences concerned are fraudulent insurance claims regarding staged road traffic accidents. If we're right, the amount involved could run into millions. Quite a few millions,' he added with a grin. 'I'll be sure to let you know how things develop.'

* * *

Their meeting with Becky Pollard, editor of the *Netherdale Gazette*, was equally positive, once she cleared up a misunderstanding.

'Clara thought your meeting with Alondra last week was so you could compare notes about me,' Nash told her.

Becky laughed, scornfully. 'Don't flatter yourself, Mike, it had absolutely nothing to do with you. The reason Alondra hasn't told you what the meeting was about is that I asked her not to mention it until we were ready to proceed, but I can reveal it now. We're planning to run a series of articles featuring local celebrities, and Alondra's name is high on that list. Not just because of her stature as an artist, but also her backstory. I've even got a title for it. I'm planning to head it "The Evolution of Catwoman".'

Nash smiled at the reference to Alondra's nickname, bestowed on her because of the iconic trademark signature, an image of a cat, on all her paintings. 'That's great news. She'll be delighted at the publicity, but I'd better explain why we're here.'

Half an hour later, leaving behind the two images of the Eastern European siblings, which Becky promised to feature in the paper's next issue, they drove back to Helmsdale.

'I reckon that's been a good morning's work,' Nash told Clara as they headed up the stairs.

'Yes, although it could have been even better. Let's hope the chief succeeds in pitching your idea for getting Sinclair out of prison. If the threat you made, implicit though it might be, does the trick, it might give us the lead we're hoping for.'

The first thing Nash and Mironova noticed on entering CID was their colleagues staring fixedly at their respective computer screens, so deep in concentration they didn't even turn when the door opened. Nash motioned to Clara, signalling towards the coffee machine whilst simultaneously miming someone eating. Clara got the message and nodded, pointing across the street, before turning to exit the office.

When she returned, fifteen minutes later, she distributed sandwiches to accompany the mugs of coffee Nash had already provided. He pointed to his office. Clara smiled as she followed him inside and closed the door. 'They've taken the task to heart, that's for sure,' she said, in little more than a whisper. 'I only got a muttered thanks for the sarnies.'

Nash smiled. 'You did better than me. I didn't even get that for the coffee. But I have got a note from Lisa. It says they discovered Felicia's landlord had sold up and moved away. Unfortunately, no one knows where.'

'Well, I have news for you,' Clara said. 'When I went to order the sandwiches, Elsa Franks was in the shop chatting to her husband. Joe introduced me to her, and Elsa asked if I would give Lisa a message. She isn't certain, but she believes Demetra mentioned the name of Felicia's brother once. She thinks he was called Costin.' Clara glanced at their colleagues in the outer office. 'I'll tell Lisa if, and when, she ever surfaces from the internet.'

They had only just finished their lunch when Nash's phone rang. He listened for a couple of minutes and then said, 'OK, Steve. Lisa can't be disturbed. She and Viv are tied up with something very important. Clara and I will attend to it, and if you get any more calls for CID, don't ring upstairs, phone our mobiles.'

He replaced the receiver and told Clara, 'We're off to Bishopton. Free Willy's struck again.'

CHAPTER EIGHTEEN

As they were getting into Nash's car, he told Clara a little more about the incident. 'Steve told me our exhibitionist got a bit more than he bargained for this time. The lady concerned was offered a female support officer, after he chose to display his wares to this her morning, but she refused. Apparently she was laughing as she spoke. We've to meet her in the café in the high street.'

There were quite a few customers in the café, but Clara gestured to a lady seated on her own at a table by the window. She had a mug of coffee in front of her, and the floor alongside her was taken up by a trio of large shopping bags. She appeared to be quite calm, even smiling as they approached her table.

'Mrs Gascoigne?' Nash asked.

The woman nodded, and having introduced themselves and showed their warrant cards, Nash signalled to the waitress for two coffees. Once these arrived, he asked the lady, who told him her name was Sylvia, if she could describe the man who had exposed himself.

She grinned, which surprised the detectives, as she responded, 'You want a full description? OK, he was white, in his late twenties or early thirties. He was wearing dark-coloured jeans, a grey, long-sleeved polo shirt, and black trainers. His hair was untidy, and it was mousey in colour.'

'Did he speak to you?'

Sylvia laughed. 'I didn't give him chance. As soon as I saw his prick I told him I'd just bought some cocktail sausages with more meat on them that his pathetic little thing. Then I told him to go home and have a wank.'

Clara clamped her lips together in surprise and tried hard not to laugh.

'You don't seem too upset by what happened. Might that be delayed shock?' Nash asked, trying hard to remain professional.

'Hardly, Inspector Nash, I've been married and divorced twice, had several boyfriends, and now have three adult sons. After all that, the sight of another dick certainly doesn't faze me.'

Clara made a note of the description, along with Sylvia's details, explaining she would have to go to Helmsdale station to make a formal statement, if that was convenient. She may also be required to attend an identity parade once the culprit had been arrested, if he didn't admit the offence.

Sylvia thought about this final statement for a few seconds before telling them, 'If an identity parade becomes necessary, I ought to add to the description I gave you earlier. The guy who flashed his todger hasn't been circumcised.'

She laughed as she spoke, and the detectives smiled, even as Nash told her he didn't think that exposing the genitalia would form part of the identifying process. They thanked Sylvia for her assistance and departed.

As they drove back to Helmsdale, Clara commented on Sylvia's reaction to what would have caused many women great distress.

'I think you're right,' Nash agreed, 'which makes catching this guy a priority. Next time he might pick on someone less resilient.'

Their upbeat mood generated by the positivity of the witness was enhanced when they returned to the CID suite, where Viv and Lisa gave them more good news.

* * *

'We think we might have identified strong candidates for two of the victims from Layton Woods,' Lisa explained. 'Viv had a bright idea, which helped considerably.'

Nash winked at Clara. 'There's a novelty, Viv having a bright idea. How did that miracle come about?'

Far from being upset by the insult, Pearce grinned as he told them, 'We were having a lot of difficulty getting potential matches, because the images Mexican Pete sent through were lacking detail. I amended them by adding hair and eye colouring from a series of MISPER photos. We examined each one, discarding the non-runners where appropriate. There were a lot of failures, because even using the parameters you suggested, we still had a fair number to go at. By the time we'd finished, we had three potential matches for one of the victims, and four for another of them. I've printed the amended images off for you to look at, together with the details of each candidate. Sadly, we couldn't find any likely matches for the other skeletons, so we're a bit stuck there. We wanted to know what our next move should be.'

'Clara and I will take a look at what you've got for us, and then I'll give Mexican Pete a call. If you email the details of the likely candidates to him, he can get the forensic odontologist to contact dental practices in the relevant parts of the country. If we're lucky, we might soon be able to identify two more of the victims and we can then visit the next of kin. That might give us our first really positive lead, so well done to both of you, that was really excellent work.'

Nash paused and then told the detective constables, 'While you were busy, Clara and I went to Bishopton, where we interviewed another of Free Willy's targets, a lady who was unmoved by his display and was able to give us a full description.' He smiled as he added, 'A very full description, in fact.'

'What does "a very full description" mean?'

'Don't even go there, Lisa,' Clara warned her. 'Believe me; you really don't want to know.'

One thing that puzzled Clara, as she remarked to Nash, was they had only managed to get possible matches for two of the victims from the MISPER list.

'That might be because the others have never been reported missing,' he replied. 'There are hundreds of thousands of people who go missing every year, and not all of them are reported. They might not have close relatives or friends to become concerned about their welfare. Then there are the ones who simply vanish without leaving any indication that they are going to be off the radar.'

'What do you mean?'

'Suppose someone tells people they intend to go to London to live and work, but does not leave a forwarding address or contact number. How would anyone know if they're safe and well, or if they're lying at the bottom of the River Thames with lead weights keeping them from resurfacing? Even in these days of mobile phones, the lack of contact could easily be put down as a change of service provider, or the phone being lost or stolen.'

It was, Clara acknowledged, a powerful testimony to the vulnerability of people who had nobody to miss them, or in extreme cases, to mourn their passing. Nor did it make it any easier for those determined to bring justice to victims of horrific crimes, but that didn't in any way weaken their resolve to do so, and to punish the evil characters who caused such suffering. She vented her feelings, and was surprised by Nash's response.

'What you said just now echoes the motto over the Central Criminal Court at the Old Bailey. It reads, "Defend the children of the poor and punish the wrongdoer" He grinned. 'However, a visitor once said it should be changed to, "Abandon all hope ye who enter here".'

This was by no means the first time Clara had experienced Nash's fund of knowledge. Keen to test this out, she asked, 'Where did that pessimistic sentence originate?'

'It's a quotation from Dante's *Inferno*, and is supposedly the inscription over the gates to Hell.'

'How did you come by it?'

Nash grimaced. 'Latin lessons at school. Our teacher was an aficionado, and foisted stuff like that on us. I can recommend it as an extremely good cure for insomnia. As for the quotation, in the case of some notorious criminals who ended up in the Old Bailey dock, I reckon it's entirely appropriate, because with any luck, they should be on the way to Hell.'

* * *

There was a further period of inertia as the team waited for feedback regarding the potential candidates Viv and Lisa had put forward. Clara was reminded of something Nash had once said during the course of a previous enquiry. "Sometimes, detective work is a bit like a building site. You can pass by a partly constructed building time after time without there being any noticeable change, or anyone working on it. Then there's a sudden flurry of activity, and just when you think the job is almost complete, it all goes quiet again".

Nash's analogy might be accurate, but it did nothing to ease their frustration at the current lack of progress.

The rest of the week passed without any developments, but the following Monday brought the action Nash had predicted. It began with a phone call from Ruth Edwards. The chief constable announced that she had received the go-ahead, and Nicholas Sinclair was to be moved from Frankland to the custody cells at Netherdale. 'The transfer will take place as soon as they can arrange transport and security, probably on Saturday,' she told Nash. 'Of course, this will mean you'll be working over the weekend. But I'll let you know in good time, because I guess you'll want to be in Netherdale to welcome him.'

'I certainly will, and thanks for your effort, Ruth.'

'It's good to tell there's no one in earshot. You're only allowed to call me Ruth in private.'

'Yes, ma'am.' Nash laughed as he put the phone down.

No sooner had he replaced the receiver when it rang again. This call was from their pathologist. 'The teeth from the skeletal remains have been compared to those your team picked from the missing persons list, and we now have two matches. I've sent an email to DC Pearce with the details. When you do contact next of kin, don't forget you must collect DNA samples. Only when I have positive familial indicators will I be able to confirm identity, categorically. To this end, my colleague has stressed the need for discretion with the relevant dental practices.' Then, with his usual attitude to Nash, he finished by saying, 'And no doubt you'll want the DNA samples fast-tracked?'

Nash was smiling as he said, 'I will have those samples to you as soon as possible. Thanks for your work on this, Professor, and please pass on our gratitude to your colleagues.'

After ending the call, Nash went into the main office. 'There should be an email from Mexican Pete in your inbox, Viv. He and his counterparts have matched two sets of dental X-rays with patient records. We'll need to find the next of kin and obtain saliva samples for DNA analysis. The results will be compared to the victims before the professor will give positive identification. Of course, this must be handled with complete discretion.'

He turned to Mironova and told her, 'I also got a call from the chief. She's got the go-ahead for the Sinclair transfer, and will let us know beforehand so we can go to Netherdale to interview him. Don't make any plans for the weekend. In the meantime, I'm going to phone the prison governor and put our plan into action. I want him to make sure news of Sinclair's transfer reaches the media, albeit a severely edited version. It will contain the supposed reason behind the move — Sinclair's responsibility for six more murders.'

Clara shook her head. 'I seem to remember God once saying you could give Machiavelli lessons in deviousness. How right she was.'

Nash smiled at Clara's reference to their retired chief constable, Gloria O'Donnell, known to one and all by her initials.

* * *

After Pearce printed off four copies of the email from the pathologist, and attached them to the relevant missing person's report, the detectives studied the paperwork. The first of the victims was a twenty-six-year-old woman by the name of Cassie Harris. She lived alone in a rented apartment in Manchester, where she worked as secretary to two partners in a large solicitors' practice. There was no mention of her being in a relationship, or having had a romantic involvement in the years prior to her disappearance. She was reported missing simultaneously by her employers and also by her brother, who lived and worked in London. Having tried and failed to contact Cassie by phone, he had contacted the solicitors, who confirmed they had already reported her absence to the police. This all took place seven years ago, when Sinclair was securely locked away — further, conclusive proof of his innocence.

'We'll need someone to visit the brother and collect a DNA sample,' Clara suggested.

Nash smiled. 'Fancying a trip to the big city, are you? I don't think the chief will allow that expense. It would be a waste of time and money for one of us to travel all that way when someone from the Met can do the job far quicker and easier.'

They turned their attention to the second file. This concerned another single woman, by the name of Lucy Fowler. Lucy was twenty-nine years of age at the time she vanished, and like Cassie Harris, had no known romantic relationships. Lucy had held down several jobs in her late teens and early

144

twenties, but had then retrained to become a nurse, working in a Sheffield hospital.

She had been reported missing five years ago by a senior member of the hospital staff. This was confirmed by her parents, who had been unable to get replies to either phone calls or emails. Her parents had retired early to live in Portugal, six years before Lucy disappeared. A file note added later stated that Lucy's father had since died, and her mother subsequently sold the property and returned to the UK to live in Sheffield.

'At least we won't have to travel as far in order to speak to Lucy's mother,' Clara said, glancing at Nash. 'And South Yorkshire has far nicer scenery than London.'

Lisa Andrews was concentrating on another aspect of the reports. 'These women have quite a lot in common,' she said. 'Both of them are single with no known attachments, which seems rather strange, because they're both very good-looking. The both lived alone, and appeared to have few, if any, close friends. They had good jobs, not the sort that would be likely to get them into a difficult situation. And, in both cases, the only family members lived a long distance away.'

'What does that suggest to you?' Nash asked.

'If their social life was as near to non-existent as these reports suggest, might they have wanted to change that? Whether it's relevant to how they vanished is hard to judge at this point.'

'Going on from what Lisa has said, there is one thought that is puzzling me,' Nash told them. 'How do two young women from Manchester and Sheffield, respectively, come to end up buried in Layton Woods? That is, always assuming the identification turns out to be correct. We're a long way from both those cities, and this area isn't exactly a hub of social activity.'

'We need that DNA sorted ASAP,' Clara said, 'because until we get that, we can't begin asking questions of people close to these women. I'm speaking of family and work colleagues, because there doesn't appear to be anyone else.'

'Speaking of the DNA, I think our best bet would be to ask Jackie Fleming to organize the testing for us. When we get the results, we'll have chance to interview the families before we see Sinclair. Hopefully, we can get more from him than he gave us when we visited Durham. If he tells us anything this time round it will be a bonus, because last time we got zilch.'

'Is there anything specific we can do in the meantime?' Clara asked. 'I'm getting a bit fed up of sitting twiddling my thumbs, and rereading all these files.' She gestured to the boxes.

'Keep going, Clara. You may just find the key to this whole case.'

* * *

The next morning, several TV channels and at least three newspapers shared the same lead story, under the title, *Double Murderer Sinclair to be quizzed over more killings*, which was almost word for word what Nash had asked the governor of Frankland prison to let slip to an eager pressman.

Reading the headline gave Nash an idea. He rang Jackie Fleming. 'I think it might be as well to ensure there's a reasonable contingent of uniformed officers on standby for when Sinclair arrives. If the media continues to stir things up like this morning, they might well be needed for crowd control.'

Clara, who was listening, turned away so Nash couldn't see her smile. At no point during the discussion had Nash reminded Jackie of the fact that he was the one who had provoked the media reaction. Clara's mention of Machiavelli had been right on target.

When the detectives received the DNA test results, they confirmed beyond question the identity of the two victims, Cassie Harris and Lucy Fowler. 'Now we have to brace ourselves for the task of delivering the bad news to the next of kin,' Nash told Clara. 'That's the aspect of our job I detest most of all. When we appear, it's as if the last vestige of hope, however remote, has been snatched away. First, we'll have to make travel arrangements. Cassie's brother lives in London, and Lucy's mother in Sheffield. I think it makes sense to try and combine them into one day, so I'll contact Tom Pratt and he can look into train schedules. Once I've got a potential itinerary, we can contact the relatives and ensure they're available. It would be unfair to delay seeing them when they've been asked to supply DNA. They'll be anxious to hear any outcome.'

CHAPTER NINETEEN

Alondra drove Nash to Netherdale station, collecting Mironova en route, and the detectives were in time to catch the early morning service to London. There, they interviewed Neville Harris, a forty-year-old chartered accountant, at his home. They gained little from the meeting, or so they thought at the time, but one remark they heard later gained greater significance.

In response to Nash's question about Cassie's personal life, her brother told them it was virtually non-existent. 'I used to tease her about it,' he said, his voice reflecting his sadness. 'Although it wasn't her fault. When she was eighteen she got involved with a man, but later discovered he was married, and had a reputation as a serial womanizer. She was badly hurt, and it put her off men for years.'

'I can't say I blame her for that,' Nash responded. 'You said it put her off men. Does that mean she'd begun to change?'

'I believe so, but I can't be sure. When I was teasing her, just a few months before she vanished, she told me she might be going to try one of those online dating sites. Whether she went ahead or not, I can't be sure. She never mentioned it again, so I assumed she'd given up on the idea.'

'It's a shame we can't access her computer or laptop, or whatever device she used, because that might tell us whether she did go on one, but I suppose all her belongings have long since been disposed of.'

Harris thought for a moment and then told them, 'Actually, I think I've still got her laptop somewhere in the depths of my garage. I never bothered to switch it on because the machine was an old one, and I have far more up-to-date computers of my own. Whether you'll be able to get it up and running after all this time is a different matter. One thing that puzzles me, though — how come the media are linking that man Sinclair to Cassie's murder? Surely he was in prison long before she disappeared?'

Nash shrugged. 'We have no control over the media, and I'm afraid the press will print anything that grabs attention.'

'I quite agree, Inspector Nash.'

'Going on from what you told us about Cassie's laptop, we'd like to take a look at it. It's standard procedure in this sort of inquiry. Would you mind having a look for it?'

The detectives left soon afterwards, the laptop secured in Nash's briefcase. As they travelled north on the second leg of the journey, discussion centred on Harris's comment about the dating website. 'Do you think that's how the killer made contact with a woman who lived and worked so far away?' Clara asked.

'It's a strong possibility. It'll be interesting to see what Lucy Fowler's mother can tell us. With luck, she might know more, because for one thing, a woman is more likely to reveal her personal life to her mother than a male relative. And Lucy's disappearance is more recent, being only five years ago. I have one concern, though. If Mrs Fowler is getting on in years, her memory might not be as good as it should be.'

As they began talking to Alice Fowler, it soon became apparent that Nash's fears were groundless. Lucy's mother was a sprightly, alert, sixty-three-year-old, who greeted them with a welcome coffee and a slice of cake. Although visibly distressed by news of her daughter's death, she answered their questions promptly and rationally.

The reason for her composure became clear when Nash told her, as gently as possible, that DNA analysis confirmed the body to be Lucy's. 'That only tells me what I already knew. There could be no other explanation for Lucy to go five years without contacting me, or her father before he died, bless him.'

'I know you were living in Portugal when Lucy vanished, but were you in regular contact prior to that?'

'Yes, we spoke pretty much every week, and we were able to see her, because Raymond, my husband, used one of those video call things. Skype, or something like that, I think it's called. I just let him get on with it, because I'm useless at such technicalities. I'd wait until he'd made contact, and then we could chat away. It was great, almost as if Lucy was in the same room.'

'Can you remember how long it was before her disappearance that you last spoke to her?'

'Only about ten days, I think, but I can't be certain, because we were so worried about her.'

'Did she have a boyfriend, or anyone she was really close to? Or didn't you talk about that sort of thing?'

'She had one or two when she was a teenager, but nobody really significant. She told me she wanted to find someone special, the right man. But none of the boys she dated lived up to her expectations, so she ditched them.'

'Had there been anyone more recently?'

'There was nobody that I was aware of, although that might have been about to change. The last time we spoke, she told us she'd signed up for one of those online dating sites like you see advertised on TV.'

Nash and Mironova exchanged glances, a signal that didn't escape Alice's notice. She looked directly at them and asked, 'Do you think that might have been what happened? Did she meet someone online and he killed her?'

'We're not sure of anything at this stage, but you must remember, although Lucy went missing five years ago, her body has only recently been discovered, so we're in the very early stages of the investigation. However, it is a possibility we're not ruling out.'

Clara could guess Nash's next question before he asked it. 'I assume after Lucy disappeared, her apartment would have been cleared by the landlord. Do you know what happened to her belongings? Were they sent to charity shops, or disposed of some other way?'

'They certainly weren't — Raymond and I wouldn't hear of that. We arranged for the landlord to put them in storage, and they've remained there ever since. Raymond was convinced Lucy would turn up sooner or later, but as time went by, that seemed less and less likely. After Raymond died, I almost got rid of them, but I hadn't the heart to do it.'

'Have you a list of what's in that store? I'm not thinking of clothing or anything like that, we're more interested in her computer, tablet, or mobile phone, that sort of thing.'

'There's a laptop, I believe. But I don't think there's a phone or anything else of that nature.'

'Would you grant us permission to take the laptop away and check what's on it? I promise we'll keep it safe and return it as soon as we've finished with it.'

'I think that would be OK. I'll have to make arrangements to get it,' Alice replied, adding, with the first touch of humour they'd seen, 'I suppose I can trust you.'

Nash handed her his card. 'If you call me when you have it, we'll send one of our colleagues to pick it up.'

As the detectives were leaving, Alice put her hand on Nash's arm. 'I know it's what you call a cold case, but please do your best to find the evil man who killed my Lucy. If you can put him behind bars for life, I might begin to believe in justice again.'

'Rest assured, we will leave no stone unturned in trying to find the killer.'

Once they boarded the train for the final leg of their journey, they discussed Alice Fowler's reaction to the news, and her revelations during the interview.

'She was remarkably composed,' Clara said. 'But I guess that was due to her having already accepted the situation. She was only awaiting confirmation.'

Nash was surprised. 'I thought you'd have looked beyond the surface. Alice Fowler might have put a brave face on things, and said some comforting platitudes, but beneath all that, her heart is breaking. She lost her husband three years or so back, and now the hopes she held of the daughter she loved being found alive have been dashed. How does any mother cope with such terrible news?'

'I didn't think of it that way,' Clara admitted. 'Do you want me to depute Viv or Lisa to travel to Sheffield and retrieve Lucy's laptop?'

'Send Lisa. She can do the tea and sympathy bit, and might just hear something more that will help us. Besides, Viv's going to be busy,' — he tapped his briefcase — 'he's got a laptop to work on.'

'I think it's getting to look more and more likely that the girls met their killer online, don't you?'

'That certainly seems the favourite option. How else do you explain the distance between where they lived and where their bodies were found? However, despite having what appears to be our first major clue, we're a long way from identifying the killer. And we still have two unidentified victims. Three, if you include the John Doe at Kirk Bolton.'

'Are you going to let Superintendent Fleming know what we've found out tonight, or will you leave it until morning?'

Nash glanced at his watch. 'It's a bit late to call Jackie tonight. She'll probably be propping up the bar at the Horse and Jockey by now, downing her third pint of *Theakstons* while she chats up Jonas Turner.'

Nash's ridiculous suggestion made Clara laugh, causing one or two of her fellow passengers to stare at her. Absurd though it was, the picture his remark conjured up was the brightest note in an otherwise difficult day, reinforcing his comment about the upsetting nature of the task they had been performing.

In contrast to the intense frustration of the previous weeks, the news brought by Nash and Mironova brought a buzz of excitement amongst their colleagues, from the chief constable down to the most junior ranks. Any further irritation caused by the delay until the computers had their contents analysed was offset by a distraction, albeit a welcome one.

* * *

On Saturday morning, Nash, along with Mironova, Fleming, and Edwards, watched from the chief constable's office window as the prison van crawled slowly and carefully through the milling throng surrounding the main entrance to the headquarters building. Once it had passed through the electronically controlled gates leading to the custody suite car park, the vehicle reversed to the entrance, where its bulk obscured the view to anyone except perhaps a drone operator. Anyone entering or exiting the building would be invisible to the press photographers with their telephoto lenses, the TV crews with their high-definition cameras, and the crowd of onlookers provoked by the news item.

'It looks as if your strategy worked a treat,' Ruth Edwards told Nash, 'I just hope it turns out to be worthwhile.'

For quite a time, it appeared that this was not to be the case. To begin with, Sinclair was defensive and somewhat aggrieved by the way he had been treated, or as he saw it, mistreated.

'Why am I here?' he demanded angrily, as soon as Nash and Mironova walked into the interview room.

Nash held up one hand, signalling him to wait. Once Mironova had activated the recording, she asked if Sinclair required the services of a solicitor.

Sinclair rolled his eyes. 'I've told you lot before, I can't afford one,' he said angrily.

Nash then asked Sinclair to repeat his first question, but the prisoner lapsed into sullen silence.

'OK, you asked why you had been brought here. That question baffled me, because I'd have thought the answer was blindingly obvious. Do you not read newspapers or watch TV in prison? If you did, you'd be well aware of the reason for bringing you here. The purpose of the move is to question you about six more murders, in addition to the two for which you've already been convicted.'

Nash paused and waited for a reaction, but Sinclair stared at the table in front of him, still unwilling to respond. Nash bent forward, staring at Sinclair as he continued, 'When I said we were going to question you about those six murders, that wasn't strictly correct. We already know you must have committed them, because the media told us so — and they're never wrong, are they?' he said, pointedly. 'We just need you to enlighten us with a few of the mechanics of how you went about it.'

Still no reaction, so Nash went on, 'What we're most anxious to find out is how you managed to sneak out of the maximum security wing of Frankland, meet up with your victims, travel all the way to Layton Woods, kill and bury them.'

Sinclair looked up, as Nash continued, 'I'm speaking about the women who were murdered in the years since your incarceration. We'd also like to know where you've hidden the murder weapon and the spade you used to dig the graves, plus whose car you used for transport. If you did all that and then returned to your cell unnoticed, you must be a latter-day Houdini.'

Sinclair lifted his gaze further and saw the detective smiling at him. He was puzzled, still speechless, but this time it was surprise that was striking him dumb.

Taking advantage of the continuing silence, Nash asked, 'One other point for clarification, Nicholas. Could you explain why you were kneeling down when you stabbed the man found at Kirk Bolton? Our pathologist has examined the original PM reports and told me the angle of the wounds suggest that only someone much shorter than you was capable of delivering the blows that killed him. So I ask you again, why were you kneeling down? That's pretty much all we need you to tell us.' Nash then added, 'Because if you can't provide a rational answer to those relatively trivial questions, we will have to consider the ridiculous and unthinkable alternative — that you might actually not have committed any of those murders.'

His final words brought a gasp of astonishment from Sinclair, as he realized that in a few sentences Nash had taken a sledgehammer to the seemingly irrefutable evidence against him, leaving only a few shattered remnants. After another long silence, Sinclair spoke for the first time. 'You actually believe I'm innocent?'

'Of course I do, and now we've got that nonsense out of the way, Nick . . .' Nash paused. 'Would you prefer to be called Nico, or is that only for Demetra to say?'

Sinclair uttered one word, 'Nick.'

'OK, so why don't you tell us about what really went on back in the day? Though I should warn you, we do have an alternative suspect for the Kirk Bolton murder you are convicted of. Along with that, we are beginning to wonder if the death was actually murder, or an act of self-defence. Because I think the only way to explain how Demetra's DNA got onto his outer clothing, and how the murder weapon with the victim's blood found its way into your flat, is if she killed him.'

Nash paused to allow this to sink in, and then said, 'I certainly don't believe he was Demetra's lover. In fact, I don't believe she had a lover. Even if what the witnesses have told me is incorrect and she did have an affair, I definitely don't think she would choose someone old enough to be her father to carry on with. No, considering every aspect of that argument, I'm forced to the only feasible conclusion, that Demetra was loyal to you throughout. That also leads me to wonder if that was the reason she ran away, because she was frightened of the consequences of her actions. Was she afraid the police would jump to the wrong conclusion, just like they did with you? Or was it something or somebody else she was scared of, like the Layton Woods killer, for example?'

There was a long agonized silence, until Sinclair told them, 'I only wish I knew. I have asked myself that question over and over, day in, day out, for the past sixteen years.'

Clara noticed there was no rancour in Sinclair's voice, no bitterness in his expression, only deep sadness, combined with yearning for the woman he'd lost. Whatever Demetra had or hadn't done, and whatever had happened to cause her to disappear, Clara was becoming convinced that Sinclair knew absolutely nothing about it. Either that, or he was hoping to make them believe it. Even as she had the thought, Clara dismissed it, because there was no way Sinclair was such a good actor. If he did know something, why was he not prepared to reveal what had really happened to Demetra?

As usual, Clara's primary role was that of observer. Over the years they had developed a synergy, with their different skills melding to form a highly efficient unit. On several previous occasions, it had been her talent for picking up and recognizing reactions from those being questioned that had led them to either pursue or discount a suspect.

As Sinclair formulated his reply to Nash's twin questions, Clara was startled to see tears glinting in the corners of his eyes. As she pondered this, Clara wondered how hard it must have been for this man, locked away for a decade and a half, having been convicted for crimes he knew he hadn't committed. Along with that awful knowledge, Sinclair suffered the torment of not knowing what had become of the woman he loved, unsure if she was safe and well — or if something dreadful had befallen her.

To top all that distress was another agonizing thought. What had become of the child they had conceived together? If Demetra was alive, had the baby been born, survived, and was now well on the way to adulthood — or had something bad happened to them both?

CHAPTER TWENTY

Although Sinclair had now been made aware of facts that proved his innocence, he seemed either oblivious to them, or uncaring. With that, Clara realized the subject wasn't even of the slightest interest to him. His only concern, now, as always, was for the welfare of his wife and their child. Nothing anyone could say or do would ease the heartache Sinclair was enduring, the misery that had been his constant companion since the day he returned to his flat to find Demetra gone, the place wrecked. That torment would continue unless something happened to break the deadlock. As matters stood, Clara couldn't see anything short of a miracle resolving the impasse.

After a silence that seemed to drag on for ages, Sinclair shuffled in his chair and spoke, his voice little louder than a whisper. It was so quiet, Clara wondered if the recorder would be strong enough to pick up what he said. 'They accused me of dreadful things at my trial, and they implied Demi was little better than a slut. I didn't care what they said about me, because I knew none of it was true. I didn't believe their accusations about Demi either. She would never have behaved like they implied. What I didn't know then, what I don't know to this day, is what happened to her. I pray with all my heart, as I have done every day, that she is alive and well somewhere.'

Emotion threatened to overcome him, but he gulped, shook his head as if to clear his mind, and then continued, 'For some reason, Demi left me, left the life we were planning together. I have no idea why she did that. Something must have happened, of that I am certain.'

Sinclair smiled, but it was an expression of sadness rather than humour. 'Was it something I said? Something I'd done? I don't know, and not knowing simply adds to my torture.' He stopped suddenly, as if the effort of talking about the past and the emotional strain caused by his recollections was too much for him.

Into the silence, Nash asked a question, picking up on one of Sinclair's remarks in a way many, Clara thought, including herself, would have missed. 'What did you mean when you said, "something must have happened, of that I am certain"?'

'I could tell Demi was worried about something, and it wasn't anything trivial, but I have absolutely no idea what the problem was, because she wouldn't tell me. I'd been working away for almost a month. It was pretty much a twenty-four/seven job, so I didn't have chance for even a flying visit home. Our only contact was via a few extremely brief phone calls.'

The sad smile returned as Sinclair told them, 'The only reason I volunteered for that job was because the overtime was huge and there was a handsome bonus when the work was done. Demi and I discussed it before I put my name forward, and we thought it would be useful to put the money aside for when the baby arrived.' He laughed sarcastically. 'The money certainly came in handy. It helped to pay my legal bills.'

He paused to take control again. 'The last time I spoke to Demi was the weekend before I was due to return home. She sounded dreadfully upset about something, but wouldn't tell me what. I was tempted to abandon the job and come home there and then. I didn't, I remained on site, and I've regretted that decision for the past sixteen years.'

'What happened next?'

Clara guessed Nash's question wasn't purely seeking information, but to deflect Sinclair from becoming too absorbed in self-pity.

'When I walked in, I thought I was in the wrong place. It was a shambles, with broken furniture, shattered mirrors, the TV screen in smithereens. You've no doubt seen the photos, but in real life it was far worse. Added to that, Demi had gone. She'd taken every item of clothing she possessed. There was nothing to suggest she had ever lived in the flat. She didn't even leave me a note.'

That must have been the worst imaginable homecoming, Clara thought, but even then Sinclair could not have known the nightmare that was to follow.

'Did she take anything that belonged to you?'

Sinclair gazed at Nash, plainly taken off guard by this unexpected question. After another long pause, he said, 'I've never given that a moment's thought, but she did take something. In fact she took two things. Our wedding photo was one. Nobody noticed at the time, because the frame was there, or what was left of it, but the photo had gone.'

'And the other thing?'

'It was my stuffed rabbit. I remember telling Demi about the rabbit, who I naturally called Peter. He was given to me when I was five years old by one of my foster carers, and I kept it because it was the only toy I had.'

'Why didn't you phone her mobile to ask where she'd gone, and what had happened at the flat? And, even more important, to ask why she ran away?'

'Demi didn't have a mobile. She's a complete technophobe. She used to keep the TV instruction book alongside her chair, that's how bad it was.'

'Did you go looking for her, or check with people at the hotel where she worked, or ask her friends if they'd seen her?'

'I was about to, but almost as soon as I reported her missing I found myself in a cell awaiting trial for two murders. In the short term, I almost started believing the lies about her seeing someone else, because I'd been told them again and again. Sometimes the questioners seemed to revel in my discomfort, but then I realized they were trying a crude form of brainwashing. I was able to resist them easily, because deep down I knew Demi was totally incapable of acting so deceitfully. Once I started thinking rationally, I was able to dismiss the lies, but it got me no nearer working out what really happened, or where Demi had gone.'

Noticing how distressed Sinclair had become, Nash suggested they halt proceedings. 'I don't know about you,' he told Sinclair, 'but I'm ready for a cup of coffee. How do you take yours?'

Nash called an officer to take Sinclair to his cell and arranged for refreshments with the custody sergeant. As the detectives walked along the corridor leading to the headquarters canteen, Clara said, 'You seem to be treating Sinclair more like a witness than a suspect. Is that some deep ploy to gain his trust?'

'Certainly not, I think Nicholas Sinclair *is* purely a witness. Because as far as the crimes we're investigating are concerned, he is completely innocent. My agenda is purely to find out the extent of his knowledge. But from what I've heard so far, I believe he has no more idea than we do as to what actually happened sixteen years ago. The next part of the interview should confirm whether that is so, or if there is something he hasn't told us, either because he's deliberately withholding it, or because he doesn't realize it's significance.'

There was little conversation during the coffee break, both the detectives occupied with their own thoughts.

When the interview resumed, one of the few items, sparked by a remark made by Nash, resulted in Sinclair realizing, for the first time, how much his situation had changed.

'How are conditions in Frankland? Are you treated OK? I know there were one or two bits of trouble.'

'It isn't good, but I guess much of that is an attempted deterrent to prevent people from reoffending. I certainly wish I didn't have to go back there.'

Nash's reply stunned him to silence. 'You won't be going back. Tomorrow you'll be collected by Sergeant Steve Meadows and transferred, discreetly, to Helmsdale station. You will be the only prisoner. Sergeant Meadows will be there through the day, with another trusted officer in place overnight. We're keeping you away from Frankland for your own protection.'

Nash broke into a huge grin. 'Helmsdale station normally only operates during office hours, unless the need arises. As of Monday, all arrests will have to be dealt with here in Netherdale. Unfortunately, there is a major plumbing problem in the cells which makes them unusable, and I believe it will take some time to obtain the required parts.'

Sinclair stared at him for a moment before he realized the meaning behind the statement and nodded. 'I understand.'

Nash continued, 'So far you've refused the services of a legal representative because you can't afford one, but I suggest you contact your solicitor, James Anderson, in the near future. I'm sure Mr Anderson will agree to deduct his fees from your compensation settlement. I appreciate that solicitors don't come cheap, but even after settling his bill, you'll be extremely well off.'

'What compensation?'

'The money you'll be entitled to in recompense for sixteen years of wrongful imprisonment.'

Sinclair was stunned and sat staring at the detectives in disbelief.

Clara had puzzled over how Nash intended to ascertain the extent of Sinclair's knowledge, but his next question settled the issue.

After a short silence Nash asked, 'Does the name Felicia Baciu mean anything to you?'

Sinclair's immediate reaction was a puzzled frown. Either he didn't know the name, Clara thought, or he was unaware of its relevance. When he did reply, it confirmed the latter of her theories. 'I know her name, but I never met her. Demi mentioned her a few times. They became friends when they attended English classes at the tech. Probably the fact that they both came here from Romania helped. Why do you ask? Has she come forward with some evidence?'

'No,' Nash told him, 'but we've had facial reconstruction done on the victims found in Layton Woods. We already knew from the DNA profile that two of them, a brother and sister, came from Eastern Europe. We showed the image of the female to another student in the same class and she identified it as being Felicia.'

Nash paused briefly, then changed the subject. 'The other fact we unearthed — sorry, bad pun, is that Demetra withdrew money from her bank account, using one of their London branches. The withdrawal took place after you reported her missing. In fact, according to the date and time of the withdrawal, you were in this building being questioned about the stabbing. This went a long way towards convincing me Demetra might still be alive, or at least she was still hale and hearty after everyone presumed she'd been killed.'

There was no mistaking the jubilation Sinclair felt at this revelation. He looked, Clara thought, as if the weight of the world had been lifted from his shoulders. Demetra must be a very special kind of woman to inspire such devotion, with expectation of nothing in return.

Sinclair's elation barely diminished when Nash asked, 'Do you have any idea who the Kirk Bolton man was, or how Demetra's DNA got onto his outer clothing?'

'I haven't got a clue, but I'm certain it isn't the filthy reason everyone insinuated back in the day. Shall I tell you why I'm so certain of this?'

'Go ahead, Nick.'

'Before Demi and I made love for the first time, she told me she was a virgin.' Sinclair smiled. 'I think she was shocked when I told her I was also a virgin. I think that made our relationship even more precious, the knowledge that there had never been anyone else for either of us.'

Keen to try and alleviate Sinclair's obvious distress, Nash signalled the end of the interview by telling him, 'Although you're going to be kept in a cell at Helmsdale, that is purely for your own safety. Only two officers, sworn to secrecy, know you will be there. They have been instructed to treat you as if you were a guest. That means you'll be able to order in meals, even drinks if you so wish, and the good news for you, being a Yorkshireman, is they'll be on the house.'

Nash's remark brought a smile to Sinclair's face, and for the first time this one didn't contain even a tinge of sorrow.

CHAPTER TWENTY-ONE

Tuesday was known in Bishop's Cross as Pension Day. A large percentage of the village population were beyond retirement age, and walked to the village store, which doubled as a sub-post office, to collect the money. Even those who received the state benefit via bank transfer withdrew funds from the ATM sited on the front wall of the store. Many of them then went into the shop to spend the money. This multi-tasking saved unnecessary walking, which was a great bonus.

When the phone rang in CID, Lisa Andrews was already driving to Sheffield to collect Lucy Fowler's laptop. Nash, Clara, and Viv were discussing progress over their first coffee of the day. The internal call came from Steve Meadows. Nash listened for a couple of minutes, thanked Meadows, and told his colleagues, 'Leave your coffee. We're off to Bishop's Cross. There's been a raid on the village post office. The post-master was attacked and, by the sound of it, badly injured.'

As they began the journey, Clara phoned Detective Superintendent Fleming to tell her about the incident, only to find she was already aware of it.

'Apparently,' Clara told her colleagues, 'Jackie was in the control room when the call came in. She wants us to keep her *au fait* with developments.'

On the country lane leading to the village, the first vehicle they encountered was an ambulance heading towards Netherdale, its emergency lights flashing. Nash swung the Range Rover onto the verge to allow it to pass.

'That must be the assault victim,' Viv suggested.

Confirmation came when they drew up outside the village store, where an ambulance responder car was pulling away. The small forecourt in front of the shop was already cordoned off with incident tape. Watched by a few curious locals, they put on protective suits, added their names to the log, and ducked under the tape. Four uniformed officers were standing outside, and the senior of them gave the detectives an account of what they had found when they answered the emergency call.

'The first customer of the day raised the alarm. He arrived just after nine o'clock and the morning papers were still outside, the door was locked, the screen still across, and there were no lights on inside.'

The officer explained how the elderly customer summoned the part-time shop assistant, who opened up and found the proprietor unconscious on the floor. He pointed across the village green to a small terrace of cottages. 'She lives in number three, so we suggested they wait for you there. That way they can have a cuppa.' He grinned. 'It was also the best way to keep them out of our hair. You'll be able to inspect the crime scene without interruption.'

'What do we know about the victim?'

'His name is Arnold Clarke, and he's been postmaster here for over twenty-five years. His wife used to help him in the shop, but she died a couple of years or so ago, so now he relies on Norma, the woman who found him. He doesn't live on-site, but has the adjoining cottage.'

'OK, we'll have a look. One more thing, how was Mr Clarke dressed when you arrived?'

The relevance of the question was lost on Mironova and Pearce, and also, it seemed, on the uniformed officer. 'He was wearing pyjamas and slippers,' he replied, looking puzzled.

'Thank you. That rules out it being an inside job. If Mr Clarke had been involved in the robbery, he would have been dressed differently. My guess would be either the robbers triggered an alarm, possibly one of those motion-sensitive devices. Or perhaps Mr Clarke simply heard noises coming from inside the shop.'

Once they were in a position to view the interior, Clara whistled with surprise. 'This was no spur-of-the-moment burglary, judging by the mess and what was taken.'

'I agree, this must have been planned in advance, and the thieves would have needed a van to carry away the amount they stole,' Nash said as he looked round.

The shelves that had contained wine and spirits were empty, mirroring those behind the service counter, where cigarettes and tobacco had been kept, the screen ripped away. Sticking close to the side of the room, avoiding any potential evidence, and the blood on the floor, they approached the post-office section in the corner of the store. It was then they began to appreciate the extent of the villains' haul.

The door of the safe along the side wall was wide open, the shelves stripped clean. In addition, the thieves had prised open the rear compartment of the ATM and removed all the notes from within.

'That's why Mr Clarke was in here. The thieves needed him to open the safe,' Nash said.

'He obviously did as he was asked, so why was he injured?' Viv asked.

'Perhaps he tried to resist. We won't know until we interview him and find out exactly what went on. Viv, would you go across the road and interview the customer and shop assistant? Clara, you and I can try to figure out how they managed to do all this without the entire village turning out to watch the fun.'

Nash noticed a door alongside the cigarette shelves at the rear of the shop counter, which he guessed led to a storage area. Once he and Clara entered, they were immediately able to see how the intruders had accessed the premises. The roller shutter door on the rear wall of the building had been forced. Once inside, the mechanism key was used to raise the door, until it jammed halfway because of the damage. However, it was not the means of entry that grabbed Nash's initial attention. 'I think we're going to have to raise our estimate of the amount they stole even more — and the size of the van too,' he told Clara, gesturing to one side of the storeroom.

She followed his pointing finger. Along the side wall was a pallet she guessed might have contained beers, wines, and spirits, but which now stood empty, shrink-wrap and cardboard strewn over the floor. Above it, the shelves were also devoid of contents. Nash's twin theories about the amount of loot and the size of the van were becoming ever more viable, as was his suggestion that this had been a carefully planned, well-executed raid.

'How many do you reckon? I guess it would have taken at least three.'

Clara was puzzled momentarily. 'How many what? Oh, you mean how many villains were there?' Seeing his nod, she thought for a second or two and then agreed, 'I'd say there were certainly three, possibly even four or five. They'd want to be in and out as quickly as possible, and would have needed someone to keep lookout in case they were disturbed. Which could also explain why Mr Clarke was attacked.'

'We'd better clear out and make way for CSI,' Nash suggested. 'But I reckon they'll have a wasted journey. I doubt very much if they'll find anything useful. This looks far too professional for the thieves to make such an elementary mistake as leaving fingerprints or DNA behind to help us. Let's go see if Viv's got anything interesting out of the shop assistant.'

As they were about to re-enter the main shop section, Nash saw a bank of switches on the wall. He stopped, staring at these for a moment. 'Clara, take a look inside and see if any of the lights come on.' He then switched them in turn to the on position.

'No joy,' she reported. 'Even the chiller and freezer cabinets aren't lit up.'

Nash ducked under the roller shutter to the outside, and looked along the back wall of the building. Clara followed, and together they stared at the cable running vertically down the brickwork. 'That'll be why the alarm and the lights failed to activate,' Nash told her.

The cable had been sliced through, the cut clean enough to suggest a very sharp implement had been used. 'It also means the electricity supplier will have to be contacted to repair that cable before all the frozen produce gets ruined. Added to that, there's no point in us trying to retrieve CCTV footage from within the shop. Yes, these were definitely professionals at work.'

Clara followed up on his mention of CCTV. 'We ought to check around the village and see if anyone has an exterior CCTV system. Any camera might have picked up the thieves' van as they either arrived or left the scene.'

'That's an excellent idea, Clara. We'll act on it once we've found out what Viv has to report, if anything.'

They exited the shop, disposed of their protective gear, and were halfway across the village green when Pearce emerged from one of the cottages, accompanied by a young woman and an elderly gentleman. The man turned aside and walked slowly, stiffness in every stride, towards the far end of the green. Pearce introduced the young woman, who Clara reckoned to be around the thirty-year mark. 'This is Norma Blake, Mr Clarke's assistant. She has something to tell us which could be quite important.'

'It's to do with the amount of cash on the premises,' Norma told them. 'Today is when people collect their pension, even those with direct banking withdraw some cash. It's paid on a lunar month basis, and this just happens to be the day. On Monday, a security van delivers extra cash. I don't know the amount involved, because Arnold, Mr Clarke that is, he deals with all the post office side of things. I only attend to shop customers. But judging by the number of people who usually come to collect their pensions, it must be quite a considerable sum.' She paused. 'Can you tell me how Mr Clarke is? The gash on his head and all the blood . . . it looked terrible.'

As she was speaking, Nash's phone rang. He listened and then said, 'Thanks, Jackie, that was perfect timing.' He smiled at Norma. 'Superintendent Fleming has just been to Netherdale General. Mr Clarke's injuries aren't life-threatening. No doubt they must have looked worse than they actually are because of the blood. He's recovered consciousness, and apart from some stitches, and no doubt a blinding headache, he should be none the worse for wear.'

When Norma had left, her stated mission to get her car and go visit the shopkeeper, Clara asked Nash what the lunar month reference was about. 'It means people actually get their money every four weeks, which equates to thirteen times a year. Now, you and Viv can go for a walk, while I talk to the boffins.'

Pearce looked puzzled, but Clara guessed Nash's meaning immediately. 'You want us to go round the village looking for CCTV cameras, don't you?'

'That's right, and I'd be particularly interested if you find any on houses between here and the main road. They'd be in a prime position to record vehicles coming in and out of the village. If we get lucky, they might have an image which would give us the make and model of the van our robbers used. And if we strike really lucky, it might be clear enough to have recorded the number plate.'

'I think you'd need one with night vision capability for that,' Pearce replied. 'Mind you, most of them have that nowadays.'

Having met with the forensic officers and briefed them on what to expect inside the store, Nash walked back to his car. He was joined soon afterwards by Clara, who had news. 'I found a CCTV camera on a house at the end of the village green, where the road narrows before that bridge we came over. The good news is, because of the position of the house relating to the road, the camera is pointing almost head on down the village green. At the moment, the householder is showing footage from last night to Viv. The guy is quite young and is a bit of a geek, so I left them to it, as I don't speak Nerdish.'

Nash chuckled, but asked, 'Have they seen anything that might be useful?'

'I believe so, but without a translator I can't be sure. Although, as I was leaving, they were talking about image enhancement capability.'

'That sounds promising. If we only get a make and model, it will be a big step forward.'

Five minutes later, Pearce rejoined them, bearing great news. 'I've asked Alec to email me the footage from his CCTV. It contains very clear images of the van, which is a Ford Transit, and even shows the registration number.'

'Great work, Viv. Phone the details through to Steve Meadows and ask him to do an ANPR check. Let's hope it wasn't reported stolen before last night. We'd better wait here until we get the results in case the raiders are locals.'

Only seconds after giving Meadows the details, Pearce had the result. 'I think we can return to Helmsdale, Mike. The van is registered to someone with an address in Hunslet, Leeds.'

'OK, let's go, and on the way, Clara, you can phone Jackie Fleming and update her, and get her to ask Leeds City police to raid those premises.'

Fleming's response was positive, to such an extent that she phoned back and told Clara that Leeds CID had requested a copy of the video in order to confront the suspects. 'Ask Viv to send it to me and I'll pass it on, and tell him well done,' she added.

On reaching Helmsdale, Viv's first task was to upload the CCTV footage to his computer and forward it to Superintendent Fleming. Less than an hour later, as Nash was pondering whether to get a coffee, his phone rang. He listened for a while, and then Clara heard him tell the caller, 'That's wonderful news, and a great team effort, both here and in Leeds, I'd say. I just wish we could get such good results as easily as that on some of our other cases.'

'That was Jackie Fleming,' he explained to the others. 'When she gave Leeds the name and address it triggered an alarm. The men are well known, so they sent what sounds like a posse to the address in Hunslet. There was no sign of the van so they hung about, waiting for it to arrive, keen to nab the villains in possession of the loot.' He grinned. 'Apparently, the post office raid must have made the robbers hungry, because they stopped off for breakfast before returning. Our colleagues sat about for ten minutes or so, and the van pulled up with all the stolen gear in the back. Four men got out of the vehicle and were immediately detained. They are now in cells, and Leeds detectives are about to conduct searches of their homes. Depending on whether they find evidence of more serious crimes on their patch, the prisoners will be transferred to Netherdale tomorrow. They're hoping to find goods stolen in other, similar robberies, but one way or another, we're definitely flavour of the month in Leeds.'

CHAPTER TWENTY-TWO

When Viv arrived in the office the next morning, he was presented, ceremoniously, with Lucy Fowler's laptop. 'Here you are, oh great one,' Lisa said.

Viv shook his head, as Nash said, 'Use my office, Viv. You won't be disturbed in there.'

'Do I get a pay rise if I'm working in there?' he asked with a grin.

Nash just looked at him.

'OK, boss!' he said, and hurriedly closed the door behind him.

It was mid-afternoon when he revealed his analysis of both Cassie Harris and Lucy Fowler's laptops. As they had suspected, both women had joined dating websites, albeit different ones. Resulting from this, they had each been on one date. However, when asked repeatedly to record their experience of these, neither woman had responded. Nor had they accessed the sites since.

'Probably because they were already dead,' Mironova commented.

As they looked for further common denominators, the detectives were surprised to see the names and personal details of the men they had met. Although they had also been asked for an account of how the date went, they had also failed to respond.

'We need to check out these men as a matter of urgency,' Nash told them. 'That's down to you and your IT skills, Viv. I suspect it will be no easy task. Lisa can give you a hand. I'm going downstairs, to check on our *"plumbing problem"*.'

Viv turned and headed for Nash's office.

'Er, Viv, where are you going?' Clara asked.

'Back to work.'

She pointed at his desk. 'I think you'll be more comfortable there.'

'Can't blame me for trying,' he mumbled. 'Mike's chair is more comfortable than mine.'

'Yes, and he has a larger desk. It comes with the rank.'

As Pearce and Lisa began their research, Nash reappeared and Clara followed him into his office. 'Do you believe these names mask the true identity of the killer? That they are the same person?'

'I'm absolutely certain of it, and what's more, I'm prepared to bet when Viv comes back with the results of his search, he'll tell us those men don't exist.'

'I thought dating websites put very strong measures in place to protect their members from predators?'

'I believe they do, although I've no direct experience of how those sites work. However, if someone is as knowledgeable, determined, ruthless, and cunning as the man who lured these poor women to their death, they'll have ensured the false information they fed those websites will pass even the most stringent scrutiny.'

It was early evening when Pearce reported back, and one glance at his unhappy expression told Nash and Mironova the search had been unsuccessful. His opening remarks merely confirmed this, and also echoed Nash's prophecy almost verbatim. 'Nothing. Those two men are ghosts. They appeared for a while and then vanished.'

'What exactly do you mean?'

'Taking the address info from the dating site, I did a property search, one which gave the history of both locations. That gave me the contact details for the letting agents in the area. So I spoke to them. They both told me the same story. A man rented a house from them on a short-term tenancy. This covers the time during which we know both women were reported missing. Both agents also said their man had done a moonlight flit, thereby forfeiting the bond he was required to pay up front.'

'Is there any trace of the names elsewhere, after they did a runner from those houses?' Clara asked.

'No, that's what I meant about them vanishing. They simply ceased to exist. Lisa did unearth one interesting fact, and that is those names were registered on the voter's roll almost as soon as they began the tenancy of those houses. But there's no trace of them being recorded at another address in the UK at a later date.'

'That would be to add authenticity to the ID. It also suggests the details given to the dating website, the letting agents, and the local authorities were completely spurious. That, in turn, argues very careful planning. Neither of the men ever existed, except in the warped mind of a sadistic killer. They were characters created for a specific reason, and that was to lure defenceless, vulnerable girls to their death, girls who set out on those dates hoping to meet Mr Right.'

Nash's summary deepened their already intense gloom even further.

* * *

First thing next morning, having reported the failure to Superintendent Fleming, Nash told her, 'We had such high expectations of the computer contents, but this swine is too cunning to be caught so easily. In fact, I'm beginning to think we need a miracle to have any chance of solving this case.'

'In that case you'd better start praying, Mike, and I'll do the same.'

As things transpired, it wasn't long before their prayers were answered, in two separate and totally different ways. The first of these happened almost immediately after Nash ended his call with Fleming. He was in the act of replacing the receiver when he remembered the elusive comment that had been plaguing him for several weeks.

During one of their discussions, Nash had mentioned the remoteness and inaccessibility of the clearing in the woods where the bodies had been buried, plus the difficult terrain requiring a four-wheel drive vehicle. At that point, Jackie Fleming had asked, 'Is that track the only way to reach the clearing?'

Tying her question in with the local knowledge required to identify a burial site secluded enough to make discovery of the bodies unlikely, there was one element to the investigation that had been completely overlooked. That oversight had to be rectified at once.

Nash called the team together and explained what was required and why. He began by offering an apology, 'I ought to have thought of this a long time ago. Granted, nobody else did, but that's why I'm paid what Clara is fond of referring to as my "vastly inflated salary".' Ignoring Mironova's cheeky grin, he continued, 'We need a list of everyone connected to the Layton Estate, from the management to the workers, plus outside contractors and casual labour. To get that, we need to contact the owner of the estate.'

Nash was surprised when Lisa Andrews laughed. 'Good luck with that, Mike,' she told him. 'Layton Hall is virtually unoccupied these days — has been since Piers Layton kicked the bucket. His son, Cornelius Layton, inherited the estate, but except for very fleeting visits, he's rarely at the Hall. In fact, by what I've heard from time to time, he's rarely in this country. Layton is some sort of financial big noise and spends most of his time travelling abroad. This is only hearsay, but rumour is he owns properties in France, America, and Australia, plus his own private jet. Whether that last part is true or just gossip, I can't say, but I reckon your best bet would be to speak to the estate manager. I can get his contact details from our friend Barry Dickinson. If you recall, Barry is gamekeeper on the Winfield estate, Layton Hall's next-door neighbour.' Lisa grinned, adding, 'By next-door neighbour, I mean the houses are only about five miles apart.'

'If you would do that please, Lisa, and if we get a list of employees from the estate manager, Viv can start checking them out. Unless, something totally unexpected takes precedence, in which case all bets are off.'

Later, Clara marvelled at the accuracy of Nash's prophecy, albeit an unintentional one.

CHAPTER TWENTY-THREE

Some teenagers spend their school holidays participating in a range of outdoor activities. A far higher percentage can be found hunched over a gaming device, staring at the screen on their laptop, tablet, or mobile.

Very few of them, unless compelled to do so as punishment for some demeanour, pass their time doing household chores. However, one of those who undertook the task voluntarily was no ordinary teenager. Conscious of the long hours her only parent worked to earn a meagre wage, and knowing the majority of the pittance went to educate, feed, and clothe her only offspring, to the girl it seemed only fair to repay such a sacrifice.

It was during the polishing marathon that a minor accident occurred, the consequences of which led to a discovery that would change the lives of a number of people, for better or worse. All this occurred because of a loose attachment to a piece of cheap furniture.

The teenager was polishing a chest of drawers in her mother's bedroom when one of the knobs on the top drawer came away in her hand. She stared at it in dismay for several seconds, before realizing the fault would be relatively easy to repair. All she needed was a screwdriver, but first she had to retrieve the screw that had worked loose.

She removed the drawer contents and set about the repair. Having done so, she glanced down at the interior. One edge of the lining paper on the base had become crumpled during her maintenance work. She went to straighten it and noticed the corner of something beneath it. Curious, she peeled back the corner. It revealed a rectangular piece of folded stiff card. Her curiosity had now gone into overdrive. Why had her mother secreted it away?

She lifted it out and examined the blank facade, then turned it over and noticed some printing and handwriting on the back panel. Her English was good — she was among the top pupils in the subject at her school. It was not perfect, though, so she spelled the printed words out slowly, saying them aloud, 'Net Her Dale Stu Dios.'

Opening the cover revealed a photograph. She stared at the image, her mouth wide with surprise. The subjects were a happy, smiling, young couple, both in formal attire. The woman was dressed in white and held a small posy of flowers, suggesting they had just become husband and wife.

The woman was easily recognizable. It was her mother. Therefore, the handsome man staring adoringly at the bride must be the girl's father. She didn't recognize him; how could she when she had never seen him, or a photograph of him? Her mother said he had died before she was born, killed in an accident at work.

The girl's eyes filled with tears. Why had her mother kept this photo from her, when it was all she had of the father she had never known? Why, on the rare occasions when she had plucked up courage to ask about him, had her mother instantly changed the subject?

Without conscious thought she looked at the back of the cover again. What was Net Her Dale? Was it a place, or a person's name? Stu Dios she did understand. A studio — perhaps this was the place where the photo had been taken, or the photographer's business name. Perhaps Mr or Mrs Net Her Dale had been commissioned to record the happy event?

Her attention switched to the handwriting, which was in pencil and had faded with the passage of time. Despite this, and the scrawl that challenged her to decipher the message, she was eventually able to read the details, '*Nicholas and Demetra Sinclair*', followed by a date sixteen years previously.

Nicoleta Zamfir gasped aloud. All possibility of error had now gone. Obviously, by naming their daughter Nicoleta, Demetra had been honouring Nicholas' memory. Eventually, when her fresh bout of tears subsided, Nicoleta became even more puzzled as to why her mother had concealed the photo, and why she never spoke of her husband, Nicoleta's father.

Another realization brought a second wave of shock. Her own name was no longer accurate. She was not Nicoleta Zamfir — in fact she never had been. She was Nicoleta Sinclair. Now she was keen to know more about the man whose name she bore, the man who had joined with Demetra to create her.

There was one simple way, but it was barred to her. Her mother's sadness, the tears in her eyes when the subject of her father was brought up, meant that Nicoleta could not, would not, raise it again, except if absolutely necessary. How long she sat on the edge of her mother's bed, puzzling over the problem before a possible solution came to her, Nicoleta wasn't sure.

Perhaps, if she typed his name into the search box on her laptop, something about him, possibly relating to the accident in which he died, might be revealed. But this had happened sixteen years earlier, maybe nothing would show up — unless perhaps he'd been a famous footballer or celebrity. Nicoleta giggled at this absurd notion of her father, but then, she was a teenager.

As she acknowledged the slim chance of finding anything, Nicoleta had a brainwave. If she linked the name

Nicholas Sinclair with those three words Net Her Dale, it might work. She looked at the back of the photo cover again, and realized perhaps she'd been wrong. Maybe it was all one word, not three. There was only one way to find out, and that was by trying both.

She replaced the clothing, closed the drawer, abandoned the rest of the housework, and went to her bedroom. Having switched her somewhat decrepit laptop on, Nicoleta sat cross-legged on her bed and waited. The connectivity was agonizingly slow, reflecting the age of the machine, its less than high-end software, and the lack of broadband speed in their remote location.

Eventually, she began by entering the Christian name Nicholas, and after typing the first three letters of the surname SIN, was surprised to see there was already a flood of results. She clicked on the first of these and was rewarded by a stream of articles about someone with a similar name to her father. Her English might be good, but for this she switched on the translator and dismissed these items as irrelevant. No way could these, referring to a man described as a psychopathic serial killer, have anything to do with her father, who died before she was born. The very idea was ludicrous. No way could her mother have married someone so evil. Equally important, this monster was alive — and in prison.

As her eyes scanned the results, Nicoleta saw another word alongside the name. She read the headline aloud, her trepidation increasing, '*Serial Killer Sinclair to be brought to Netherdale for further questioning*'. Nicoleta rushed to the toilet and was violently sick.

A long time later, when she had at last regained her composure, she began to read more of the articles. Her mind was such a jumble of emotions that she was barely able to take in the full horror of everything she was reading.

Deserting the laptop again, Nicoleta began pacing the floor of her tiny room, her agitation apparent in every step. Question upon question flooded her brain. Less than an hour ago, she had assumed her surname to be Sinclair, not Zamfir, but perhaps, if what the article insinuated was true, she was not entitled to it. If the allegations in the papers were correct, Nicholas Sinclair was not her father. She was the bastard child of Demetra and her lover, a man as yet unidentified, the man Sinclair had stabbed to death.

There was one strange anomaly in this reasoning, however. If those facts were correct, why had her mother named her child Nicoleta, the feminine form of Nicholas? It didn't make sense. Perhaps the papers had got it wrong. Maybe she should try reading a different article. Nicoleta selected another search result, and immediately saw a familiar name and face towards the end of the article. Reading the contents carefully, she became even more confused. She tried yet another piece, and found virtually identical details. How could this be so inaccurate? Both newspapers alleged that Nicholas Sinclair had also been convicted of killing his wife, Demetra. They had even printed a photograph of her mother, confirming to Nicoleta that the person referred to was not someone with an identical name. If they had got one fact so wrong, might they have got even more details incorrect? Her mother was not dead. So, were the other allegations against her father equally false?

Nicoleta studied several more articles, referencing the discovery of the skeletons. One included a name and photograph that hadn't appeared in the others. Alongside was the description, *Detective Inspector Nash, lead detective in the new Sinclair Investigation*. Nicoleta stared at the image of the man who held her father's fate in his hands. She thought he had a nice face and kind eyes. Perhaps he might help her reach the truth. At that moment, however, such possibilities were extremely remote.

Another series of perambulations across her bedroom floor brought a solution to the immediate problem. To resolve the impasse would involve a confrontation with her mother. That could not be avoided, and to be fair, Nicoleta knew it was what she wanted. In order to prepare her quest for the truth, she needed ammunition. That was simple to achieve. Back at the laptop, Nicoleta pressed several keys, and the printer on her tiny desk alongside the window began spewing out sheet after sheet of paper.

* * *

It had been a long, tiring shift. The restaurant where Demetra worked had been extremely busy. The tips left by some of the grateful customers almost made up for the weariness — almost, but not quite. As she climbed the hill towards her family home, the house that was her parents' legacy to her, she was glad she had this retreat to return to. It had been a refuge in more ways than one many years ago. But that was part of her past she refused to dwell on. There were many things she regretted, things she would rather not recall. In all that had happened, and in everything she had done, she had only one regret.

Putting that to one side, as firmly as she closed the door on her previous life, at least she had compensation awaiting her when she reached the house. Except for the fact that she'd probably be sound asleep by now.

Her initial surprise came when she opened the door to find a light burning in the sitting room. Surprise turned to shock when she heard her daughter's greeting, delivered in English.

'Good evening, mother,' Nicoleta smiled, but with little humour. 'Or would you prefer me to call you Mrs Sinclair?'

Bereft of speech, Demetra stared open-mouthed at her daughter, unaware this was merely the first in series of devastating revelations Nicoleta had in store for her.

'Should I also be called Sinclair? Or perhaps you could tell me the name of your lover, if he is my father? Did you run away from England because of the affair, or were you afraid your husband would kill you, like he did your lover? Or perhaps you knew that the man whose name you gave to me was actually a monster, a serial killer. Is that the reason you never want to speak about him, or to tell me anything about him?'

Nicoleta paused to catch her breath, staring at her mother. 'One other thing puzzles me, *Mrs Sinclair*. How come you're standing in front of me, when everything I've read says you were murdered sixteen years ago in England? If so, how come I was born?'

Glaring at her mother, and with tears streaming down her face, she continued, 'Because of what I have learned today I am ashamed of you. Ashamed of the man I thought was my father, and ashamed of myself for being connected to someone so evil.'

Nicoleta turned away in disgust.

Demetra sank onto the sofa and after a long, constrained silence, gathered her jumbled emotions sufficiently to speak. 'Yes, your father is Nicholas Sinclair. But I have no idea where you got the rest of that nonsense. Nicholas is not a serial killer. He is not capable of being wicked.'

Nicoleta spun round and flung a sheaf of papers at her. 'If what you say is true, then perhaps you will explain that. You still haven't told me how come you're alive, when all these reports say you're dead.'

Shock quickly turned to horror as Demetra read the newspaper articles. As Nicoleta watched, she noticed her mother's hands trembling, as tears coursed unchecked down her cheeks.

Eventually, Demetra spoke, but she was not addressing her daughter. 'Oh, Nico, my poor, poor, Nico, what have I done to you? I know you must hate me now, but everything I did was to protect you and our child.'

At last she turned to Nicoleta, using the pet name she had given her when she was still a babe in arms. 'Nicola, please, please, ignore all this rubbish.' She brandished the paperwork. 'Your father did none of those horrible things. He is the kindest, gentlest person I ever met and I loved him deeply — and still do, although he must detest me for everything I have brought upon him.'

Demetra stopped suddenly as an awful thought struck her. 'Oh no, Nico probably believes I am one of those poor women found in the woods.'

She stared at the papers again, then a look of determination crossed her face. 'I must return to England and face the consequences of what I have done. I must do so for Nicholas, your father, even though I will either end up in prison — or dead.'

She took Nicoleta's hand, squeezing it tight as she pulled her down beside her. 'Your father did not kill that man. Nor was that man my lover. The only man I ever loved, have ever loved, was your father. That is why you bear his name, and why you should be proud of it, Nicoleta. You might ask why I am so certain your father did not kill that man.' She turned her daughter to face her. 'The answer is because I killed him.'

Nicoleta stared at her mother.

Demetra continued, 'I do not regret that. If I hadn't stabbed him and escaped, you would not have been born. That is the reason I left England, the reason I deserted Nicholas, because we were in terrible danger, and that peril extended to you, my child.' She slipped her arm around Nicoleta. 'Let me tell you what really happened, and why I must go back, regardless of my fate.' As she explained, Demetra had to stop several times as either she or Nicoleta were overcome by emotion.

As she listened to her mother's story, Nicoleta's reaction showed a strength and maturity far in advance of her tender years. In responding to Demetra's determination to follow this path, Nicoleta put forward an amendment which would have far-reaching consequences for both of them. It was an idea that troubled Demetra to begin with, but her daughter's resolve was difficult to withstand.

'If you go to England, I will go with you.' Nicoleta saw her mother was about to object. 'No, please, let there be no argument. I cannot be left here alone if anything happens to you. And if there is danger, we face it together. I learned an English expression at school. It says "a trouble shared is a trouble halved", and now I understand what that means. I wish to meet my father. The father I have missed for fifteen years — the father who does not even know I exist. Together, you gave me life, and I have always regretted never having him to turn to for help or guidance.'

She paused, emotion almost getting the better of her. 'When you told me he had died, I accepted it, and I saw how sad even talking about him made you. I didn't want to add to that by asking questions. It made me unhappy when I saw other children with their fathers. Now I want to learn all about him, and hope he wants to know me, and that one day I can make him proud of me.'

'Let me think about this.' Demetra headed for the kitchen and made them a drink, trying to allay the exhaustion from her work and the late hour. She realized she had little choice but to accede to her daughter's demand.

She returned with the mugs, saying, 'OK, but first we need to obtain lots of things. Travelling to England isn't like catching a bus to the next town. We will try and make plans in the morning.'

It was one thing making such a huge decision, but putting it into practice was another matter entirely. Even making basic arrangements involved difficulties Demetra could not have envisaged. The major stumbling block involved documentation. Demetra's was long since out of date, whereas Nicoleta's was non-existent. Another, far larger problem became apparent. In making the glib announcement that they would undertake the journey, they had failed to take into account both the practicality and expense involved in travelling from Romania to England.

Eventually, Nicoleta came up with a possible way out of their difficulty, but was unsure how to proceed. She told her mother, 'I have an idea. Someone I think will help us, and deal with you fairly. Perhaps you should see what I've found out about him.'

'Who is this man?'

'His name is Detective Inspector Nash. He is in charge of the new investigation. I saw his photo in the papers.'

'We must make certain he is someone we can trust,' Demetra replied.

Mother and daughter examined the results on Nicoleta's laptop. 'He certainly seems to be very successful,' Demetra agreed.

Nicoleta gestured to the photo on the screen. 'He has a nice smile, Mamă, and kind eyes. I think he's the sort of man we can trust. Shall we ask him to help?'

CHAPTER TWENTY-FOUR

Steve Meadows was waiting for Nash when he walked into Helmsdale police station. 'There was a phone call for you earlier, Mike. Actually, the phone was already ringing when I opened up at eight o'clock.'

'Who was it from, Steve, Insomniacs Anonymous?'

'I've absolutely no idea, except that it was a woman and she sounded foreign.'

'What sort of foreign? Are we talking Europe, Africa, Asia, America, or Down Under?'

Meadows scratched his head. 'Difficult to tell. Her English was pretty good, but accented. If I had to guess, I'd say somewhere in Europe. She would only speak to you, and so I explained you hadn't arrived yet because it was too early, and she said she'd forgotten about the time difference. Said she'd call again' — he glanced at the clock — 'in about half an hour.'

When Clara arrived, Nash told her about the mystery caller. 'Oh dear,' she responded. 'I do hope it isn't someone from your wicked past, I don't think Alondra would be at all pleased.'

'Don't take the piss, it's insubordinate. For that impudence, you can go and set up the coffee machine.'

Before Clara had chance to do so, Nash's phone rang. She remained in the doorway, keen to see if the caller was the mystery woman.

'OK, Steve, put her through,' Nash said. He waited a moment, before confirming, 'Yes, I'm Detective Inspector Nash. How can I help you?'

There was a longer pause as he listened, and Clara saw his expression change from one of curiosity to astonishment, and then what appeared to be downright disbelief. Eventually, he said, 'I understand. But this call must be costing you a fortune. Why not give me your number and hang up? I'll call you back immediately. When I do, I'm going to put you on speakerphone so my deputy, Detective Sergeant Mironova, can also hear you.'

There was another pause, before Nash said, 'Yes, that's correct, her name is Mironova. Clara's from Belarus originally, but doesn't like to admit it.'

He scribbled a number on his notepad, repeated it to the caller, and rang off. He glanced at Clara, and as he was keying in the digits on the handset, he told her, 'I bet you can't guess who the mystery woman is? And before you say anything rude, it isn't someone from my past, but from another person's.'

Clara was baffled, guessing that had been Nash's intention. Before she could speak, the ringing tone was replaced by a woman's voice saying 'hello', very cautiously.

'It's Mike Nash calling back. I'll do everything I can to help you. Tell me what you need.' He made a scribbling gesture with his free hand, so Clara reached over and took possession of the jotter and pencil, then waited.

His first question was, 'How do you spell Nicoleta?' Having established that, he asked, 'And what surname would you prefer, Zamfir or Sinclair?'

Clara's eyes widened in surprise as she listened to the instantaneous and resolute reply, 'Sinclair, most definitely Sinclair for both of us.'

'OK, and can I reach you on this number at any time?' Nash and Clara heard a whispered conversation at the other end of the line, before Demetra said, 'That would be difficult, I work in the evenings. I need to get money together. Nicoleta says you could have her email address and then you will be able to send her a message when you need to call.'

'That's a good idea.'

'Hold on, Inspector Nash, I'll put her on.'

Nicoleta recited the email address, and passed the phone back to her mother.

Nash then told Demetra, 'Clara has written down everything you need, so I'll email you as soon as possible with a progress report.' Before ending the call, Nash told her, 'There are a couple of things you should know. Most important, we are now absolutely certain Nicholas didn't commit *any* crimes. And I think you are very brave to return to England. In the circumstances, from what you have told me, we will ensure you are kept safe from danger and any possible prosecution.'

There was an audible gasp of surprise, which they guessed was brought on by the depth of Nash's knowledge, and the interpretation he had put on the facts at his disposal. He grinned at Clara before adding a footnote that was all Demetra wanted to hear, 'We're looking forward to meeting you — but not half as happy as Nicholas will be. I'm also looking forward to telling him the good news. Rest assured, Nicholas has never stopped loving you. Oh, and before I ring off, I have to ask if you're intending to bring Peter with you?'

The silence was momentary, until Demetra caught the allusion. 'Nicholas told you I'd taken his stuffed rabbit, didn't he?'

'Yes, he was actually pleased you'd done so, because he felt sure that proved you were still alive, despite all the newspaper reports.'

'In that case, I will certainly bring Peter along, if Nicoleta will allow it.'

Nash put the phone down, looked at Clara, and asked, 'What did you make of that?'

'To be honest, I'm still trying to convince myself it really happened, and that I haven't dreamed it.' She thought for a few seconds and then asked, 'How do you think we should set about obtaining the things we need to get Demetra and her daughter to England?'

Nash looked at her in mock surprise. 'I'm going to do it the same way as you infer I tackle any difficult problems, by getting someone else to do the work for me. In this case, I think we should go to Netherdale and consult higher authority. Grab your coat while I make a quick phone call to ensure Ruth Edwards is available. If so, we'll enlist her help. Anything like this will be easier for someone of chief constable rank to achieve. She's got far more clout than me.'

* * *

The chief constable was in her office talking to Jackie Fleming when the detectives arrived. They were speculating as to the reason for Nash's visit, but their guesses were completely wide of the mark.

'What is it you think so important that you can interrupt our delightful study of next year's budgetary requirements?' Edwards asked.

Nash recognized the mock seriousness in her voice, and responded likewise. 'I'm truly and deeply sorry about the intrusion, when the matter is of little consequence, but I think your reading will have to be delayed for quite some time, in the light of the phone call Clara and I have just taken.'

'I hope it wasn't bad news,' she said, as she laid her pen on the desk.

'It was definitely not bad news, particularly for Nick Sinclair. There were actually two callers, Nick's wife Demetra, along with their fifteen-year-old daughter, Nicoleta.'

'What?' the two women voiced in unison.

'Yes. They rang because they want to return here from Romania, and need our help with such things as passports, visas, and travel arrangements.'

Clara reckoned that if the band of the Coldstream Guards had marched through the room, their instruments blaring loudly, neither Ruth nor Jackie would have noticed.

'Are you serious?' Ruth managed to splutter out the question after several seconds.

Nash grinned. 'I certainly am, ma'am. April Fool's Day is long past.'

* * *

By the time Nash and Mironova returned to Helmsdale, Steve Meadows had told Lisa and Viv about the mysterious phone call, so their colleagues were in a fever of curiosity.

'Go on, Mike, tell us who the mystery woman calling you at all hours is. Not one of your old flames, I hope?' Lisa asked, mirroring Clara's earlier comment.

Nash ensured the outer door was shut before he instructed them, 'What I am about to tell you must, on no account, be divulged to anyone outside this room. The only other people who know are the chief and Jackie Fleming, OK?'

Having elicited their promise of discretion, he continued, 'There were actually two callers, Demetra Sinclair and her daughter Nicoleta.'

Their reaction was similar to the earlier one from Edwards and Fleming. Taking advantage of the stunned silence, Nash explained what had been said, and the plan for them to bring mother and daughter to England.

Viv Pearce was first to react. 'Have you told Sinclair about the phone call?'

'No, although I was very tempted to, but I thought it better to wait until we know for certain they're en route. It would be cruel to get his hopes up, and then have to let him down should something go wrong. I'm not sure how much

191

Demetra will be able, or willing, to tell us about what went on back then, but I have a feeling this might turn out to be the break we've been looking for. I do know she's extremely wary about returning, and she admitted she's scared for her life. We'll have to ensure both she and her daughter are kept safe until we have this case wrapped up. Maybe then, she, Nicholas, and their daughter can begin a new life together, if that's what they all want.'

As Viv was sorting out coffee, Lisa gave them more news, on a slightly different subject. 'I spoke to Barry Dickinson last night as you asked, Mike, and he gave me contact details for the Layton Estate manager. We had a long chat, during which Barry told me quite a lot about the Layton family, not much of which was good. As you weren't here this morning I took it upon myself to speak to the manager, stressing that I was speaking on your behalf.' Lisa grinned. 'I might have given him the impression it was at your instruction. He's promised to send the list of what we need via email as soon as he's compiled it.'

'That's good work, Lisa. What was so interesting in what Barry said about the Layton family?'

'It was mostly to do with Piers Layton. I told you he'd died quite a while ago. Apparently, he was a really nasty piece of work. He and his wife, Moira, got divorced well over twenty-five years ago, and the split was very acrimonious. She left after accusing Piers of long-term domestic abuse, including both physical and mental cruelty. She took their son Cornelius, who was in his early teens, with her. There was a long, bitter custody battle, which she eventually won.'

Lisa paused until Viv had delivered the coffee, and then resumed. 'After his wife and son left, Piers Layton's behaviour went from bad to worse. He either sacked a lot of staff, both at the Hall and on the estate, or caused them to resign because of his boorish behaviour. At one point he was arrested and found guilty of public disorder and criminal damage at the pub in Kirk Bolton, and only a week later he was stopped for erratic driving, failed a breathalyser test, and was disqualified from driving for thirty-six months. That meant he had to employ a chauffeur, who also acted as his minder when Layton went on a bender. That happened more and more frequently, although not at Kirk Bolton because he was banned from the pub. The overindulgence eventually took its toll and he died of heart failure. That merely hastened the end, because rumour has it, the post-mortem also revealed Layton had acute cirrhosis of the liver.'

'What happened to Mrs Layton? Did she return to Layton Hall with her son?'

'No, sadly, Moira had also passed away before Piers Layton died. When she left him, she went to live in a tiny village near Pateley Bridge. She died in a house fire, along with her nephew, her sister Freda Wilkinson's boy, Aubrey, who was visiting her on holiday.'

'Where was her son Cornelius when the fire broke out? Did he manage to escape?'

'That's not how Barry told it. He said Cornelius was on a hiking holiday in Scotland at the time. He was so upset he wouldn't even return to the house. Apparently, he went to live and work in London, and only came back to Layton Hall after his father's death. Of course, a lot of this is rumour and gossip, so it might be totally inaccurate.'

'Does that mean Cornelius is the only surviving member of the Layton family?'

'Not quite, although nobody speaks about the other one. For very good reason.' Lisa grimaced as she spoke.

'Why is that?' Clara asked before Nash could.

'Again, much of this is hearsay, so you must take it with a pinch of salt. Piers Layton had a sister. She might be alive or dead, for all I know. There was a lot of trouble when she and Piers were teenagers, and soon afterwards she eloped with a farm worker off the estate. Rumour is they later emigrated to Canada.'

'What trouble are you talking about?' This time Nash got the question in first.

'The sister, Joyce, took hold of her father's walking stick and beat Piers unconscious with it. Like I say, this is all gossip. But Barry told me Piers refused to press charges, which I find deeply suspicious.'

'Was that because Joyce was his sister? Piers doesn't sound like a particularly forgiving bloke.'

'That's not the reason. According to rumour, he didn't pursue it because Joyce threatened to go to the police, alleging attempted rape.'

'Physical, sexual and domestic abuse, drunkenness and violence . . . what a lovely man,' Clara said, sarcastically. 'It's a wonder to me that Cornelius Layton turned out so well.'

'All this is fascinating, but hardly relevant,' Nash told them. 'We should concentrate on current events rather than the murky Layton family history.'

CHAPTER TWENTY-FIVE

Having only recently seen Superintendent Fleming, Nash was surprised when she phoned him shortly after Lisa's account of the Layton family. 'Paul Grant from Traffic was going to call you,' Jackie explained, 'but I've also got some news, so I thought I'd combine them in the same message.'

Nash smiled. 'Is this a cost-saving exercise?'

'Not really, it's more relaying the gratitude of West Yorkshire police on two counts. The first of those is what Paul was about to tell you. The outcome of the Winter Bridge incident is that as a result of their investigation, Leeds CID have arrested seven people who are charged with fraud involving several staged road traffic accidents over the past eighteen months.'

'That's a good result, but I think most of the credit should go to Paul.'

'Possibly so, with regard to the scams, but the other excellent result is all down to you and your team. I've just this minute taken a call from my counterpart in Leeds CID. Following your identification of the Bishop's Cross post office raiders, they searched the houses of the four men being detained and recovered a great deal of stolen property. Going from what he told me, they've already identified proceeds from three further incidents, all of which took place within the last month. The theory is they were accumulating stock in order to make it a worthwhile lot to put to their buyers.'

'I'm glad we were able to contribute,' Nash responded.

'Yes, but that's not all. In one of the raids, a shopkeeper was attacked in much the same way as the postmaster at Bishop's Cross, but he wasn't so lucky, because he later died from his injuries. Officers found a baseball bat with his DNA on it, plus that from the shopkeeper at Bishop's Cross, in the van used by the robbers. So all four men are going to face murder charges, and will be going inside for a long time. I think if it continues like this, you might be made a Freeman of the City of Leeds.'

'I hardly think so. As with the other case, it was all down to teamwork. Clara had the bright idea of checking for CCTV cameras in the village, and Viv followed it through, using his skill to enhance the image enough to get a number plate. I'll be sure to let them know the outcome was down to their excellent work.'

* * *

As he was driving home that evening, Nash reflected on the day's events, and this spawned an idea. On reaching Smelt Mill Cottage, he greeted his wife Alondra, his son Daniel, home from boarding school, and Teal, their black Labrador. He then made an excuse and went into the study. He opened his laptop and sent a quick email to the Romanian address Nicoleta had given him. That way, if there were any unforeseen problems at their end, she or her mother had his contact details to let him know. It was a far easier, less expensive solution than an international phone call.

When he emerged, Alondra was waiting in the lounge. She handed him a glass of red wine. 'I thought you'd like this, because it's obvious you've had a good day. Why the sudden dash into the study, though?'

Nash gave a sly grin. 'I was sending a message to a young girl.'

If he'd hoped to fool her, the attempt was unsuccessful. 'I assume it's connected to the case you're investigating. Work is the only thing that gets you moving so quickly — well, almost the only thing,' she amended the statement. 'Come through to the kitchen, and you can explain while I'm sorting out the vegetables.'

By the time he'd told her about the day's surprising developments and the background to the early morning phone call, it was almost time to serve their evening meal. Alondra's reaction to Nash's account of what he knew about Demetra and Nicoleta's past was one of sympathy, mixed with a touch of sadness.

'That poor girl. Growing up in the belief that her father was dead, then finding out everyone believes him to be an evil monster. You must do everything in your power to help them, but what will happen once they reach England? How will you keep them safe and out of the way of the media?'

'The media is my biggest worry. We need a place where they will be out of sight from press and public alike, and where they feel protected. I don't want to encircle them with a host of uniformed officers, because that might attract the attention we're trying to avoid. It's a temporary problem though, and what I'm really looking forward to is witnessing the reunion between Nicholas and Demetra. It's patently obvious he loves her as strongly as ever, and it will also be fun to watch him meet his daughter for the first time. Anyway, that's enough of talking shop for tonight.'

Once they were in bed, Nash reached over to switch off the bedside lamp, but Alondra put her hand on his arm. 'Leave that for a minute, I've had an idea.'

Nash smiled. 'What might that be?'

'Not the one you've obviously got in mind. Why not invite them to stay here?'

'You mean Demetra and her daughter?'

'Yes, it would mean extra work' — she patted her expanding waistline — 'but I'm as fit as can be. If I need help, there's always you and Daniel. And I'm sure Mrs Sinclair will lend a hand if I ask. Think of it, Mike, this house is remote. We're not overlooked, so they will have all the privacy they need. We have two burglar alarms, one electronic, the other with four legs and a very loud bark. And there will always be at least two people on hand to help protect them, in the unlikely event that bad people find out they're here.'

Nash rose up on one elbow, smiling at her as Alondra explained her motive for making the suggestion.

'I would like to do this, because I remember a time when I was in deep trouble, with people trying to kill me, and you took me into your home and protected me. I would like to repay that debt by offering the same protection to someone else.'

Nash smiled at the memory. 'I'm not sure to this day whether I did that so I could have my wicked way with you.'

Alondra shook her head sorrowfully. 'As I recall, you had no choice in the matter. I seduced you.'

Nash put his arms around her and whispered, 'I am so glad you did. My life would be empty without you, Mrs Nash. I was lonely until you came here, and since then it's got better and better.'

Alondra smiled. 'So, can we help them?' she prompted him.

'I'm sorry, darling. It's a very generous thought, but I'm afraid it's impossible. Demetra Sinclair is involved in an ongoing investigation. If I brought her here, it could be seen as prejudice, and compromise any prosecutions.'

'Oh, of course, I didn't think of that.'

'But don't you worry. I'm sure they will be happy to take all the help they can get. And you have given me an idea.'

* * *

Nash told Mironova about Alondra's suggestion and the possible solution that had occurred to him. Her reaction, although it contained an element of surprise, was a positive one. 'I think it shows how fortunate you are to have such a kind-hearted wife.'

'You don't have to tell me how lucky I am, I count my blessings every day. So I made a visit on my way in to work and got confirmation it would work, and now I'm off to see the chief.'

Ruth Edwards was equally positive. 'I've spoken to the powers that be again, and they're pulling out all the stops to get Demetra and her daughter back to England. I used your blackmail-style bargaining tool. I pointed out that every day Sinclair is in detention causes the amount of compensation for wrongful imprisonment to mount. I should have positive news for you soon.'

She smiled. 'I'm delighted you've managed to solve the accommodation issue, and it will save the need, and cost, for a security team. Especially as no one will know Demetra is even in the country. At this stage,' she pointed out, 'you have no idea if Demetra will be able to tell you anything useful, and whether she will turn out to be a witness or not.'

There was more optimistic news later that morning, when Lisa confirmed she had received the list of Layton Hall employees and contractors from the estate manager. 'I'll work with Viv and check if any of them are on our system, shall I?'

'Please do so, Lisa, and let me know if either of you turn up anything juicy.'

By the end of the day, Pearce reported back, and the result was disappointingly negative. 'We did find one or two motoring offences, including an uninsured driver and an out-of-date MOT, but nothing that could be seen as relevant to our case.'

'Those might get Paul Grant excited, but they do nothing for me,' Nash responded. 'I'm not at all surprised you didn't turn up anything useful, because the man we're after is far too careful to leave any obvious markers for us to follow. Now you've finished that job, I've another for you tomorrow. This one could prove equally unrewarding. It will also be a good deal more difficult. Now we've got an idea as to how two of these women were lured to their death, via the dating site, I wondered if we could try and identify the other victims using different websites. There may be others who have suddenly failed to respond in the same way. If you are able to get the site administrators to cooperate, which will involve explaining the reason for your request, it might pay dividends to compare any results with the facial recognition images we have.'

'OK, Mike, I'll get on with it, first thing.' Pearce grinned. 'As long as you explain to Lianne why I've been on dating websites, should she find out.'

'I'll tell her you did it to keep her on her toes, shall I?'

'That wasn't quite what I meant.'

* * *

Two days passed before Ruth Edwards phoned Nash to report success. Having noted down the details she supplied, he sent an email, followed by two phone calls, advising both it was all systems go.

Then he summoned Clara into his office and explained how they were going to proceed. 'It will mean a late finish for both of us, but well worth it, I reckon. I think the time is right for us to go downstairs and deliver the good tidings, don't you?'

When they entered the open cell, Sinclair was seated at a small table, watching a portable television, both supplied by Steve Meadows. The expression on Sinclair's face was a mixture of sadness and a wary anticipation of what the meeting was about, Clara thought. She hoped the news he was about to receive would change all that.

'Good morning, Nick,' Nash greeted him. 'I thought you'd be interested to know that DS Mironova and I are travelling to Leeds tomorrow.'

Although the statement was quite straightforward, it obviously had Sinclair completely baffled. Before he had chance to ask what he was talking about, Nash continued, 'Leeds Bradford Airport has expanded rapidly over the past few years, and we're going there to meet a flight from Bucharest that arrives in the early evening. We're going to meet two passengers from off that plane.'

Nash smiled as he saw Sinclair's expression change from doubt to hope, and added, 'One of the passengers is Demetra. The other is Nicoleta Sinclair — your fifteen-year-old daughter.'

Tears of joy flooded down Sinclair's face, and Nash waited for the emotion to settle before telling him, 'I have a message for you. Demetra wants me to tell you how dreadfully sorry she is for all the unjust punishment you've suffered. She didn't explain why she ran away, and it was only by chance, after Nicoleta found something about you online, that she learned what had happened to you. She contacted us immediately to tell us you are innocent, and we've only been waiting for the paperwork to be sorted before bringing them here.'

Nash had to pause again, as Sinclair was all but overcome, and then continued, 'The message from Nicoleta is to say how much she is looking forward to meeting you and hopes you will allow her to become part of your life. I think the fact that Demetra named her daughter after you shows the strength of her love, but she is now afraid you will hate her for what she has put you through.'

Before they left, twenty minutes later, by which time Sinclair had regained a measure of his composure, Nash gestured to Mironova, who produced two sheets of paper and passed them to Sinclair. 'Nicoleta emailed these to us yesterday. I asked for them so you could see what to expect.'

Sinclair studied the images of his wife and daughter, his tears threatening to return, despite the beaming smile on his face.

'Once they arrive here, we're going to set up a video link so you can see them and speak to them. Unfortunately, we can't arrange a face-to-face meeting yet, because we need to keep them safe, and out of reach of the media. You know how reporters often get things wrong.'

Sinclair laughed, and told them, 'Please tell Demi there is nothing to forgive. I would go through it all again, if it meant being able to hold her in my arms, and to meet my lovely child.'

CHAPTER TWENTY-SIX

Nash had taken the precaution of sending a copy of his and Clara's photo-ID warrant cards as an email attachment, so Demetra and Nicoleta had no difficulty recognizing them when they emerged from airport arrivals.

He greeted them and introduced Clara. He then gestured to the other member of the welcoming party and told them, 'This is my wife Alondra, who prompted the idea of where you can stay.'

They heard a gasp of surprise from Nicoleta, who was staring at Alondra in awe. 'Did you say Alondra, Mr Nash?'

'That's correct.'

Nicoleta spoke in an awed tone, barely above a whisper as she asked, 'You are Catwoman, yes?'

It was Nash's turn to look surprised, until Alondra confirmed it, and Nicoleta had explained. 'I am art student. I see many of your paintings in school during lessons. They are beautiful.' She turned to her mother. 'You did not have to describe North Yorkshire to me, because I already know it, from Mrs Nash's wonderful landscapes.'

As Nash was stowing their luggage in the rear of the Range Rover, and Nicoleta was asking Alondra about her paintings, Demetra seized the opportunity for a quiet word with Clara. 'It is very generous of Mr Nash to make all the arrangements. Is this normal for an English police officer?'

'Certainly not, but Mike Nash is no ordinary police officer. He is totally trustworthy and an absolutely brilliant detective, although I wouldn't dream of telling him so.' She smiled. 'You'll be completely safe staying near Mike and Alondra.'

During the journey, although Nash concentrated on driving, he listened with interest to the conversation taking place in the rear seat, where Clara was recounting the discussion of the previous day, and Sinclair's reaction to the news of Demetra's return, and learning that he has a daughter.

'He does not hate me, then? I worried he would, because of all I have done, all he has suffered because of me.'

Clara reassured her on this point, relayed Sinclair's messages, and seeing mother and daughter were in tears, added, 'Of course, Nicholas might ask to borrow a pair of handcuffs to prevent you running away again.'

Demetra's laughter contained a strong element of relief, so Clara continued, 'I gave him the photos you sent, and he is desperately keen to meet his daughter when it is safe and you can be together.'

Alondra turned and told them, 'In the village where you are staying, word has been spread that you were guests at a wedding of friends, but now the couple are on their honeymoon, you were invited to stay with family. If anyone sees you, they will accept the gossip.'

Nash dropped Clara at home, and it was dark when they pulled up in Wintersett village, where a cottage was brightly illuminated. The front door opened and the visitors saw an elderly man and a teenage boy standing in the gap, with a small terrier seated alongside, tail wagging furiously.

'This is Mr Jonas Turner,' Alondra explained. 'He is a very good friend of ours and you will be completely safe here. And this,' she added, as she reached out and slipped her arm around the boy's shoulder, 'is Daniel, our son. I hope you like dogs. Pip is very well behaved,' she paused and added, 'and so is Jonas, most of the time.'

Once they were inside, Alondra was interested to see the shy smile on Nicoleta's face and her slightly heightened colour, clearly brought about by Daniel's look of undisguised admiration. Alondra made a mental note to issue a word or two of caution to thirteen-year-old Daniel on the subject of the younger guest. She did not believe Daniel would misbehave, but it was better to be safe than sorry.

After several cups of tea, and before Jonas showed them to the spare room they would share, Nash told them, 'I think you should have a lazy day tomorrow, give yourselves time to recover from the travelling. Although I have arranged one thing I believe you will enjoy. Daniel is going to come here and use his laptop to set up a video link. That way you can both see, and speak, to Nicholas. We'll discuss other matters later,' he said, staring at Demetra, 'when you're fully rested.'

Demetra nodded. The message had clearly got home.

As Nash led Daniel out to the car, Demetra asked Alondra why they were going to so much trouble for complete strangers. 'Mr Nash said it was something you said that gave him the idea for us to come and stay here with this gentleman. Opening his home to people he had never met is extremely kind of him.'

'Several years ago I was in a very bad position, with people trying to kill me. Mike saved my life, and he and Daniel took me into his house and kept me safe. During that time I fell in love with him, and so, when he told me about you, I felt sympathy, and wanted to help in the same way as I had been.'

'So Daniel is not your son?'

'No, he was nine years old when I met him. His mother died when he was six, but Mike had never seen him until then. Daniel was born in France, and Mike didn't even know he existed. His mother could not stay in England after her twin sister was murdered. When you think about it, our two families have much more in common than outsiders might imagine.' She smiled. 'Remember, I am only at the other end of this lane. Although you must stay here, as though you are friends of Jonas, I am only a phone call away.'

Alondra climbed into the Range Rover for the short journey home as Nash said, 'I think that went well.'

'Yes, I'm sure everything will be OK. At least they both speak English and we don't need an interpreter.'

'You might be wrong,' Daniel piped up. 'They may need one for Mr Turner's dialect!'

* * *

It was late on the following morning when the chief constable phoned Nash to request a report on the video call between Sinclair, Demetra, and Nicoleta.

'There were times when I thought I'd have to send someone out to buy a fresh box of tissues,' he joked.

'Was Sinclair crying that much?'

'It wasn't just him. Clara and Lisa were also close to tears watching on the interview video link.'

'It seems your assessment of Nicholas Sinclair was absolutely spot-on, Mike. He comes across as a warm-hearted individual, a million miles away from the monster being portrayed by the media. It makes a pleasant change, you getting things right,' she joked, in attempt to goad him.

Ignoring the slur, Nash responded, 'I'd better phone Alondra and get a progress report about the other end of the phone call. Going from what you've just told me, I reckon she might have sent Daniel to the village shop for some tissues while she mops up the flood on Jonas' floor.'

'You ought to warn Mr Turner to expect visitors tomorrow,' Ruth advised him. 'We need a formal statement from Demetra, so Jackie and Clara will come and sit in while you interview her.'

Ruth was surprised by Nash's reply. 'Actually, I won't be conducting the interview. I intend to leave that to Clara, with Jackie alongside her.'

'Why are you doing that? I thought you'd want to take the lead in such an important case.'

'Normally, I'd agree. But there might be parts of what Demetra experienced she might be reluctant to reveal to a strange man, things she would be happier divulging to a woman.'

'Is that because you believe she was the victim of a sexual assault?'

'It's a strong possibility, because I can't think of any other reason for someone who comes across as gentle as Demetra to stab a man to death, except in self-defence, can you?'

'That's good thinking, Mike, so we'll let Clara conduct the interview, with Jackie keeping a watching brief. By the way, I think your definition was totally accurate — the one where you described yourself as being a strange man.'

'Have I missed something on the calendar? Should today be marked as "Get at Mike Day"? If so, I ought to have been informed!'

The chief constable was still laughing when Nash put the phone down.

He delayed making his phone call to Jonas for an hour or so, guessing the emotions at the cottage would still be running high. When Jonas answered, his opening sentence confirmed this. 'After ye left 'em last night, they were both in a bit of a state, so ah got 'em off t' bed. They were a bit better this mornin'. An' now they're out in t' garden, cryin', talkin' an' laughin' after that weird session young Daniel set up.'

'So you don't know what was said?'

'Only parts they told us abaht. Ah know you'll need t' talk to Demetera official like—'

Nash interrupted, 'Demetra, her name's Demetra.'

'Aye, that's what ah said, Demetera. But ah don't think t'day would be a good time. Better give 'er chance t' recover a bit.'

'I'm going to do that, and we've arranged for Clara and Superintendent Fleming to come over and conduct the interview tomorrow.'

'Crikey! Comin' to mi house?' He stopped speaking to Nash and called out, 'Pip, Pip, did ye 'ear that? Sergeant Miniver is comin' 'ere. Ah'd better find a cleaner tie t' wear.'

Nash hung up, shaking his head at the old man's regular mispronunciation of words. He then phoned Alondra. 'I've heard Jonas's version of this morning. How did it really go?'

'It was very emotional. I kept out of the way, but I could see their faces. There were lots of tears, tears of happiness, I think.'

'Did Daniel manage the set up without problems?'

'Yes, he was fine, although I did send him home while they spoke. When he returned to claim his laptop, he suggested Nicoleta could go for some fresh air when he takes Teal out. Oh, by the way, I had a quiet word with him while we were alone. He's promised to behave himself where Nicoleta's concerned. I don't think he would have done anything wrong, but they are both teenagers, and I understand hormones can become rampant at their age.'

Nash whistled with surprise. 'I never thought of that.'

'Luckily, I saw the expression on his face when he was introduced to Nicoleta, so I was able to warn him.' Alondra started to laugh.

'What's so amusing?'

'Daniel's reply, he told me, "I leave that sort of behaviour to an expert, like my Dad. That was before he met you, of course".'

'I was right, today is definitely "Get at Mike Day",' Nash grumbled.

* * *

Next morning, Nash waited for Clara and Jackie to arrive at Jonas' cottage. Alondra, who seemed to regard it as a social gathering, had supplied cake and biscuits for his house guests and visitors alike. She had left Nash with Jonas and Demetra, and taken Nicoleta to Smelt Mill Cottage to visit her studio.

'She will be out of the way while her mother is making her statement. I can distract Nicoleta by talking about art. By the way,' Alondra added, 'she has asked us all to call her Nicola. She thinks Nicoleta is too formal. A bit like Michael instead of Mike, I suppose.'

'Or Alejandra rather than Alondra,' Nash retaliated. 'OK, Nicola it will be from now on.'

As it transpired, Nash's carefully thought-out plan for Clara to conduct the interview was scuppered at the very beginning by Demetra, who had her own ideas on the subject. After explaining she could have a solicitor to represent her if she felt the need, Clara and Jackie had accompanied her into the sitting room, but as Jackie was closing the door, Demetra asked, 'Where is Mr Nash? Why isn't he here?'

'He suggested this arrangement, because he thought you might prefer talking to a woman,' Clara explained. 'In case there are parts of what you have to tell us that are delicate, and would embarrass you having to repeat them in front of a man.'

'That is extremely considerate, but not necessary. I would prefer him to be present, if that is in order.'

'He's in the garden with Mr Turner. I'll go and fetch him,' Jackie volunteered.

Before he joined them, Clara had explained to Demetra that she would record the interview for the contents to be typed up into a formal statement. She stated the date and time, their location, and who was in the room. Then she asked Demetra to state her name, and nodded to Nash, who started by asking exactly what Clara would have done. This was hardly surprising, as he had briefed her beforehand.

'Why not tell us exactly what happened to make you run away? Was it connected to Felicia Baciu?'

Demetra stared at him, open-mouthed with astonishment. 'How did you know this?'

'Mr Barratt, your English tutor, had told his wife of the coincidence that two of his Romanian students should vanish. Another student, Elsa, mentioned Felicia had a brother who lived and worked in Netherdale. We know from DNA that two of the skeletons we recovered hailed from Eastern Europe, and were siblings.'

Demetra stopped him. 'Please, what does this word "siblings" mean? I am not familiar.'

'"Sibling" means two people with the same parents, and I'm sorry, but we believe we have found Felicia and her brother.'

Demetra looked shocked. 'Oh, no, poor Felicia.'

'This convinced us we were on the right track. One other thing you should know. Within weeks of Felicia's disappearance and then you vanishing, Mr Barratt was murdered. I believe the murders are connected, so please tell us all you can, Demetra, so we have some facts to work with, instead of theories. Hopefully, we might then be able to put the evil man who has caused so much suffering where he belongs, behind bars.'

CHAPTER TWENTY-SEVEN

Demetra was clearly upset by the news of her friend and former tutor's death, and the inference of it being linked to her story. It was a while before she was able to tell them what had happened to her.

'You are correct, Mr Nash, it all began with Felicia. At one of our English classes, I could tell she was excited about something. She had no family, apart from her brother, and her few friends were back in Romania. She was very lonely, in a strange land, with different language and customs. I knew what that felt like, but luckily, soon after I arrived here I got a job and I met Nicholas, so I had all I needed. Felicia craved friendship, and something more, something similar to what Nicholas and I had. She told me she had met someone online who seemed really nice.'

'Online? Was that through one of those dating websites?'

'That's what she told me, yes.'

'OK, so what happened when Felicia went on this date?'

'I don't know. I never saw her again. After the lesson, we left the college and I saw Felicia meet a man. I watched her get into his car, and I remember thinking, "I hope it all turns out right for you". I didn't give it another thought until she failed to turn up for the next lesson. Even then, I wondered if she was somewhere with that man . . . er . . . enjoying herself. When she failed to arrive for the following week's class, I got really concerned, but I didn't know what to do.'

'What happened to change your mind?'

'I saw a photograph of the man in the *Netherdale Gazette*. I recognized him immediately. It was the man I saw her meet, but there was something wrong. Felicia had told me the name of the man, and it was different to the one in the newspaper.'

'Are you absolutely certain it was the same person? Might it not have been someone similar, given that your sighting was during the evening?'

'This was in early June, so it was still daylight. Also, I was standing only two or three metres away from them.'

'OK, Demetra,' — Nash glanced sideways at Clara, who was waiting, notebook and pencil at the ready — 'can you remember what the names were?'

Demetra told them. The first name meant nothing to her audience. The second clearly did, given by the stunned silence that followed.

Nash, who had been the least surprised by the revelation, asked, 'What did you do next?'

'I went to the flat she shared with Costin, her brother, and asked him where Felicia was. He told me he didn't know. The last time he'd seen her was before she set off for the English lesson. She'd told him about the date, described the man she was going out with, even told him the man's name. He'd been searching for this man, Frank Drake, but with no luck. He was horrified when I told him what I'd seen in the newspaper. I think we both knew something really bad must have happened. Costin told me he was going to confront the man, and he would let me know the outcome. That was the last time I saw Costin. When I hadn't heard anything for another week, I went back to his flat. The door was unlocked, and the apartment was a mess. There were overturned chairs, one of them broken, a mirror had been smashed. It looked as if there had been a fight.'

'What happened next?'

'I didn't know what to do. I was now worried about Costin as well as Felicia. My only thought was to consult Nicholas and ask his advice, but he was working away. Someone must have been watching me leave Costin's flat and followed me home. As soon as I unlocked the door, a man pushed inside and attacked me. I fought as hard as I could, but he was far too strong. He tied me up, put me in the back of his car, and said he was taking me somewhere secret. Somewhere I would be punished for being an interfering nosey-parker.' She screwed up her face. 'Is that the correct expression?'

Nash nodded, and Clara asked, 'Is this the same man you saw Felicia with?'

Demetra shook her head. 'No, I hadn't seen him before. He told me other girls had been taken to the place, and described what had happened to them.' She shuddered at the memory.

It was several minutes before she gathered her composure to speak again. 'When he stopped the car, we were in the middle of a forest, but it was almost dark. He dragged me from the car and through the woods into a tunnel to some sort of cave — then I was alone. I was desperate, I knew I would have to try and escape. I was wearing Nicholas' gilet because I'd left mine at work. His Swiss Army knife was in one of the pockets. When the man came back, hours later,' she hesitated, 'he untied me, then I stabbed him.' She bit her bottom lip, took a deep breath, then continued, 'There was a lot of blood, and I felt certain he was dead, but I didn't care, all I wanted was to get out of that horrible place.'

Nash was puzzled. 'I don't understand. The man's body was found at Kirk Bolton.'

She shook her head. 'I wasn't in Kirk Bolton.'

'Can you tell us where you were?'

'No, but I might be able to take you.'

'Perhaps you can describe your surroundings. That might help.'

Demetra thought for a moment. 'There were trees all round, so it must have been close to where he stopped the car. That's all I can remember — apart from the water.'

'You haven't mentioned water before. Does that mean there was a lake or river nearby?'

'The cave was behind the water.'

Nash looked at his colleagues, who seemed as confused as him. 'I think you'll have to explain that, Demetra.'

'The cave was inside a . . . er . . . oh, I don't know the English word. In Romania it is called *cascadă*.'

'Cascade? Got it. The cave is behind a waterfall, right?'

'Yes, yes, a waterfall.'

'And the waterfall is surrounded by a forest, which I guess is quite a distance from Netherdale, am I correct?'

'That is right.'

'So how did you escape from the cave?'

'I could see daylight, ran towards it, but there was no way I could get out, I would have fallen to my death. I went back through the cave and found the tunnel. Then I followed a track away from the waterfall, and walked a long way. I came out of the forest and onto a road. There was a junction, I think the word is, and a sign. It said Netherdale was eight miles away, so I kept walking until I reached our flat. I knew what I had to do to keep out of danger, to keep Nicholas safe, and protect our unborn child. The man had told me I was a threat, because I'd recognized the man who had been with Felicia. That meant I was still not safe. I thought that if the bad men couldn't find me, they couldn't kill me. As Nicholas was away, he would not be in danger. I didn't think anyone would suspect Nicholas of anything bad. I decided my only option, was to return to my family home in Romania and stay hidden. In addition to the danger I faced, I'd killed a man.' She stared at Nash, fear in her eyes as she whispered, 'I had committed murder.'

Demetra paused, emotion once more threatening to overcome her. 'I knew if the man who had ordered my execution came looking for me, or sent more of his men to kill me, Nicholas would have defended me. I could not put him in such danger. My only choice was to go away, go as far as possible from here, leaving behind everything I loved.'

'So you packed your things and caught the first train to London, yes? Tell me something, though, how did you get out of Britain? There was no record of your departure when the police checked at airports, ferry terminals and other ports?'

Demetra smiled slightly, which in the circumstances surprised Clara. 'That's because I committed another crime before leaving Netherdale. I wanted there to be no trace of me for someone to find, so I went back to Felicia's flat and found her passport. She and I are . . . were . . . very similar in appearance, so nobody questioned the document when I produced it.' She frowned slightly. 'How did you know I'd gone to London?'

'Because you withdrew a large sum from your bank account at a London branch. Did you go straight from there to Romania?'

'Yes, I had to hide my tears until I reached home. I had to face up to the terrible things I had done. I had to get used to living with the knowledge that I would never see Nicholas again, and he would never get to meet the child. I remained at my parents' house, which now belonged to me. But when the money I had brought from England ran out, I had to take a job as a waitress at a local restaurant. The wage was small, but I had to eat, and more importantly, I had to feed and clothe Nicoleta.'

After Nash terminated the interview and signalled to Clara to stop the recording, Demetra asked, 'Will I go to prison now?'

'Certainly not, Demetra.' Superintendent Fleming spoke for the first time. 'The only crime you committed was stealing your friend's passport, and that is not a serious offence. When you stabbed that hideous man it was clearly an act of self-defence, and there are no witnesses to contradict your account of what took place, so you are not going to be charged with any crime. Our only reason for keeping you from meeting Nicholas, and our only reason for not releasing him yet, is to prevent the truth from coming out before we are ready to put the guilty person on trial. That will happen soon, believe me. Mike is going to ensure justice is served. He has orchestrated every move since we knew Nicholas to be innocent, so you can trust him to try and get it done as quickly as possible.'

When the meeting ended, Demetra left to find Nicola. Jackie Fleming waited until the door closed, and then turned to her colleagues. 'Once the statement has been typed up we need it signed, and I think that should be done on police premises, witnessed by someone without an axe to grind regarding this case. Now we've learned what Demetra knows, we have a prime suspect for the murders, but I'm concerned as to how we should proceed in view of their identity. With nothing more than the unsupported allegation of a witness any defence lawyer could categorize as biased, we're going to need far more by way of evidence before we could consider making an arrest.'

'I have an idea as to how we can get Demetra onto police premises without any eagle-eyed media representative recognizing her, and it might kill two birds with one stone,' Nash replied, before explaining what he had in mind.

'That's a good idea, but what about our other priority?'

'I want Pearce to do some research on the man Demetra saw with Felicia, plus people close to him. When we know more about our target, we can think of ways of trying to bring him to justice. I also think we should revisit Layton Woods along with Demetra, and take a look at the cave where she was held captive.'

'That might be risky if the media are lurking about, surely?'

'Not if we adopt the same tactics as we're planning for getting her into Helmsdale police station.'

Jackie smiled. 'Yes, I think that would work rather well. Let's go for it. If I take the audio recorder back with me now,

I can get Tom Pratt started on typing it up. I told Demetra we wouldn't lose any time, and I ought to keep my promise.'

Although it was now early afternoon, Clara left shortly after Fleming, having received detailed instructions from Nash. The first of these was merely confirmation of his earlier suggestion. 'I want you to call in at Helmsdale and get Viv and Lisa working on what we've learned this morning. Viv can work his computer magic to download everything he can possibly find about the man, including his family, friends, failed or current relationships, career progress, even what he was given as a tenth birthday present.'

Clara saw him smile and guessed the implication of his final sentence. 'In plain English, you want anything and everything, whether it seems relevant or not, correct?'

'Absolutely spot-on, and while Viv's busy with that, try and distract Lisa from daydreaming about Free Willy by getting her to contact every dating site that was operational sixteen years ago.'

'I thought Viv had already done that, without success?'

'He did, but this time it's different. Viv had nothing to give them, whereas Lisa can ask them if Felicia Baciu was ever enrolled as a member. If we get confirmation of that fact, we can request a warrant and examine her file.'

'I hadn't thought of that. I'll get them on it immediately.'

'And when they've done that, tell them they can take tomorrow off, seeing as it's Sunday. I'll cover while I start organizing a sightseeing trip for one of the guests.'

CHAPTER TWENTY-EIGHT

Two days later, Nash, along with Mironova and a CSI team, entered the track leading to Layton Woods. Lisa Andrews followed behind in her partner's Land Rover, accompanied by a WPC. Forensics had been requested in response to a supposed tip-off from a member of the public, alleging knowledge of a cave. Their visit had been timed to take place as soon as daylight permitted, in order to avoid attracting attention. This proved to be a wise decision, for a completely different reason.

Despite the early hour, there were several bystanders loitering alongside parked cars on the road leading to Kirk Bolton. Clara recognized one of them, a reporter for a local radio station. Once they were clear of onlookers, the small convoy of rough-terrain vehicles moved slowly along the narrow, twisting path, made even less accessible by a further spate of heavy rain, which had pooled in the ruts created by unprecedented levels of traffic.

As Nash carefully negotiated a particularly boggy section, Clara told him, 'At least we'll be safe from prying eyes, because the cars our journalists were using would never make it this far. The only way we could be spotted is via a drone.'

'Don't tempt providence, Clara.'

They waited at the edge of the glade they now referred to as 'the car park' until their colleagues reached them. As they climbed out of the vehicles, Nash was speaking to the female officer, who asked him, quietly, 'Ought I to salute you, Mr Nash? I don't know how these things work in England, and I didn't think to ask before we set off.'

He smiled at her. 'That's no longer necessary. We did away with saluting, except on special occasions, several years ago.' He led her along the track to the clearing. 'Does this place look at all familiar?'

Demetra stared long and hard, her eyes roaming from one side of the clearing to the other as she tried to recall any distinctive landmarks, before replying. 'I'm not sure. It is like the place where I was taken, but all forests are very much alike to me. I was born and brought up in a town.'

'OK, let's walk across to the other side and see if that makes a difference. Remember, just stick with me, Lisa or Clara, but don't speak to any other officer, or they may recognize you — or pick up on your accent.'

Nash signalled to his colleagues to follow, and with Demetra, Clara, and Lisa alongside, he walked slowly and carefully avoiding tree stumps remaining after felling activity. As they passed a couple of posts driven into the ground with pieces of material and incident tape attached, Demetra noticed the mound of freshly dug earth alongside. She shivered as she realized what those markers represented.

They were almost two thirds of the way across the clearing when she paused, her head tilted slightly as she listened. Nash and Mironova waited for her reaction. 'I can hear water. From over there, I think.' She pointed towards the line of trees in the distance that marked the edge of the clearing.

'That's right,' Nash told her. 'The sound you can hear is from a waterfall called Black Fell Foss, a tributary of the River Helm.'

Demetra looked confused, so Nash explained. 'A tributary is a stream that runs into a larger river. Black Fell is the mountain you can see beyond the trees, and foss is an old Viking word meaning a waterfall.'

'I think this must be the place that horrible man brought me.' Demetra gestured towards the markers. 'Are these where those women were buried?'

Nash nodded, and Clara put her hand on Demetra's in an attempt to ease her obvious distress. 'If I hadn't been wearing Nico's gilet with the knife in it, I would never have been able to escape, and I would have ended up in one of those graves.'

'You didn't end up here because you were brave and resourceful,' Nash told her. 'And now, your determination and courage will help us bring justice to these poor victims. Let's move on, shall we?'

Encouraged by Nash's words of support, Demetra strode forward. When they reached the line of trees, the trio stopped. 'This is definitely the right place.' Demetra pointed to the waterfall. It was impossible to make out anything unusual behind the screen of water cascading down the near vertical hillside. The spray, created as the plummeting flood collided with rocks and boulders, rendered the task even more difficult.

After staring at the waterfall for what seemed an age, Clara noticed something in her peripheral vision. She moved her head slightly before saying, 'I think I can just about make out a small gap on this side of the cliff, but I could be wrong.'

'I don't think you are,' Nash told her. 'I can see it now. I reckon that could be the tunnel entrance.'

He turned to Demetra, his arm outstretched as he pointed to the place they'd seen. 'Is that the way you escaped?'

'I think it is, Mr Nash. I was so desperate to get away, and panicking because of what I'd done, I didn't look round.'

Determined to lighten the mood, Nash gestured to the police uniform that was Demetra's disguise and whispered, 'You can call me Mike if you want. You're not on duty today.'

He signalled to the CSI team, who began putting on the protective clothing they had been carrying.

Nash turned to Lisa, and speaking loudly, said, 'Can you take your trainee out of here, please? This may not be suitable viewing.'

Lisa nodded and led Demetra away, avoiding eye contact with the Forensic team as they gathered up their equipment to start work.

Nash spoke to the team leader, demanding, 'Why the hell wasn't this found before? This area is supposed to have been checked thoroughly.'

There was a long silence before the new boy, Holmes, spoke up. 'I'm sorry, sir, but we were instructed to look at the ground for bodies, not the hillside.'

'That's all very well, but let's just hope there's some evidence in that cave that hasn't mysteriously vanished.'

'Why do you think it might have vanished?' Clara asked.

'There has been a mountain of publicity connected to this neck of the woods. I reckon the man we're after is too careful to take chances. He's likely to remove anything that could incriminate him at the first opportunity. The advantage we've got is he doesn't know we're aware of the cave's existence.'

There was a long wait before they received a progress report via two members of the CSI crew, one of them the leader. 'We've made what could prove to be a very important discovery inside the cave,' he told Nash and Mironova. 'There's a bed at the back with manacles welded to each corner. On the bed is a mattress, and although the light is by no means good, by shining our torches, we could see a large number of stains. Some of these appear to be blood, but there are others which might be different bodily secretions, such as vaginal fluid and semen. We've got a plan for removal of the mattress, but before we do that, our first job is to take photos of it in situ. That's part of the reason we've come back, to collect the equipment we need for the removal, and for Mr Clever Clogs there to pick up the camera he left in the van.'

His colleague looked suitably embarrassed, but Nash wanted to know how they intended to remove the mattress.

'It doesn't take two of you to carry a camera, surely?' he joked.

'No, we're going to wrap the mattress in plastic sheeting to protect it, and keep it in place with duct tape. Then we can carry it without compromising any potential evidence. Once we've got it out, we can take it back to the lab for DNA and other tests.'

'Isn't it possible to take samples on site without going to such extremes?' Clara asked.

The officer shook his head. 'No, there are way too many of them, and with the length of time they've been there, some of them might have degraded. In addition to that, many of them are intermingled, and we need to ensure we obtain every piece of evidence possible.'

It was late afternoon before the combined party began the return journey from the clearing. By then, Nash had supervised the retrieval of the potential evidence. He updated Superintendent Fleming. 'It's too late today for the other expedition we had planned, so I think that should wait until tomorrow.'

* * *

Next morning, Nash drove to Helmsdale. He was following a squad car driven by Clara Mironova, along with two uniformed female officers. They drove into the car park at the rear of the building. Once they were safely inside, Nash escorted one of the WPCs to the cells, where Superintendent Fleming was waiting alongside Sergeant Meadows.

'We'll leave you in peace for a while, and then we'll bring Nicola to meet her father.'

Nash and Fleming went upstairs, having watched the emotional embrace between Nicholas and Demetra. In Nash's office, Clara introduced the second spurious female officer, Nicola Sinclair, to Ruth Edwards.

'How's your supply of tissues holding out?' she enquired of Clara, as they entered the room.

'I've brought some more in, so we should manage,' Clara laughed.

'Good, but if you hear an alarm go off, it's probably to warn of flooding in cell number one.'

The chief gestured to Nicola's costume. 'That was a brilliant idea, Mike, disguising Demetra and her daughter as police officers.'

'Yes,' Clara said, 'the press jackals barely glanced at the car when we drove right past them.'

'Let's hope the return journey proves just as uneventful.' Nash turned to the girl and gave an encouraging smile. 'Your mum and dad are having a chat right now, but they want you to join them soon. I think at present they're making plans for the future, a future that will see you together as a family.'

'Thank you, Mr Nash, for all your kindness to us.'

'Don't mention it. I spend so much time chasing down bad men and trying to prevent nasty things happening, that it's been a real pleasure dealing with good, honest, and decent people.'

By the time the reunion between Nicholas and Demetra was over, and he had met his daughter, it was almost lunchtime. Having introduced the pseudo-policewomen to the other members of their small team, Clara took them to the rest room for refreshments, while Nash received updates from his colleagues. The first, from Viv Pearce, took the form of a thick folder. 'That contains everything I could find online about the Layton family going back three generations,' Pearce told him as he handed the file over.

'Good work, Viv. And what have you to report, Lisa?'

'Nothing much, I'm afraid, Mike. I've been contacting dating websites operational sixteen years ago, but I've had no luck in finding any reference to Felicia Baciu.'

'You'd better not let Alan know you've been on a load of dating sites,' Nash teased her. 'He might get jealous.'

Lisa smiled complacently, which puzzled Nash slightly. 'I don't think I need to worry about that,' she replied.

Before leaving, Demetra read and signed her formal statement, with traffic inspector Paul Grant co-opted to countersign as independent witness.

'Now I understand why the *plumbing problem*' — he made air quotes with his fingers — 'is taking so long to repair. You should hear the complaints at HQ custody suite.' He laughed. 'Just wait till they find out why. Don't worry, your secret's safe with me.'

When they arrived back at the cottage, Jonas, Alondra, Daniel, Teal and Pip came to meet them. 'I was going to ask how it went,' Alondra greeted them. 'But I can tell from your faces it was more than OK.'

Mother and daughter were both smiling, their delight obvious.

'I'm longing for the day when Nico is free and we can begin a life together as a family. It is a future I never believed could happen, and almost all of it is thanks to Mr Nash and his officers.'

'That is so true,' Nicola said. 'And I am also looking forward to spending time with my father, to make up for the years when I didn't know he was alive.'

Demetra turned to Daniel and told him, 'You must be really proud of your father, just as Nicola will become proud of Nicholas. It is a joy to discover so much good in the world to counteract all the evil I have had to endure.'

CHAPTER TWENTY-NINE

At home that evening, Nash made an excuse and retired to the study, where he began reading through the Layton family file compiled by Viv Pearce. There was a lot to take in, as members of each generation seemed to have two prime objectives in life. The first of these was the accumulation of as much wealth as possible, by whatever means they could. This had resulted in the Layton clan becoming one of the county's wealthier families. The second aim, possibly an inherited trait, appeared to be enjoying every aspect of life, particularly the pleasures of the flesh.

Having already been given a heads-up from Lisa Andrews on the rumour, scandal, and gossip surrounding one member of the dynasty, what he read came as no surprise. It was as he neared the end of the paperwork, and was considering closing the folder and opting for an early night, that he noticed something he felt looked out of place.

Nash went back several pages and withdrew a photograph, comparing the image with the other two he had seen. Puzzled by what was in front of him, he decided he needed a second opinion, from someone whose profession gave them a distinct advantage. He left the study and went to the lounge, where Alondra and Daniel were discussing which bedroom would make the best nursery.

'Alondra, I've been looking through a file, and I found something odd. I wonder if you'd take a look and see what you think.'

Daniel got to his feet. 'I suppose that means I'm *persona non grata*. I'm off upstairs.'

Nash started at his son and blinked.

Catching his father's expression, Daniel laughed. 'Well, you pay the school fees.' With that, he left the room.

Alondra shrugged. 'He's right — you do.'

Nash sat alongside her, showed her the photos, and explained what was puzzling him. After studying them for a while, she agreed with his line of thought, albeit not whole-heartedly. 'I can see what you're thinking, but I wouldn't go so far as to call it conclusive. It might simply be a trick of the light when these photos were taken. Is it important?'

'I don't suppose it is. I just thought it was a bit peculiar. If it does turn out to be relevant, there is a way to find out. I'll know one way or the other soon enough.'

Nash was still pondering whether or not he had found an anomaly in the file when, next morning, Lisa Andrews entered his office. Her pace, only marginally short of a gallop, plus her excited expression, told him she had news, and it was good. How good it might be soon became apparent.

'I've found Felicia Baciu's name on a dating website. What's even better, when I told the site administrator why I was enquiring, she was extremely cooperative, even waiving the need for a warrant. She's emailed me the details, and, like the other victims, Cassie and Lucy, Felicia only had one date, and she also failed to report her experience afterwards.'

Lisa placed the paperwork on Nash's desk and continued, 'Likewise, the man she dated never reappeared on their site again.' She gestured to the sheet of paper. 'His details are on there. Viv's checking the address out as we speak, but I think you'll find the name he used interesting — very interesting.'

Nash looked down at the page and whistled with surprise. 'The cocky bastard,' he muttered. 'That's arrogance of the very worst kind.'

Half an hour later, having received confirmation from Viv that the address given to the dating website by the man was yet another short-term tenancy, Nash held a conference call with the chief constable and Superintendent Fleming.

'I think this is a clear indication of guilt,' he told them. 'But, unfortunately, it is totally worthless in court. If we were to present it without any supporting evidence, a defence barrister would tear us to shreds. Our prime suspect, identified by Demetra, is Cornelius Layton. His full name is Darius Cornelius Layton, and to pass himself off on the website, he used the spurious name David Clayton. He obviously felt certain enough nobody would trace the details, and even more confident they wouldn't link it to him.'

'I agree we can't arrest him simply on the basis of this, even with Demetra Sinclair's eyewitness statement, so what next?' Ruth Edwards asked.

'We should wait for the forensic evidence from that cave,' Jackie Fleming suggested. 'If we get a familial match to the DNA we hold on file for Layton senior from his criminal activities, we should be home and dry.'

They agreed. None of them even considered the idea that she had just invoked Sod's Law.

* * *

Given the potential for even further delay, Nash suggested Demetra and Nicola might want a further video call with Nicholas. In the event, this was held in abeyance when the detectives received some disturbing news from the Forensics team.

'We've analysed the specimens from the cave,' their leader told Nash. 'There was blood and vaginal fluid from five contributory sources recovered from the mattress. The DNA tallied with that of the five female victims found in the nearby forest.'

The officer then delivered his main piece of information. 'We have also identified semen stains on the mattress, all from the same provider. DNA extracted from the semen has been checked against our database and there is no match. I'll let you have written confirmation via email.'

He was about to ring off when Nash said, 'Are you absolutely certain?' Before the officer could protest, Nash continued, 'Would you please check your findings against one specific sample I know to be on record, and call me back with the result. The subject on file is Piers Layton, and I'm looking for a familial similarity. Layton's offence took place almost twenty years ago, I believe, leading to his DNA being recorded on our system.'

Three quarters of an hour later, Nash received the update he'd requested. 'There is absolutely no familial similarity between the DNA of Piers Layton and that extracted from the mattress within the cave.'

Seconds later, the dialling tone in his ear alerted Nash to the fact that the Forensics officer had ended the call. He sat for what seemed like an age, trying to make sense of the news which had turned their case on its head.

DS Mironova, who had been called to a reported burglary, returned a while later and noticed Nash seated in his office, a brooding look of concentration on his face. She waved a greeting, but got no response. She wondered what was occupying his thoughts, but knew him far too well to interrupt. He often became abstracted when he was trying to solve a crime, or when he was attempting to make sense of something he'd seen or heard. That surely couldn't be so in this instance. They already had their prime suspect. All they needed was confirmation from the science.

She waited a further ten minutes, and when he hadn't emerged, or even moved from his chair, she deemed it time to interrupt. 'Is there a problem?' she asked, as she walked into his office.

Nash smiled, but with little evidence of humour. 'That has to be the understatement of the year, if not the century.

Take a seat and I'll explain. You'll want to be sitting down when you hear this.'

Clara sat down as instructed, but Nash's opening sentence caused her to leap to her feet, staring at him in dismayed astonishment as she said, 'You're telling me there is no familial match between the DNA from the cave and that of Piers Layton?'

Nash nodded, and Clara began pacing up and down the room, her agitation evident from her stride, almost that of a marching soldier. 'So that means Cornelius Layton cannot be the serial killer, and all our theories are unfounded?'

'Actually, that's not entirely accurate. There is one possible explanation we haven't previously considered.'

'What might that be?'

'Perhaps we're correct, and the killer is Cornelius Layton, but Piers Layton wasn't his father. Maybe Piers Layton's wife was in a relationship, and her lover fathered the child. Let's face it, if only half of what we've heard of Piers Layton's violent and abusive conduct is accurate, she'd have every excuse for seeking solace elsewhere.'

'Trust you to think of a sordid explanation,' Clara told him. 'So, have you worked out where we go from here?'

'Not yet, I'm still in shock.'

'Join the club.' Clara thought for a moment. 'I don't suppose there's any chance Forensics got it wrong, is there? The sample provided by Piers Layton must be knocking on for two decades old, and maybe testing techniques weren't as sophisticated as they are today.'

'That's a very good point, Clara. Unfortunately, they compared it to the record on file, not a sample. Our boffins are convinced they haven't got it wrong, but they could be working on inaccurate data.'

'How can we check that? Piers Layton has been dead for ages. You're not thinking of having his body exhumed, surely?'

'I don't think we need to go to such extremes. I was considering asking the Mounties to help.'

'Who are you talking about?'

'The Royal Canadian Mounted Police, referred to as the Mounties. Piers Layton's sister Joyce emigrated to Canada. Trouble is, she ran off with a farmer. I believe they got married, but I have no idea what his name was. If she's still alive, or had children, there is bound to be some familial similarity in their DNA structure. To enlist the Canadian police's help we need to get Ruth Edwards on board. I was just girding my loins to deliver the bad news when you returned. Perhaps if we put forward the plan to her it might soften the blow slightly — or maybe not.'

The resulting phone call was as difficult as Nash had predicted, but at least, when it was over, the chief had agreed to go ahead with his idea.

It was only as Nash was driving home that another possibility occurred to him, based on something else he'd read in the Layton file. It was a wild idea, but it offered an alternative solution. If all else failed, they might have to go down another route entirely, and if it proved fruitful, it would alter their perception of events beyond measure. What they'd learned that afternoon had turned the case on its head. Nash's idea would send it spinning yet again.

* * *

As soon as DC Pearce entered the CID suite next morning, he was summoned immediately into Nash's office. Viv was concerned he had done something wrong when he noticed the sober expression on Nash's face. Fortunately, Nash's opening words laid his fears to rest. He listened carefully to the instructions, but then asked, 'I thought I'd done all that, have I missed something?'

'Certainly not, but I want you to extend the search parameters beyond the original remit I gave you.' Nash explained what he required, and Pearce promised to set about the task without delay.

When Viv had returned to the general office, Clara, who had been listening in puzzled silence, asked Nash the purpose behind his request. He told her what he had in mind, and his explanation left her staring at him, her expression a mixture of disbelief and horror.

Eventually, when she had recovered the power of speech, she told him, 'I know I've accused you of harbouring some outlandish theories from time to time, but this one has to be a world record, even for you. How on earth did you dream it up?'

Nash gestured to the Layton folder on his desk. Something I saw in there — or rather, something I didn't see — got me thinking. So I consulted an expert. In other words,' he added with a smile, 'I asked Alondra to look, and she confirmed my suspicions. That, I hasten to add, is all they are. I have absolutely no evidence to back them up, so we must hope Viv finds something that will enable us to settle the issue one way or another. If by chance I am correct, we stand a chance of solving these murders. If not, as Ruth Edwards said, we're back to square one.'

It was lunchtime when Pearce returned to Nash's office and laid a sheaf of papers on the desk. 'I've done as you asked. What's this about?'

'I'll explain to you all when Lisa appears, then I don't have to repeat everything. In the meantime, let's look at what you've got.'

Nash examined the paperwork. 'For a while I thought we were going to be out of luck, but the last page shows we still have a chance of obtaining what we need, as long as the person concerned is prepared to cooperate,' he said, before handing it to Clara.

She held up the piece of paper in question and asked, 'Is this what you were referring to?' Seeing Nash's nod of agreement, she passed the sheet to Viv, who began to laugh.

'What's so funny?' Nash demanded.

'Are you proposing to visit this place? If so, can I come along and bring my camera, because I want to take photos. The sight of you inside a convent is far too good to miss.'

Lisa's return coincided with Viv's final remark. She wondered why Clara and Viv were laughing uncontrollably, while Nash scowled at them in annoyance. 'I have been to one before,' he stated.

The two detective constables listened as Nash explained his reasoning, and there was no doubt both Viv and Lisa were appalled by the implications.

Once they were alone, Nash told Clara, 'We have to settle this once and for all, so I want you to contact Rowandale Abbey and seek an appointment with Moira Layton's sister, Dorothea, who is a nun there.' Nash smiled slightly as he added, 'In a strange way, her name might turn out to be highly appropriate.'

Clara looked baffled, until he explained the meaning of the name.

CHAPTER THIRTY

The village of Rowandale was situated towards the northern edge of the county, a journey of more than an hour from Helmsdale. Nash and Mironova arrived late the following morning, having secured a promise that Sister Dorothea would be available to meet them.

The building was nothing like Clara's mental image of a convent. To her, it appeared more like a stately home from the Regency period. She mentioned this to Nash, and listened with interest as he replied.

'That's probably how it started life. Many religious establishments such as monasteries and abbeys were destroyed during the persecution of Catholics. It started with Henry the Eighth, and his daughter, Elizabeth the First, continued the vandalism. Later, Oliver Cromwell was determined not to be outdone, so he did his best to add to the devastation. Once Catholics were free to return to their traditional way of worship, finding new premises would have been their first priority.' Nash paused, 'Sorry, priority was a bad pun.'

'Yes, it was pretty bad, but I'll forgive you on this occasion, as it was obviously unintentional.'

Sister Dorothea was an elderly woman, who nevertheless belied her age, both in her sprightly movement and mental alertness. She was waiting in a large room alongside the imposing entrance hall. The room they were ushered into contained a series of tables, flanked by long wooden benches, from which Clara guessed it to be the refectory.

Sister Dorothea was accompanied by another woman, who introduced herself as the abbey's Mother Superior. Nash and Mironova introduced themselves and showed their warrant cards. Having inspected these, the Mother Superior asked the purpose of their visit. 'In your phone call, you mentioned something about unsolved crimes, which both intrigued and puzzled me. Because I cannot imagine how an establishment such as ours, or the sisters who worship here, could have any connection to something evil.'

Her final word gave Nash the clue he needed. 'It is precisely to solve a number of such evil deeds, and to prevent further ones happening, that we need Sister Dorothea's assistance.' Nash smiled as he asked her, 'I assume you know the meaning and origin of your name? In Greek, it is "Gift of God", and I believe it to be highly appropriate to our mission.'

'Did you look that up?' Sister Dorothea asked.

Nash shook his head. 'I didn't have to, I learned it at school.'

'Then I would say you're extremely erudite and well educated. Tell me, Inspector Nash, are all police officers as well read as you? I need to know, because I haven't had many dealings with law enforcement. Do you carry a magnifying glass and wear a deerstalker hat?'

Sister Dorothea, it seemed, had a wicked sense of humour, which Clara thought might prove helpful. Nash explained what they required and why, which shocked his audience into temporary speechlessness.

Having first made *signum crucis*, the Sign of the Cross, the Mother Superior told Sister Dorothea, 'I believe it is your duty to do as Inspector Nash requests, if only for your own peace of mind.'

'I know that,' the nun responded. 'And I will gladly do so.'

Half an hour later, having achieved their objectives in obtaining a DNA sample, and her family background, the detectives began the return journey, the blessings of the nuns being their last memory of Rowandale Abbey.

As they were leaving, the Mother Superior remarked, 'I believe we should remember you and Sergeant Mironova during our devotions, and ask God's guidance in your quests. If our prayers can assist in your battle against evil, we must give every effort to the cause.'

Once they were en route, Nash told Clara, 'Now, we have a potential ID for Kirk Bolton man, and I think we should call at the lab in Netherdale before returning to our office. We need to deliver the goods as soon as possible.'

* * *

On this occasion, the delay was nowhere near as long as previously. Forty-eight hours later, Nash travelled to headquarters to deliver their findings to the chief constable and Superintendent Fleming.

Before leaving Helmsdale, Nash phoned Alondra, and asked her to visit the Turner residence and pass a message to the house guests. 'Please tell them we now have everything we need to close the case, and their wait will soon be over.'

He also asked Lisa to make a phone call. When he explained who he wanted her to speak to and why, she asked, 'Does that mean your theory is correct?'

Nash's nod confirmed this.

When Nash entered the chief constable's office, she had news to impart. 'I've had word from Canada. Canadian police tracked down Piers Layton's sister Joyce from early immigration records and obtained a DNA sample, and as with her brother's, there is no familial similarity to those from the cave. So it looks as if I was right, and we're back to square one, sadly.'

'I didn't expect them to tally, and we're certainly not back to square one. We now have a prime suspect for nine murders, probably ten.'

Ruth Edwards and Jackie Fleming stared at Nash in horror. 'Ten murders!' Jackie exclaimed eventually. 'Does that mean you've found four more bodies in Layton Woods?'

'No, the other victims are buried elsewhere. Let me explain . . .'

Nash had just finished telling the senior officers what they'd discovered when his mobile rang. 'Sorry, ma'am, I have to take this.' He listened to the message for a moment, before saying, 'Thank you, Lisa, that is extremely good news.'

Nash looked up and said, 'We will be able to arrest our suspect in two days' time, before which we need to obtain a search warrant.' He looked at the chief constable. 'Will you organize that for us, please?'

Ruth Edwards gave him a mock salute. 'Aye, aye, sir.'

* * *

Before leaving work the following day, Nash ensured everything was in place for the arrest they were to make. Satisfied on that score, he phoned the *Netherdale Gazette* and spoke to Becky Pollard. 'Hi Becks,' he greeted her. 'Do you fancy a bit of fun?'

Her reply made him chuckle. 'Have you forgotten you're a married man now? Or has Alondra seen sense and thrown you out? Is that so, or aren't you getting enough at home?'

'That's not the sort of fun I have in mind,' he told her with mock severity. He explained his idea, and heard Becky gasp with surprise. 'OK,' she agreed after a second or two, 'I'll ensure I have someone available for the first part, and I'll attend to the second myself. I promise not to release anything until you give me the go-ahead.'

When he reached Wintersett, he stopped to speak to Demetra and Nicola, telling them what was about to happen, adding that if everything went to plan, their ordeal would be over within twenty-four hours. 'Then you'll have to face another ordeal, but this will be more pleasant, and it's one you will be able to share with Nicholas.' Seeing their puzzled expressions, he said, 'I'm talking about the media attention, which will be focussed on you as they try to get your stories. You might not like being in the glare of publicity, but it will only be temporary, and I think it's a price worth paying.'

Shortly after 9 a.m. the next morning, Nash ensured he had the relevant files secured in the Range Rover before the team of detectives departed. In convoy was a van containing uniformed officers and another with a CSI crew, who all arrived at their destination simultaneously. Along with Mironova, Andrews, and Pearce, Nash went to the imposing front entrance, where he rang the bell.

The sonorous tones were audible even through the thick oak door. They had barely died away when the call was answered. The middle-aged woman standing before them confirmed that she was the housekeeper, and that her employer was in residence. She asked the purpose of their visit, and was shocked when the number of officers, ignoring her question, entered the building.

Ten minutes later, with their detainee handcuffed and in the back of the van, ready to be transported to Netherdale, Nash signalled the officers and Forensics team to enter and begin searching the premises. The housekeeper protested, concerned by the potential for breakages. 'I wouldn't worry,' Nash reassured her, 'Your employer won't be returning here — ever. If I was you, I'd be more concerned about finding a new job.'

It was an hour into their search when the two Forensics officers, accompanied by DC Pearce, descended into the basement. Before they could enter the cellar, they had to open twin locks, using keys removed from the man they had arrested. As Nash watched, he turned to the housekeeper and asked if she knew what was in the basement.

'No,' she replied, 'I've never been allowed down there. In fact, I've never seen that door open.'

That in itself was strange, Nash thought, and his suspicion as to what they might find below stairs was soon justified, when Pearce summoned him. The first item of interest was a briefcase, covered in dust, bearing the initials AB. On opening it, they found papers belonging to Arthur Barrett, the murdered English tutor.

Nash looked at Clara, who had just joined them, and said, 'I think that's game, set and match, don't you?'

She agreed, but before long, further discoveries yielded even more ammunition for their case, in the form of plastic bags, six in number, containing clothing and possessions of five females and one male. Leaving the specialist team to deal with them, Nash, Pearce, and Mironova returned to the ground floor, with Lisa Andrews remaining to assist with the continued search of the property.

Nash directed Pearce to the study, pointing to a laptop on the desk. 'Will you tell Forensics you're taking that? But begin to work your magic on it while you're here. Clara and I are going to Netherdale to interview our suspect.'

They were nearing the junction with the Bishopton road when Clara got a call. She listened for a while and then said, 'Great news, I'll tell Mike.' After ending the call, she said, 'That was Viv. He's already found loads of stuff on the computer, all to do with dating sites and the girls our man dated. And the search team have also found some identification details within those bags, mobiles, jewellery, and such, so we should be able to put names to the remaining victims. They also found an old passport hidden away, which might be enlightening.'

'Ring Viv back. Ask him to get an officer to bring that passport to Netherdale, now.'

When they reached the headquarters building, Nash took the file from the boot of his car and walked into reception, to find Superintendent Fleming waiting for them.

'Our suspect's in interview room one. His solicitor's waiting for you in room two, threatening lawsuits and dismissals — left, right, and centre. How did it go at the house?'

Nash told her, before he and Mironova braced themselves for the disclosure meeting. As Jackie Fleming had predicted, the solicitor was outraged, and vented his spleen on Nash. As soon as they entered the room, the lawyer told Nash, 'This is an absolute disgrace, bringing my client here in handcuffs, exposed to the full view of the media circus outside. I'll ensure you lose your job for this. Whatever you believe my client might, or might not, have done, treating him like some low life is totally unacceptable. I'll have you know that Cornelius Layton is a highly respectable, extremely influential citizen. Now, before we leave, you must apologize for what is clearly a disastrous mistake.'

Nash listened patiently to the tirade, and when it was over, his response left the lawyer speechless. 'Do shut up, you're beginning to bore me. As for your little rant, I agree with one thing you said. I don't believe Cornelius Layton ever committed a crime, but your client might be able to confirm whether that is correct or not.'

Seeing the solicitor was about to speak, Nash held up his hand for silence. 'Allow me to explain. The man you have been asked to defend, is *not* Cornelius Layton. He is a very cunning, violent, and evil criminal who has committed at least nine murders to my certain knowledge, probably more.'

He put his file on the table and removed several sheets of paper. 'I think these will clarify the situation for you. I will soon have in my possession a passport. A passport which I'm sure will have a strong bearing on this matter.'

The solicitor headed for interview room one to speak to his client before he signalled to the detectives to join him.

Nash walked into the room, purposefully, his expression implacable. 'Before I begin, Detective Sergeant Mironova will commence the interview recording.'

Once that was done, Nash turned to the suspect, who was now beginning to look distinctly uneasy. 'You must have thought you were safe after all this time. I guess in the beginning you were worried the impersonation would be exposed. But with all your relatives dead, who was there left to challenge you? Unfortunately, like most criminals, you made one big mistake — because one of your family members *is* still alive, and she told us quite a lot about you. This was before she gave us a DNA sample which will confirm your real identity beyond question — Aubrey.'

The detainee had been desperately avoiding eye contact as Nash was speaking, but when he heard the name, his head jerked up like a marionette at the command of the puppeteer. He stared at Nash, who had begun addressing the lawyer. 'His DNA taken today will not only confirm his true identity, it will also tally with samples removed from a crime scene where five women were raped and murdered.'

Nash gestured to the prisoner. 'Allow me to introduce you to Aubrey Wilkinson, first cousin of the late Cornelius Layton, another of his victims. With his own parents dead, plus his aunt Moira and her ex-husband Piers Layton, Aubrey obviously believed his impersonation had been successful. However, the mistake which proved his undoing, was he forgot that his mother, Freda, also had another sister — Aubrey's Aunt Dorothea, who entered a convent many years ago.'

Nash paused, but only for breath, then continued, 'When we interviewed Sister Dorothea, she told us quite a lot about Aubrey Wilkinson, and I believe it explains why he began his murderous career.'

Still ignoring Wilkinson, Nash continued, 'Sister Dorothea told us how, in his late teens, Aubrey's life was torn apart when his father committed suicide after he had become penniless as a result of a series of bad investments. Many of which were made at the suggestion of Piers Layton, who then refused to help when the Wilkinson family became destitute. Sister Dorothea also told us how her sister Moira, Piers Layton's ex-wife, took pity on the boy, and gave him a roof over his head after his mother died. A roof we believe he later burned down, killing Moira and Cornelius. According to Sister Dorothea, Aubrey and Cornelius were very much alike in appearance, more like brothers than cousins. With no other means of support, Aubrey had begun work as an apprentice electrician. The house fire in which Cornelius Layton and his mother died was ascribed to an electrical fault, although the investigators at the time didn't rule out arson.'

Nash turned to look at Wilkinson. 'And then, there was Quentin, a school friend of yours. Isn't that so, Aubrey?'

Wilkinson looked at the floor, anywhere but at Nash.

'Quentin Hamilton.' Nash let the name hang in the air before he continued, 'Dorothea told us the boy was homosexual, disowned by his upstanding family, and had formed a strong friendship with you. She always felt you had a hold over him. Of what, she wasn't sure, but I think I know. You kept his secret, and he did your dirty work, literally with a spade. Disposing of the girls you'd selected and burying the evidence in Layton Woods. Of course, when you found him dead in the cave, you had to dispose of him — dumping his body in an alleyway in Kirk Bolton. Some friendship!'

Nash had apparently finished, but he had one more shock in store for the lawyer, a seismic shock for his client. 'Sister Dorothea was reluctant to tell us this, but in the end, her sense of duty prevailed. Apparently, at the age of fourteen, Aubrey was suspected of attempting to rape a girl who attended the same school. The case never went to trial because Aubrey's father paid the victim's parents a huge amount in compensation, money he could ill afford.'

Clara, who had been holding a watching brief as usual, could tell that long before Nash ended his narrative, the prisoner knew the game was up. Evidence from Layton Hall, which Nash outlined, merely put the seal on it. The final blow came when he added, 'We have also a familial match between Sister Dorothea's DNA and semen found at the crime scene, the cave in Layton Woods. Although that DNA links the killer to the murders, there is no connection to the Layton side of the family, merely the Wilkinson line.'

There was a knock on the door, which Clara answered, stating for the benefit of the tape that she had received an evidence bag containing a passport in the name of Aubrey Wilkinson.

It was at that point Nash began his interrogation of the prisoner, fully expecting the usual 'no comment' response. However, having been advised by his solicitor that being truthful may be to his benefit, he began to answer Nash's questions. It was two hours before the detectives took a break. After a further two hours, they left the interview room, having secured Wilkinson's full confession to ten murders.

Nash's parting shot, aimed at the solicitor, left the lawyer speechless. 'You might want to ask your client how he intends to pay your exorbitant fees, because, as far as I'm aware, he is now completely penniless. There's always Legal Aid, of course, and he's certainly going to need that.'

As they walked along the corridor, Clara said, 'I'm glad that's over, but it was worth sitting in on the interview, because that's the first time I've ever seen a lawyer at a loss for words. I thought Wilkinson was going to resist, but when you questioned him about the death of the man he'd paid to inform police about Sinclair's car going into Layton Woods, he must have realized the extent of our knowledge was too much to be challenged. The only downside of the prolonged interview is we're running late for the next scene in the drama.'

Nash laughed. 'I'm sure the audience will think the wait is worthwhile.'

* * *

The media conference organized by Ruth Edwards was scheduled to take place in Netherdale Community Centre, the most suitable venue for an event of that size. To ensure a full complement of reporters and cameramen was present, Ruth had informed the press officer to tell them they would be announcing an arrest in respect of the Layton Woods murders, plus other equally serious crimes.

The hall was crowded as the press waited for the detectives to arrive. Conscious of the drama they were about to unfold, Clara thought the theatrical setting was extremely apt. She and Nash arrived in the wings, where they met the other members of the contingent. Having spoken to them, confirming what they had achieved, Nash nodded to Ruth Edwards, who led them onstage.

The chatter from the media representatives died into stunned silence as they recognized one member of the group.

Before they had chance to recover, the chief constable introduced Nash and invited him to lead the briefing.

'As you've probably already noticed,' Nash began, 'the gentleman alongside me is Mr Nicholas Sinclair.' On hearing his cue, Sinclair raised both hands aloft.

'As you will see,' Nash continued, 'Mr Sinclair is not wearing any form of restraint, nor is there an officer guarding him. The reason for that is he is currently on bail.'

Cameras flashed and questions were being called from the press.

Nash ignored them. 'An application has been made to the Court of Appeal, where it is anticipated his wrongful conviction will be quashed. We now have the guilty party in custody, confirming Mr Sinclair's innocence of all charges. Furthermore,' — Nash raised a hand to quell the murmur from the body of the hall — 'he is equally innocent of all the other crimes you, the media, have accused and found him guilty of. That fact will be of great interest to Mr Sinclair's lawyers, and might elevate the blood pressure in your legal departments.'

Once the hubbub had again died away, the media waited, expecting further dramatic revelations. They were not disappointed.

'Allow me to introduce the two ladies seated alongside Nicholas. One is his wife, Demetra, the other is their daughter, Nicoleta. As you can see, both are hale and hearty. You may recall mentioning in your works of fiction the person referred to as Kirk Bolton man. It was alleged that he was Demetra's lover, and that Nicholas had stabbed him. Neither of those facts bears the slightest resemblance to the truth. Demetra stabbed him in self-defence, for which she will not be punished. If it was not for her courageous act, and her evidence of what she'd seen, we would not have been able to solve this case. We owe her a huge debt of gratitude, and so does Nicholas.'

Cameras flashed and questions were hurled at Nash, who, given the constraints of the forthcoming court case, answered as many as was practical.

'In light of all the rumours, I can now confirm that we have recovered, in total, six skeletons from Layton Woods.

Details will be released when we have confirmed identification of them all, and have notified the next of kin.'

One pointed question came from Becky Pollard, who had been primed by Nash to ask it. She was already aware of the answer. At that moment, the lead article for the *Netherdale Gazette* was coming off the printing press. 'Is it true that you have arrested Cornelius Layton?' she asked.

Again Nash had to let the murmurs settle. He had already seen the Forensics' team leader enter the body of the hall and stand behind the media contingent. He'd raised one thumb, while nodding his head, enabling Nash to respond.

'The answer is yes — and no. If that seems confusing, I will explain. Yes, we have arrested the person known as Cornelius Layton. However, that name is an alias. The real Cornelius Layton is buried in Stonefall Cemetery, Harrogate, alongside his mother. They were killed in a house fire, which I can now confirm was arson, and therefore murder.'

Nash allowed that to sink in, before continuing, 'With the help of DNA, we have arrested someone in connection with ten murders, and that person has confessed to them. Other than those in Layton Woods, the victims were Moira Layton, her son Cornelius, and an English tutor who asked too many questions, by the name of Arthur Barratt. Plus a man paid by our suspect to commit perjury. The murderer of these unfortunate people is actually called Aubrey Wilkinson.'

It was at this moment the chief constable got to her feet. 'Gentlemen, and lady,' — she nodded at Becky Pollard — 'this case has involved a great deal of work from our local team of detectives, with Inspector Nash at the head. Without their diligence, more murders could have been committed and buried in the woods, unknown, and unmourned. I trust you will treat all those victims with the respect they deserve.' She turned and left the stage, followed by the others.

* * *

For several days, the team were kept busy collating and preparing the case for the Prosecution Service. The wealth of evidence from the cave behind the foss on Black Fell, Layton Hall, plus Aubrey Wilkinson's confession, made the outcome a foregone conclusion, causing Lisa Andrews to suggest they were wasting their time.

'I know you'd rather be out there looking for Free Willy,' Nash teased her. 'But this is far more important. We need this guy behind bars, preferably on a whole-of-life sentence.'

At Jonas Turner's cottage, life had returned to normal, as the Sinclair family had moved into Demetra's old workplace, The Golden Bear Hotel. Accommodation there had been paid for by one of the Sunday newspapers in part-payment for the rights to an exclusive they were already advertising as *Not Guilty as Sin*.

A week after the arrest, Lisa Andrews was late reporting for duty. When she entered the CID suite, Nash, Mironova and Pearce were sitting drinking coffee. 'Sorry I'm late, Mike. But I had a good reason.'

'Don't tell me, you found Free Willy and stopped to take photos.'

'Nothing of the kind,' she said indignantly. 'But I do have news for you. I'll be asking for leave of absence in a few months' time.' She paused, then grinned. 'It's known as maternity leave.'

'Does that mean you're pregnant?' Pearce was shocked.

'Do you know what, Viv? We'll make a detective of you yet,' Nash told him.

A spate of congratulatory hugs all but masked Clara's comment. Without thinking, she said, 'At this rate, we're going to have to convert the cells into a crèche.'

Lisa and Viv looked at her, noting her mild embarrassment. 'Not you as well, Clara?' Viv exclaimed.

Nash began laughing. 'No, Clara's not the guilty party. I was waiting until we'd got rid of the Layton Woods case to tell you. In August, Alondra and I are expecting our first child.'

THE END

ACKNOWLEDGEMENTS

Putting words down on paper is the easy part for me, getting them to make sense is a completely different matter. For this reason, I have a reader, Wendy McPhee, who tells me if the finished article makes sense, and she is always honest. She deserves my grateful thanks.

My in-house editor, the wife, keeps me in order, literally, both with my work and everything else. For this, I am eternally grateful.

The staff at Joffe Books, too many to name, are all dedicated professionals and are a pleasure to work with.

THE JOFFE BOOKS STORY

We began in 2014 when Jasper agreed to publish his mum's much-rejected romance novel and it became a bestseller.

Since then we've grown into the largest independent publisher in the UK. We're extremely proud to publish some of the very best writers in the world, including Joy Ellis, Faith Martin, Caro Ramsay, Helen Forrester, Simon Brett and Robert Goddard. Everyone at Joffe Books loves reading and we never forget that it all begins with the magic of an author telling a story.

We are proud to publish talented first-time authors, as well as established writers whose books we love introducing to a new generation of readers.

We have been shortlisted for Independent Publisher of the Year at the British Book Awards three times, in 2020, 2021 and 2022, and for the Diversity and Inclusivity Award at the Independent Publishing Awards in 2022.

We built this company with your help, and we love to hear from you, so please email us about absolutely anything bookish at feedback@joffebooks.com

If you want to receive free books every Friday and hear about all our new releases, join our mailing list: www.joffebooks.com/contact

And when you tell your friends about us, just remember: it's pronounced Joffe as in coffee or toffee!

ALSO BY BILL KITSON

THE DI MIKE NASH SERIES
Book 1: WHAT LIES BENEATH
Book 2: VANISH WITHOUT TRACE
Book 3: PLAYING WITH FIRE
Book 4: KILLING CHRISTMAS
Book 5: SLASH KILLER
Book 6: ALONE WITH A KILLER
Book 7: BLOOD DIAMOND
Book 8: DEAD & GONE
Book 9: HIDE & SEEK
Book 10: RUNNING SCARED
Book 11: THE BLEEDING HEART KILLER
Book 12: CHAIN REACTION
Book 13: CUT-THROAT
Book 14: BURIAL GROUNDS
Book 15: SKELETONS IN THE CLOSET
Book 16: GUILTY AS SIN